I0674005

CLOCKWORK
GYPSY

NOVELS BY JERI WESTERSON

Paranormal

ENCHANTER CHRONICLES SERIES

The Daemon Device

Clockwork Gypsy

BOOKE OF THE HIDDEN SERIES

Booke of the Hidden

Deadly Rising

Shadows in the Mist

The Darkest Gateway

MOONRISER WEREWOLF MYSTERY SERIES

Moonrisers

Medieval Mysteries

THE CRISPIN GUEST MEDIEVAL NOIR MYSTERIES

Veil of Lies/ Serpent in the Thorns/ The Demon's Parchment/ Troubled Bones

Blood Lance/ Shadow of the Alchemist/ Cup of Blood (a prequel)

The Silence of Stones/ A Maiden Weeping/ Season of Blood

The Deepest Grave/ Traitor's Codex/ Sword of Shadows/ Spiteful Bones

Historical Fiction

Though Heaven Fall

Roses in the Tempest

Native Spirit, writing as Anne Castell

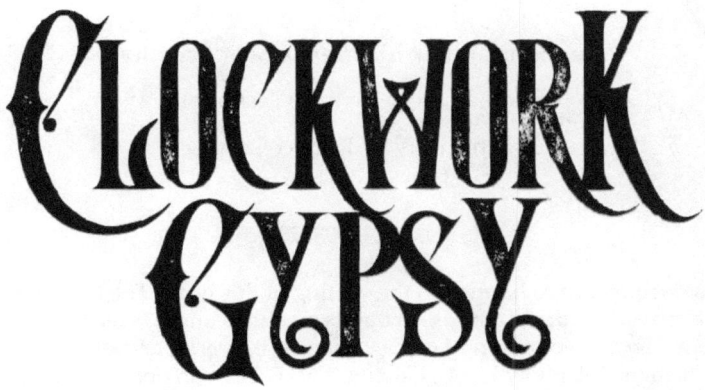

CLOCKWORK GYPSY

JERI WESTERSON

BOOK TWO IN THE ENCHANTER CHRONICLES

Illustrated by Robert Carrasco

Dragua Press

Copyright © Jeri Westerson 2020

All rights reserved, including the right of reproduction in whole or in part in any form.

This book is a work of fiction. Names, characters, places, and incidents are the products of the author's imagination or are used fictitiously. Any resemblance to actual persons, living or dead, is entirely coincidental.

Cover design by Mayhem Cover Creations

Book design by Jeri Westerson

Illustrations by Robert Carrasco

ISBN: 978-0-9982238-5-8

No daemons were harmed in the writing of this book. The Otherworld authorizes the author to write about its creatures and Ancient Ones. Any resemblance to your own plane of existence, universe, or reality is strictly coincidental. Unholy Hosts, Goblins, and Faeries do not indemnify the reader for any experienced celestial horror.

Sign up for my newsletters at JeriWesterson.com

Dragua Press
PO Box 799
Menifee, CA 92586

For Craig, *my* most unusual man.

ACKNOWLEDGEMENTS

Much thanks to Robert Carrasco for the amazing illustrations. And to Mark Luetkemeyer who gave me a terrific idea for the plot. My hats off to you both, gentlemen.

I also wish to extend my thanks to Lisa Shevin, Shaina Warshay, and Yudi Shevin for their Hebrew translations. It's very much appreciated. And to James La Salandra for his superb copy editing. Thanks very much to all.

"For those who believe, no explanation is necessary. For those who do not, none will suffice."
— Joe Dunninger, "The Amazing Dunninger", c. 1920

CHAPTER ONE

London, 1891

LEOPOLD KAZSMER, STILL flushed from his latest performance, reached for the latch of the stage door when a burst of fiery pain erupted from the tattoo on his left arm. He jerked his hand back and gasped, peering down at the All-Seeing Eye etched on the pulse point of his wrist.

With a cold feeling of horror, he was certain he had seen it...blink.

The braided double Celtic knot that ran the circumference of his wrist seemed to writhe on his skin, burning, reminding him that he was not his own man, that the gods of the Otherworld had made *two* bargains with him, and that his soul would be required in payment at any time they chose.

Not now, he begged breathlessly to the ether. *Please. Not now!*

But even in his roiling fear, he slowly came to realize that it might *not* be a call. It could be a warning of supernatural activity nearby. Was it that? He prayed again to whomever would listen that it *was* a warning...and not the other.

His quaking hand reached for the door latch again and a painful wash of heat encircled his wrist a second time. Clenching his fist and gritting his teeth, he couldn't *see* the braided knot moving but he felt it *inside* his skin, like an eel writhing in a barrel.

Definitely a warning. What could his tattoo possibly be warning him of? He'd been spending an inordinate amount of time studying the Kabbalah until his eyes ached from the strain of deciphering the tiny scratches of Hebrew, working out the spells and incantations. But it had not yet been enough. Not enough for the journey he knew he must soon undertake.

Did the squirming tattoo sense this delving into the sacred scriptures? Or…was it something closer to home? What lay just beyond the stage door?

Slowly, he withdrew the wand he kept inside his coat pocket and compressed the button that made it telescope into a two-foot long stiletto. He held it steady in his right hand and carefully closed the fingers of his left hand on the door latch. Counting to three under his breath, he yanked it open and postured in the doorway to face…nothing.

A brick wall opposite the theatre, a dark and dank alley, perhaps the bleating of a nearby cat, but nothing more. His tattoo covenant wasn't given to fancies. Something had been there. Something…not of this world. But plainly, as he stood on the landing and looked both ways down the alley, it wasn't there now.

He eased his breathing, replaced his wand, took out the multi-dimensional spectacles from his waistcoat pocket, and placed them on his nose, moving the various filters on their stalks over the lenses, and trying others. No footprints from demons, imps, or anything else. No sign of Otherworld creatures at all.

He folded up the brass spectacles and tucked them away.

There was nothing for it but to proceed as he had planned. He locked the stage door behind him, trotted nimbly down the stairs, and walked warily out of the alley to the main thoroughfare.

The fog hung like a velvet curtain. Each gaslamp glowed eerily like a will-o-the-wisp, disembodied from its post. He heard carriages — caught only the faint glow of their lamps as they passed — and the footsteps of those along the pavement, but he could not for the life of him see them.

Overhead, a city dirigible chugged, spewing its smoke and soot into the fog, making it more opaque. He knew he was near one of the dirigible stops, and there! He barely missed running into the ironwork structure. Up a few steps stood the station for the steam-powered trolleys that got about on elevated iron tracks snaking throughout the town. A few steps above that was the dirigible platform. Yes, a sickly yellow light overhead revealed it. The trolly cars had stopped running an hour ago, but the damned dirigibles continued even after their curfew. Somehow, they remained outside the law.

There was a pub not too far up the street from the ironwork, and so he moved steadily and carefully there.

The hiss of a piston didn't surprise him in the least, since both the dirigibles and the trolleys had pistons, but this one sounded different. Almost like that of Raj, his friend the automaton. If Leopold had heard the distinctive squeak of the automaton's wheels, he would have been certain it *was* Raj, but his mechanical friend never ventured from the theatre. Instead, there was the clank of steel banging on the pavement behind him in a steady rhythm, much like a footstep.

Leopold stopped and turned, looking back into the veiling fog. Pistons whooshed and the stroke of a wheel ticked on intricate gears. The hiss of a piston eased out, but there was no whirr of governors. And yet, he was certain he would have heard those sounds next. He was so used to Raj, to tinkering with the ancient automaton to understand his workings, that each sound was imprinted upon his memory.

He waited a long time, a moment made longer by the fog that yielded no difference in the passage of time, and finally he shrugged and moved ahead, certain that the pub was imminent.

And then the clank of metal again, the whirr of gears and governors, the hiss of pistons.

He stopped and whirled, wand at the ready. He didn't quite need the wand for his magic, but because it was made of the Talmudic four species—the date palm, the myrtle, and the willow, polished with the oil of the citron—it was a powerful talisman against the denizens of Gehenna. Even without it, he knew he had enough accumulated magic to defend himself in spectacular fashion after tonight's magic show, but he dreaded having to use it. Dreaded… what he might need to use it against.

The sounds stopped. He was being followed. But by whom? And…*what?*

His tattoo burned its warning on his wrist. *Something* was there.

He fumbled at his waistcoat and put on the spectacles again, peering into the gloom. But even as he moved one filtered lens and then the next, he saw nothing. They could penetrate the layers of worlds but not of fog. He tilted his head, listening to the sounds of the city, when a man came suddenly out of the gloom and ran straight into him.

"I beg your pardon," Leopold said, catching the man before he stumbled. "I'm terribly sorry."

It was an older gentleman in evening dress, a *pince-nez* perched upon the bridge of his nose, and a brush-like white mustache covering his mouth. "You damn fool. Standing in the middle of the pavement like that."

"I do apologize."

"Should know better," he harrumphed before striding on, disappearing again into the unforgiving mist.

Leopold stepped to the side. "*Átkozott!*" he swore in Hungarian, before he lit the tip of the wand, illuminating his path. He held it up behind him, trying to see farther than a few steps, but it was useless.

Moving forward, he didn't hear the mechanical noise again nor did he feel the pain in his wrist, and so concluded it might have been the dirigible lift after all.

He heard the pub before he saw it, quickly extinguished the wand, and tucked it and the spectacles away. Pushing the doors open, the place was flooded with light. What a relief it was to see things clearly...and to be surrounded by humans.

The polished wood paneling reflected back the gas flames in their sconces and from the figural lights sculpted of scantily-clad women on either end of the marble bar, the lit globes above their bronze heads casting light on all the faces of those gathered around their pints.

The pub was crowded. There were rougher patrons, but also the more genteel, sitting at booths along the walls, while the hoi polloi was packed in the center. There were private rooms off to the side for those who wished for a more sequestered meeting, but Leopold *wanted* to be among people just now. And so he sidled his way to the long bar and signaled the bartender. "Bitter, please," he said.

The barman, ginger hair parted down the middle of his pate, grabbed a glass and pulled the engine until the pint was full of amber and foam. "Thruppence," said the barman.

Leopold held up his empty hand, moved his fingers, and suddenly thruppence appeared. Those near him gasped. He set the coins on the counter.

"I know you!" said an Irishman in a double-breasted peacoat. "You're Leopold Kazsmer. He's the Great Enchanter," he said to his fellows.

Others expressed delight and gathered round him; Men in evening dress and those in walking suits, gin-bleary woman in cheap feathered hats, and other men in varying degrees of status, from clerks to businessmen.

"Show us a trick," cried a woman with too much rouge on her cheeks and a torn shawl on her shoulders.

"I say!" said a dandy in spats. "Yes, show us a trick, Kazsmer."

He rather hoped they'd ask.

"Really, gents,' he said mildly. 'I'm enjoying my beverage." He took a swig, wiping the foam from his mustache with a finger.

"Come on, Kazsmer, old chap. Show us your stuff."

"Well," he said, taking a second drink and putting the pint down. "If you insist." He raised his arm and tugged down his left sleeve revealing the tattoo. They all stared at it, as he hoped they would. He had magic left from the daemon's presence but he didn't want to use it. He decided to save it for the walk home, just in case. He'd simply perform the punter magic he was used to doing.

While they were struck by the tattoo on his left arm, he bent the wrist of his right hand and retrieved the cards from his right sleeve, presenting them in a fan.

They cheered and clapped at that mere accomplishment, but he knew that someone from the crowd would gladly participate.

"Can we pick a card?" said a woman, eyes bright and not yet dulled from drink.

"Oh, anyone can do a card trick," said a man with a stained coat. "Do something else."

"Very well." He tucked his deck away. "Have you a watch, good man?"

"I have me father's watch."

"Then may I see it?"

The man seemed reluctant until the crowd encouraged him with guffaws and catcalls. He shook his head and slowly pulled the nickel-plated watch with its chain from his pocket. Leopold took it in hand and held it up for all to see. "Now then, my man. This is a cherished watch, is it not?"

"Aye, it is."

"Then allow me to take it for but a moment." He took out a small white sack from his pocket. In it were glass and metal pieces carefully concealed, but he dropped the watch into yet another compartment, and with a bit of maneuvering, slipped the watch out of the bottom, and into his left sleeve. He bunched up the bag to look as if it contained a watch and chain. "Now observe," he said. He laid the sack carefully on the marble bar and gestured to the barman. "Have you an empty mug, my good sir?"

The barman handed Leopold a heavy glass mug.

"That will do," said Leopold. "Observe." He took the mug by the handle and slammed it down on the sack.

The crowd gasped, hands over their mouths. The man whose watch it was, yelled. Horrified and then angry, he jerked toward Leopold, but the men in the crowd held him back.

"You broke me father's watch! I'll break your neck!" He struggled in the arms of the men who held him.

Leopold doffed his hat. "My sincerest apologies, good sir. I didn't think you liked the watch all that much when you gave it away to me."

Angry tears formed in the man's eyes. "I'll slice you."

"Now really, sir. Have you no faith in magic? Don't you know I can easily restore your watch?" He took up the sack with its clinking vestiges of metal and glass, shook it once, much to the anger of the man who pulled hard at his captors, whilst Leopold tilted his sleeve, letting the watch and chain slither through to the secret compartment in the bag. He clapped the bag between his hands and molded it, grimaced at the hard work, and otherwise appeared to be pulling all the magic he could from his being. He then tipped the sack over into his hand and lifted the watch for all to see.

The angry man suddenly turned white, mouth agape. He took the watch fully restored and looked it over. "It's me watch!"

Leopold deftly stuffed the sack away, and the formerly angry man ordered another beer for Leopold.

———— ✦ ————

AFTER SEVERAL ROUNDS of beers, the barkeep finally steered the crowds away from the magician so he could drink his bounty. He chatted amiably with some of the men, those in dress coats with posher accents, those he felt he belonged with. He could forget his long-ago childhood in the Romani camps. He could forget the dirty names they called him on the streets of London as a Jew. He was the "Great Enchanter" to the punters. And that's how he liked it best.

The noise in the bar suddenly fell to a hush and all eyes directed toward the door. Leopold set down his mug and strained to see what the matter was, but he could not peer over the tops of the patrons' heads. Suddenly, the people parted. A mysterious figure walked straight toward Leopold. His jaw fell slack and he looked the figure up and down, from her laced boots to the green dress she favored with its tight, short jacket, and up to the feathers swaying on the top of her hat. She leaned on her clever umbrella. But instead of the cool gaze he expected from those dark cagey eyes, one of her eyes — the right one — was now covered with a leather and brass patch with a lens that abruptly whined as it spun, focusing in and out like a mechanical telescope. Those nearest her, backed away.

"I thought I might find you here, Mr. Kazsmer," she trumpeted. "Come, come. There's no time to waste. Let us away so that we may talk."

He moved unsteadily from the bar and when he got his voice back there was nothing he could think to say to her but a stumbling, "Why...M-Miss...Miss *Zhao!*"

CHAPTER TWO

WHY WAS IT he could chat up a barmaid or even his two identical twin assistants, but when it came to the ever-lovely and abrupt Special Inspector Mingli Zhao, he played the fool every time?

She had grabbed his arm, dragged him toward one of the private rooms, and instructed the barkeep over her shoulder to bring them brandy and glasses.

Once inside the room, she settled herself on a chair by the fire and set aside the umbrella that concealed a rapier. She rubbed her gloved hands together.

She was Chinese, but as far as Leopold was concerned it was the least interesting thing about her. She spoke with a perfect English lady's accent, had impeccable posture and verve, and an amazing capacity with sword and pistols. But her manners were abrupt, and she seemed consistently annoyed that others couldn't fathom all the intricacies of life that she was privy to.

Her black hair was piled up in careful ringlets on her head and seemed to support the hat with its jaunty feather curving artfully around her face. Her lips, slanted into a wry smile, were only slightly rouged, and her dark left eye peered his way with the amusement she always seemed to hold for him.

Yet the monstrous right eye, with its ever-adjusting lens, discomfited him almost as much as her shapely person did.

Thinking of her curves made him instantly recall the twisting tattoo that graced her slender back. It made a journey over her shoulder and down, *down* past her hip to a place he longed to see.

But there was also something of which he was certain she wasn't aware. He'd never gotten the chance to discuss it with her, for she had disappeared after their last adventure without even saying good-bye. His daemon friend Eurynomos had discovered that she herself was part daemon, and neither daemon nor man were sure that this was an entirely good thing. Still, he wanted to ask, to talk with her. He wanted…oh so many things from her.

Leopold hadn't yet sat, and she gestured toward the chair. He sank into it, barely registering that it was there. "My dear Miss Zhao. Whatever happened to you?"

"So much has happened in the last six months," she said airily. "Where to start?"

"Your…your *eye*…" He trailed off, not knowing quite what else to say on the matter.

She leaned forward with a devilish grin. "This?" And the lens telescoped and spun, focusing on him. It was terrifying. "I ran into a spot of trouble on one of my missions, all very hush-hush. I'm afraid a villain got the better of me with his rapier."

"No." He rose and found himself on one knee before her. He reached for her hands to comfort but drew back, uncertain what he was allowed to do. He was not yet that familiar with her that he could even take her hand. That would never do, and she had always been quick to throw him over her shoulder to the ground when he tried. "My dear, *dear* Miss Zhao."

"Get up, Mr. Kazsmer. I'm no weakling that I worry over a trifle like this. Besides, I've had it enhanced."

"But…but…" She had been so lovely. Well, he supposed she still was.

She took his hand in hers and finally gave him a warm smile. "Your concern is noted, Mr. Kazsmer. But you have nothing to fear. I can see quite well with this eye, even better than before. I can see great distances *and* I modified it so that it is very like your spectacles. Multidimensional, multi-functional…I am quite the modern woman."

"Well…of course. If you say so…"

"I do. Now sit down. The barkeep is here."

The man pushed through the door at that moment and set down the tray with the bottle and glasses. Mingli paid him and he quietly left.

She grabbed the bottle, pulled out the cork, and poured a share into each glass. "What shall we drink to? Reuniting? Yes, let's." She handed him a glass, clinked hers to his, and knocked it back. The feather on her hat quivered.

Leopold looked down at his glass as if noticing it for the first time. "Yes, reuniting," he muttered. He sipped his and set it down on his thigh. She had disappeared six months ago on one of her many secret missions, and he hadn't heard a word from her in all those months. Not that she owed him her time, even though they had been closely involved in a dangerous adventure. He didn't fool himself into thinking that she thought about him. She had teased him mercilessly. His inexperience with women was a painful part of his life. He had yet to learn the fine art of romance. He had kissed one of the Romani girls back at the camp when he was a boy...well, *she* had kissed *him*. He hadn't the least idea what to do except from cheap books and penny dreadfuls. He wondered about asking Eurynomos, but the mere thought of it nearly sent him into paroxysms of pure misery. Was he such a sorry man that he had to get romantic advice from a daemon?

"You were gone six months," he said, not expecting to say it. Nor the next part when he blushed and said, "and you never wrote."

"Oh yes, how are our friends? Eurynomos, Raj, and Inspector Thacker? I hope you are all well."

Leopold slammed the glass onto the table, startling her. "You were gone *six* months! And you never said a word. Not before, and not in all the time since. And now here you are, blithe as you please."

She sat back with her second brandy and sipped, peering over the rim of her glass. "And what's your point?"

"My...my *point* is, your friends care about you, were worried about you."

She leaned forward again, that teasing smile on her lips that he both despised and thrilled to. "Were *you* worried about me...Leo?"

"I bloody well was. Pardon me." He took a swig of his glass and promptly choked, coughing until she reached over and slapped his back a few times.

He wrestled himself to his feet. "Stop it! You behave as if you were merely on a jaunt, a Cook's Tour. And here you are with a missing eye and...and..."

She set her glass down and rose to meet him. "Mr. Kazsmer, you truly *were* worried about me. Do forgive me. I never thought to contact you. I assumed you'd be as busy as I was. And it wasn't as if I were at liberty to tell you what I was doing and where I was. I am still a *Special* Inspector, Mr. Kazsmer. That comes with particular responsibilities. And discretion. I thought you'd know that."

Now he felt foolish. *Again.* He sank to his seat. "I...didn't think."

"Well...if you must know...I did think about you. From time to time."

He lifted his face. "You did?"

"Of course." She smiled in that wicked way of hers. "Did you think I'd forgotten about you?" Abruptly, she pulled her gaze away and retrieved a small notebook from a pocket in her jacket. "I definitely need your expertise to investigate something."

To investigate. Oh. Is that all? He sighed, sat back, and drank his brandy.

Out of her small notebook she took a paper and unfolded it. Flattening it on the table she gestured toward it as if it were the most important document in the world. When he looked, he found that it was like any number of ordinary leaflets tacked to posts and glued to walls about London. It advertised the new railway line with the World's Fastest Steam Engine. Hieronymus Pratt and Eustace Sinclair, perhaps the wealthiest railway barons in England, had joined forces for a new railway system that promised London to Edinburgh in *two* hours. It had opened only a month before, with several lines already running, the first station in London being near Piccadilly.

"I've seen this leaflet before."

"Oh, *have* you?" She twisted her lip and tilted her head forward. He jerked his head away from the disarming feather. "But do you *understand*?"

"Understand what?" He stared at the leaflet again. An engraving of the two barons shaking hands above a foreshortened image of a black smoke-spewing engine coming at the viewer, with steam billowing out at the steam cocks near the wheels and clouds of black smoke and fire from the smokestack in front of the engineer's cab. In headline type in a swooping curve, the leaflet declared; "Kobold & Hob Railway!" and below that, a map of the current and proposed routes.

"I don't know what is so mysterious about it. Although I've never heard of a 'Kobold' or 'Hob' city. Are they in Scotland, by any chance?"

She sighed and pulled out a translucent paper vellum, unfolding it. It had a map imprinted on it and she carefully laid it upon the leaflet, lining up her map with the one on the printed bill. Her lines matched perfectly the route lines on the railway map.

"And so?" he said, still feeling lost.

"Leo," she said confidentially. It caused a shiver of pleasure running up his spine when she used the familiar of his name. "*My* map is a map of England's alignment lines."

He stared again at the overlay on top of the leaflet. "Alignment lines? You don't mean to tell me you believe in that nonsense."

In answer she raised her chin and narrowed her eye. "Nonsense, is it? You certainly dismiss that which you are not familiar with. Where is the scholar I know you to be?"

He held his breath. While it was true that he had become an expert on the art of summoning Jewish daemons and on his study of the intricacies of the Kabbalah and the many levels of Gehenna, he had found himself dismissing other more outlandish forms of spiritualism, like alignment lines and druid henges. There simply was not the scholarship to support them. It was fakery, like ectoplasm drawn from the mouths of false spiritualists, trying to get money out of the punters in dramatic séances. He couldn't abide it.

"Well," he began carefully. He had no wish to be the brunt of her rage. "I've made it my life's work to study Kabbalah and Hebrew mysticism. I find that quite fills my time."

She stared at him, even while she poured herself more from the bottle. Sipping the brandy, she never tore her gaze away. Even without the scrutinizing lens, he had always found her judgmental glare discomfiting.

"Then allow me to instruct." She set her glass down and took up the vellum, shaking it toward him. "I *have* made supernatural studies the core of my education. You do recall my association with the gods of my logogram?"

Her tattoo. Her words had been burned on his memory; "*The 'yuan gui',*" she had said. "*The Chinese term can be translated to 'ghost with a grievance.' I was marked to save me...and to curse me. For I am haunted by the spirits of persons who died wrongful deaths and I must constantly strive to make it right. And they protect me, too, so that I may carry out my mission, for however long the gods wish it of me.*"

"I remember," he said softly.

"Then you must also be aware that I study *all* supernatural sources, not just Oriental ones, for I have found that one never knows what might become useful. Now." She stabbed at the leaflet. "It might also interest you to know that there is no location in all of Great Britain called 'Kobold' or 'Hob'."

"Yes, I did wonder about that..."

"And in fact, that the railway system was built in an extraordinarily short time. Unlike any other."

"I do recall something of —"

"And that those who opposed this railway — members of the House of Commons, commissioners of various sorts — had died...under mysterious circumstances."

"Well, that I had heard briefly from —"

"Precisely! And another thing. Neither Hieronymus Pratt nor Eustace Sinclair have been seen in public for at least the last six months."

"Surely Scotland Yard has been —"

"Of course they have —"

"Miss Zhao," Leopold rushed to put in, "Do you possibly think you can allow me to finish a sentence or two?"

"Oh. My apologies, Mr. Kazsmer. I wanted to make certain you were fully versed in the seriousness of the situation."

"I can appreciate that. Now." He pulled at his collar. "You say these two men have disappeared?"

"I haven't said that. I *said* that they haven't been *seen*."

"Then perhaps we must start there."

"Have you no curiosity about the alignment lines? And that these railway lines seem to follow them directly?"

"I don't…but I suppose it is too much to hope that you will not tell me."

She turned away before he could fully detect her smirk. "I believe that these men — or someone who has done something *to* these men — have devised a railway system taking advantage of the alignment lines. Alignment lines enhance magical power. Or didn't you know that?"

"That's what I'd heard," he said sourly.

"But to what end? Why would someone need to use alignment lines for their railway?"

"To get from London to Edinburgh in two hours, I imagine."

"Hmm." She narrowed her eye, thinking.

He rose, smoothing out his coat. "We must surely start with the investigation of these men. Talk to them. See what they might be up to."

She rose and grabbed her umbrella. "I agree. But I should first like to examine one of the rail lines. Piccadilly is closest. Shall we go?"

"What?" He glanced at the clock. It was midnight. "Now? I thought we'd start in the morning…"

"No time like the present."

She whirled and threw open the door. His heart gave a sputter. He had to admit, at least to himself, that having her back caused a thrill to run through him. He grabbed his hat from the table and hurried to follow her outside.

The fog was even thicker than it had been earlier in the evening. It seemed impossible to navigate to where they needed to go.

"Perhaps a cab…" he said, stumbling over the kerb.

"Nonsense, Mr. Kazsmer. Even cabs can't navigate in this. We shall have to go by careful calculation." She flipped open the top of her umbrella handle, revealing a compass. "Of course," she muttered, "I'm not precisely certain of the coordinates but the Piccadilly station can't be far."

Leopold did his best to peer into and past the fog, but it was quite impossible. He did withdraw his wand just in case they ran into trouble, a likely event in the company of the still mysterious Special Inspector.

Mingli did little to watch the street before her. Either she was assured that Leopold would assist her if she were in danger of a collision, or her supreme confidence in her own capacity rose above all else. Instead, she concentrated her left eye as well as her enhanced one on the small compass on her umbrella handle.

She directed him down the pavement, but abruptly darted across the street. The specter of a carriage suddenly loomed out of the mist and the horse reared back.

"Bloody hell!" yelled the cabby. "You should know better than to do a damn fool thing like that on a night like this. Leave it to a bloody woman."

Without tearing her eyes from the compass, she whipped out her badge so quickly, even Leopold wasn't certain she hadn't used some sort of sleight of hand. "I'm a special inspector from Scotland Yard. I recommend you slow your pace, sir." She tucked it away again as she reached the other side of the street. Leopold hid his wand as he shrugged an apology to the cabby and he hurried to catch up to her.

The street signs were too far up the walls to be seen in the mist, and Leopold relied on Mingli's diligence with the compass. When the recognizable building suddenly emerged from the fog, he wondered why he ever doubted her. As she turned her face toward him with a magnificent smile all his ire was forgotten.

Piccadilly station had all the most modern conveniences and design. Of course, none of it could be detected in the dense fog surrounding it, even the spire on its glass-domed roof was invisible. As they climbed the wide stairs the vast array of double doors revealed themselves, and Leopold stepped up smartly to pull open the doors closest to them. He yanked, but they remained steadfastly shut.

"Dash it," he muttered. "It appears to be closed."

Mingli slapped the lid of the compass shut and leaned on the handle of her umbrella. "We do need to get in."

Leopold glanced around out of habit. Surely if they couldn't see anyone, no one would be able to see them. He opened his hand, concentrated on the lock, and summoned the magic to him. It was only a little magic—nothing but a spark for so simple a task—and it barely left him out of breath as the lock clicked and the door swung open.

"Jolly good," she said, stepping forward and using her umbrella like a cane.

Leopold followed into the dark interior. The polished tiled floors gleamed in the blunted glow of the gas lamps outside the high arched windows, leaving the vast chamber in a sort of gray light. Above their heads, the complicated cross-hatch of ironwork trusses upheld the high ceilings, while pillars of marble did their best to add an air of elegance to a normally sooty and smelly place, though with the application of enormous ceiling fans dotting the ironwork it did do to circulate the air.

Of course, they weren't spinning now, and the air settled around them like a padlocked warehouse; stale and uninhabited.

Out of the gloom rose the W. H. Smith kiosk, its day-old newspapers, magazines, and books safe behind locked scissor gates. A little further down were the pillars and pediment of the Spiers & Pond Refreshment Room. Its door, too, was firmly shut.

Yet he felt a draft, and when he glanced over his shoulder, he could just about make out the large sign hanging from the rafters that said, "To the Platform". He walked along, his shoes clacking and reverberating across the tiles, echoing in the absence of the day's steam-puffing engines, the constant stream of bowler-topped men of all character, and women with their fascinators and ruffles, all milling about and waiting on the trains or running to catch them just leaving the station with an enormous cloud of steam and sooty smoke.

It was *they* now—he and Mingli—who were the ghosts of the station, drifting about, making their own noise, though he could almost hear the familiar call of the buskers flapping the Telegraph or the Times at the passersby or the smell of coffee and tea wafting up from the opened transoms over the refreshment room near the peanut vendors with the smell of their roasted fare. Instead, all was quiet and still... disturbingly so. Leopold had never been in an empty train station. Even when he was part of the Romani camp, they hurried to do their jobs amongst the throngs. There was nothing to be gained—nor stolen— from an empty platform.

And just beyond the W. H. Smith was, indeed, the platform, also behind scissor gates. The fog rolled in from the approaches on either side of the interior tracks. It furled over the rails like slow-moving ocean waves.

"If you don't mind my asking, Miss Zhao," he said softly, as one would speak in a church or art gallery, "what are we looking for?"

"Anything unusual."

"You can't be more specific, can you? It looks to be like any other railway station I have ever traversed."

"I assure you; it is not."

He adjusted his waistcoat and raised his face. Surely, if there was some sort of supernatural activity, his wrist tattoo would alert him. He was more attuned to it these days, having so recently doubled his contract with the Unholy Hosts of the Otherworld. But not so much as a prickle. Nevertheless, he shivered. It was damnably cold in that enormous structure.

"I say," he began, with the intention of telling her to pack it in for the night. But he stopped. Smelled…something on the breeze. It wasn't the acrid smell of *Sitra Achra*, thank goodness, but something far different. Something almost…pleasant. He walked forward slowly, toward the platform. It could have come in with the fog, but somehow, he didn't think so. A fresh scent, like…leaves. Yes. That's what it was. Like autumn leaves newly fallen from the tree. Like the days he was a carefree child, when both his parents were alive, and he would leap into the carefully raked leaves in their back garden. The smell of earth, in its purest form.

He touched the scissor gate with his gloved hand and it whined open just enough.

"Mr. Kazsmer…" said Mingli softly.

"Just a moment." Enthralled, he moved forward. The fog began enveloping the platform as it had done on the streets of London. Still, Leopold knew where the edge of the platform was, could almost hear the hum of the rails. But that was silly. The rails didn't hum, especially when no trains moved along them.

"Mr. Kazsmer." She was nearer to him, but the caution in her voice was more acute.

"Just another moment, Miss Zhao." His steps brought him to the very edge of the platform. The scent was strongest here. Strange. The steam and soot should have wiped away any earthy scent like that. But maybe the fog brought it.

He looked down at the rails, stretching off into the distance as pale unbroken lines, gleaming almost with their own iridescent glow. They curved and flowed one over the other from switched rails and turnouts to the regular lines running outward toward parts unknown. Their pale paths intrigued him, and girding himself, he jumped down from the platform to stand on the rails.

"Leopold!" called Mingli.

"There's something...something here." He followed the tracks, stepping nimbly over the ties and into the ballast. Even as it grew mistier, he walked faster. He was being drawn forward. He felt it. But he had no idea what it might be.

"Leo! Wait!" she called from behind.

But now he slowed, for the scent—the *feeling*—was strongest nearby. He could almost reach out and...

When he looked down, he gasped. Mingli's gloved hands grasped his arms from behind. "Good God," she whispered.

Leopold found himself crouching, looking at the strange object...the strange...*being*. "What is it?"

Mingli came around him and knelt. "It's what I feared."

Lying half on a tie and half in the ballast, was a small-boned human-like creature, no bigger than a rabbit. It wore some sort of leafy dress exposing the legs from the thighs down. No shoes or slippers shod those oddly long feet. The skin was gray, but Leopold somehow felt it should have been green, perhaps a pale green. The face was in repose, eyes closed, mouth slightly open...and within, tiny pearl teeth. A long face, with elongated nose and eyes, short hair, and delicately pointed ears.

Yet, the most amazing aspect of all, were its transparent wings, like a dragonfly's, rainbow colors rippling across their surface. They lay flattened beneath it, slightly bent. Useless.

"It's a faery," said Mingli with great gravity. "And this tiny immortal creature...appears, impossibly..." She looked up at Leopold. "It appears to be...*dead*."

CHAPTER THREE

LEOPOLD SCOOPED UP the little creature in his hands. Limbs and neck lay loose, the head fallen back. She—for he felt she *was* a "she"— weighed nothing at all. He gazed tenderly at the lifeless creature and his heart broke. For he knew that this was something intensely fantastic that was suddenly gone from the world.

"You knew this was going to be here," he said softly to Mingli. "How did you know?"

"I...didn't *know* exactly," she said softly. "But I suspected."

"How?"

"That explanation is too long for a cold platform. Let us take her with us."

"Where?"

"To my flat."

"Your...flat?" The revelation of the existence of faeries was momentous, but perhaps not as much as her finally inviting him to her lodgings.

He rose, clutching the creature to his breast and followed her out through the station. On the steps outside, he thought it prudent to hide the faery within his coat. Without words, he walked beside Mingli as she strode forward with sure steps through the fog.

He wasn't certain where they were, but he thought it wasn't too far from his own lodgings on Regent Street. They climbed some stairs of a terraced house and entered into a dim, tiled foyer. The tarnished brass gas light fixture above them seemed careworn and slightly bent, with one of its mantles missing. The gas hissed from the naked burner tip and the other mantles flickered their weak light.

She marched across the entry and through another door that revealed a narrow, painted staircase, like a servant's stair. They climbed that until they reached the top, just below the attic. The floor had one or two other doors, but the corridor looked unused, with paint peeling and even a bit of refuse carelessly left in the dim corners. He suddenly felt very badly for Mingli. Surely as a Special Inspector she should be receiving ample salary. But he realized for a woman of Chinese origin, this may not be the case.

She put her key in the lock of one obscure door at the end of the gallery, dimly lit by another sputtering gas lamp. He was about to offer his…what? Apologies? Condolences? All of it would seem shallow somehow. He kept his own counsel, which was probably for the best…at least if he didn't want to experience her sharp tongue.

Little wonder in the brief time he'd known her that she did not bring him here. She was probably as ashamed of her poverty as Leopold had been growing up in the Romani camps.

She opened the door and stepped in. Leopold hesitated, but when she turned up the gas within, he couldn't stall any longer.

He halted on the threshold and gawped. The room was resplendent in heavy furniture with elaborately carved legs and chair backs. Dark, floral wallpaper competed with heavy velvet and tasseled drapery, with delicate figurines in pride of place on her mantel above a fireplace made of sculpted marble with an arched opening and shiny, silver grill. A large, round window facing the street of stained glass filled the wall, reminiscent of the rosette window in Notre Dame. Candlesticks in gold, crystal decanters on silver platters, and a wall filled with horrific masks from several different tribes of Africa and Asia, all made him blink in wonder. And, lying in the center of the floor, a tiger skin rug, with the head of the beast caught in mid-snarl, its sharp teeth bared.

Every corner of the room was as clean as a whistle.

"Here, Mr. Kazsmer. Place her here."

Leopold roused himself and looked where she gestured: to an enormous mahogany desk with a maroon leather top. An ornately styled lamp in cast bronze of a naked woman that reminded him all too much of Mingli's sensuous curves sat on the leather. She pulled a cord within its colorful Tiffany shade and a series of clicks and igniting gas suddenly illuminated the desktop.

Leopold stepped over the tiger's head and laid the faery on the desk. She was about fifteen inches long, with delicate bone structure and nearly translucent skin. The wings had been hopelessly crushed by his stuffing her within his coat, and he felt some amount of guilt for that desecration. It was akin to plucking the feathers from an angel's wings.

Mingli had dropped her umbrella in its stand upon entering, and set about examining the faery with her enhanced eye.

"I believe she is young for a faery. Perhaps eighty years old, or so."

"Wait. Miss Zhao. You don't seem at all surprised by the appearance of a faery, dead or alive."

She snapped up, her spine as straight as a ramrod. She lifted her chin. "I'm not. What does surprise me is that *you* were unaware of the existence of these woodland creatures."

"I…"

"You've already told me how your research seems to only involve the Kabbalah and Jewish mysticism. I must say, I am surprised. I was given to understand that you eschew your heritage as a Jew."

Her words, as always, were abrupt enough to raise his hackles. "I have my reasons," he said between gritted teeth.

She paused, seemingly to wait for more from him. When it wasn't forthcoming, she huffed a breath. "And you will not share them. Well! It's high time you understand more of the world, Mr. Kazsmer."

"I am very well-acquainted with the world, Miss Zhao. As well as the plains of Gehenna, I might add."

"Yes, of course, but such things don't always have precedent over the world at hand. *Our* world, in point of fact, Mr. Kazsmer. There are supernatural threats that do not derive from other planes of existence. I thought I had taken pains to point that out but, apparently, you weren't listening."

"I…" But she seemed to have dismissed him again and turned away. She grasped something from her mantel and took it to the desk, setting it down. It was a large bell jar, and within seemed to be the shriveled remains of…something.

"What the devil *is* that?"

"A faery. An older one. These are very rare, as you can imagine. Because these creatures are immortal, it is very difficult to kill them."

"Did *you* kill this one?" he asked, peering in at the jar's dusky interior. He'd seen something similar in sideshows. One was a mermaid, he recalled...but that was later revealed to be a fraud. It was cobbled from the upper half of a mummified monkey sewn to the lower have of a dried bass.

She slammed her hand to the table, rattling the bell jar and startling Leopold so much that he jerked upright.

"Do you imagine for the briefest of moments that I would be capable of doing harm to these creatures?"

Seldom had he seen her so angry. He took a step back and placed his hand upon his heart. "Forgive me, Miss Zhao. I have yet to fully comprehend the whole of these circumstances. The...the nature of them. Perhaps I just assumed you were saving yourself under threat of their magic."

She blinked and softened her features, yanking on the short jacket. "I see. Then there is no need to apologize. As you say, you are ignorant of these creatures and their place in the world."

"Won't you tell me?" he asked in an appeasing tone.

She set about meticulously arranging the newly dead faery by sitting it up, knees raised, placing its arms atop its knees, and then laying the head gently on the arms. She straightened the wings as best she could, and for all the world, the little faery looked as if it were only taking a nap while perched on a mushroom.

She crossed to a chinoiserie cabinet on the other side of the room, an ornate ambry of incised black lacquer with marquetry of mother of pearl and inlaid lighter wood depicting a scene of Chinese men fishing in fanciful landscapes of willows and impossible rocks jutting straight into the air. She took hold of one of the tasseled handles, opened it, and took out an empty bell jar. When she returned to the table, Leopold gasped in shock.

"You...you aren't going to put that...that faery in that jar, are you?"

"Of course. I must not allow the elements to destroy it."

"But…that's ghastly. It's a creature. A strange one, I'll admit. But it's almost human. Isn't it?"

She carefully placed the seated faery on the wooden platform, raised the glass dome, and lowered it over the creature. She turned a handle at the top and it made a sucking sound and Leopold realized it had sealed. "I preserve all such creatures when I find them," she said. "Much as one might preserve a favorite bird or monkey. I study them. For indeed, it's beastly hard to study them in the wild when they are alive."

"I can't quite believe it," said Leopold softly. He couldn't help but lean over and examine the perfectly preserved faery. "I mean…I have encountered all manner of Otherworld creatures, but I never believed in faeries. That was just a child's tale." He looked from the pleasant one to the wizened one, and back again. "What happened to them?"

"You finally ask the important question." He hadn't noticed her move away from the desk, but she had ensconced herself by her fireplace and was just lighting the bowl of a long-stemmed brass pipe.

"Miss Zhao!"

She ignored him and puffed on the mouthpiece, blowing out perfect rings of some fragrant smoke.

"Really!" he said, affronted. "Opium?"

"Leo, you're embarrassing yourself," she said out of the side of her mouth, taking another long drag and blowing out the smoke. "It's tobacco, you silly man. I'd never indulge in anything that would cloud my mind. Tobacco sharpens it." She pushed away from the fireplace — puffing away on the long stem — and approached the cabinet again. She cast both doors wide, and Leopold saw, much to his horror and amazement, an array of similar bell jars and glass cannisters filled with strange wizened beings.

"Good God. You've been collecting them."

"Yes. And do you know that the first was collected more than ten years ago." She tapped on the glass of one on the top shelf. "But all these others," and she swept her hand among the three shelves, "were collected in the last month."

"Why is it happening?"

"That's what I need your help with."

"And the railway has something to do with it? Are they being hit by the engines?"

"We've had a railway system in this country for more than forty years. No, it can't be that. But it might have to do with that particular railway."

Leopold scrubbed at his forehead.

Just then her wall clock chimed the half hour, and he saw that it was one-thirty. He stared at it, momentarily hypnotized by the swinging brass pendulum in its wooden case.

Mingli spoke aloud what he was thinking. "It's late, Mr. Kazsmer. Perhaps it's best we resume this conversation in the morning."

"Yes. Quite right."

"Here. I want you to take this with you for study." When he turned, she was holding the bell jar with the wizened faery, her long-stemmed pipe protruding from her lips.

"Oh, I couldn't."

"Mr. Kazsmer." Impatience was creeping into her voice. "Do take it. I think it will offer a world of information to you—should you care to glean any."

He stared at the thing a long time, before politeness more than anything else made him reach out and take it from her. "Er…thank you, Miss Zhao."

She walked to a window and nudged the curtain aside. "I'm afraid it's still quite foggy out there. Perhaps you'd prefer to spend the night here."

The bell jar nearly slipped from his hands, but he wrapped his arms around it as it teetered and clasped it to his chest. "I…I…"

"My guest room is most comfortable."

He breathed again, sending all his outrageous notions to the wind. "That's very kind of you. But I must get home."

"Where shall we meet tomorrow? I should like to get Raj's opinion on the matter. At the Whitechapel lockup?"

"Oh no. Raj stays at the theatre. But we have a private place to confer with him. Yes, meet me at the theatre at nine o'clock. No one else should be there at that time."

She studied him for a moment, puffing disturbingly on the long pipe. "Let me give you a carrying case for that. You can't swan about London with that in the open."

"It's hardly in the open when the fog is so dense."

"I'd wish you'd reconsider spending the night," she said, her voice muffled with her head stuck in something like a wardrobe. She pulled out a large square leather case with a handle on top. "This should do."

She placed it on the desk and opened the latch. The top folded back and there was ample room to lower the bell jar inside. She set down her pipe and snatched the jar from Leopold so abruptly he was in fear again of dropping it, but her sure hands were able to clasp it and deliver it into the box. She slapped the lid closed, latched it, and took it by the handle. "Here," she said. "Now you may carry it incognito."

He hefted it and turned toward the door, not pleased with the idea of the walk through the fog.

When he got to the door and opened it, he peered into the less than attractive corridor. He couldn't help himself when he said, "Why do you live in such a place, Miss Zhao? Surely on a detective's salary…"

She laughed—a musical, merry sound that drew him back toward her. "You think I am *forced* by circumstances to live here? Oh, Leo. You are such a dear man. You will be pleased to note that Her Majesty keeps me very well in good English coin. I *choose* to live here for its anonymity. Who would come to such a place seeking me out? I have many enemies, and it's best they don't know precisely where I live. In fact, it was only because of the fog that we entered by the front door. I assure you, there are many secret entrances that no enemy will ever discover."

"I should have known," he muttered, glancing past her into her perfectly grand surroundings. "Forgive me for underestimating you."

"They all do…to their detriment. But Leopold…" She reached out a hand to cup his face. "It is sweet of you to be concerned."

"It's nothing of the kind. I just don't like the idea of a colleague who isn't getting her due."

"Of course." A smirk curved her lips.

He raised his topper. "I bid you good-night, Miss Zhao."

"And you, Mr. Kazsmer. Do be careful out there."

He withdrew his wand. "I intend to be."

When he glanced back at her, she was watching him as he walked the length of the dim corridor, through the door to the stairwell, and even as he closed the door behind him...

—————◆—————

ONCE HE GOT home, despite the time—and he had gotten turned around in the fog which took him much longer than planned—he found he wasn't sleepy. Thoughts of Mingli Zhao always kept him awake and, well...aroused...but he tried to forget the latter.

He put his key in the lock and opened the door to the darkened interior. The foyer lay in gray shadows, with only the shapes of table and curio cabinet identified from Leopold's dark-adjusted eyes. But even before he lit the gas, he felt that something was wrong. And then his tattoo burned and he nearly dropped the case containing the faery in its bell jar. He quickly lit the lamp and turned it up.

His drawing room was in shambles: chairs strewn about with their upholstery in tatters, tables overturned, crockery smashed. As he strode forward into the open bedroom door, he stopped again. The bolster was shredded, the wardrobe pulled to the floor, and mirrors were shattered.

And everywhere, he felt the presence of malevolent magic.

CHAPTER FOUR

HE STOOD FOR a moment wondering what to do first, when there was violent knocking on his front door.

He set down the case in the middle of the pandemonium of the drawing room and strode quickly to the foyer. He stood before his front door a moment before pulling out his wand. The presence of so much magic should have filled him, made him powerful, but it hadn't. He looked at his wand as if to blame it, but it wasn't that. This magic... It was wrong. Something was wrong with it, and he couldn't...or *shouldn't*...access it.

He stuffed the wand away into his coat and pulled open the door, closing his hand into a fist, ready to fight.

A tramp stood on his doorstep. His gray frazzled hair stuck out under his dented bowler, and his frock coat was in no better shape. The tails were caked in dried mud and his shoes gaped at the soles.

"Uncle Yanko," he said quietly relieved, casting an eye over his shoulder at the detritus. "This isn't the best of times..."

The old man's eyes lit when he saw him. "Leopold! *Kis rovar.*"

"English, Uncle," he muttered.

Yanko tilted his head down, looking at Leopold from under his ragged brim. "English? Bah! What is so good about English?"

He straightened, fidgeting with his cuff. "What do you want? As I said, it isn't the best moment... Come to think of it, why are you out so late?"

Yanko gestured to the younger man, nodding his head. "You look like a prince. A king! Your mother would have been proud."

He chaffed at mention of his mother because there would be no such mention of his father except in disdainful terms. "What do you want?"

"Your uncle visits and you don't ask him in, don't offer him tea?"

"Uncle!" he rasped. "It is late. I have no time for this!"

The man sighed. "Ah! I see. You are ashamed of me. I know this."

Leopold couldn't help looking away…and glancing once more over his shoulder at the destruction.

"But your people are not ashamed of *you*, Leopold. They remember you. They talk of you. Of the little *okos*. You left us so early, so young."

"Must we go through this again? Is it money you want?"

"Why do you always think it is money? Money, money, money. You think too much about money, Nephew. Is all *this* not enough?"

Before Leopold could answer, Yanko pushed past him and stomped onto the tiled floor. "I came to warn you... Oh! It is too late."

"Warn me." He closed and locked the door behind him. "Was this destruction the doing of the men at the camp?" A strange rage began to billow inside him. He remembered well enough the taunts of "*didicoy!*" by the other Gypsy boys. *Half breed!*

Still, he couldn't help but recall how they had welcomed him into the camp six months ago, as if he'd never left. And this time they had treated him with respect. After all, he'd helped solve a murder of one of their own. And they knew he had done well as the famous "Great Enchanter". He supposed they thought he was wealthy. Well, he was getting there, but not quite yet.

"How did you know of this?" he asked, following his uncle into the drawing room.

"*Szent Isten!*" said Yanko. He pressed his hand with its dirty fingernails to his gray beard-stubbled face. "The man was here."

"What man?"

"He came to the camp after nightfall. He was…part machine. Mechanical. Parts of him gleamed. There was a sound with him, pistons hissing, metal clanking. A ticking. He destroyed everything he touched: caravans, cooking fires. He hurt those who tried to stop him. And…he killed a man."

Leopold shivered. Those were the sounds he'd heard earlier this night, following *him*.

"Who was he?"

"We don't know. But he asked where *you* were. He knew you, Leopold. He wanted to destroy you."

He thought hard but could not for the life of him recall anything that would have to do with him. "Tell me *exactly* what he looked like."

"He was a man," gestured Yanko, opening his arms wide. "A big man with mechanical legs and arms...and his eyes! They were...they were..." Yanko shook his head, seeming to search for the right words. "They glowed with the fires of Hell. It was difficult to see the rest of him in the firelight and with the commotion. But he said your name. Said that he would get his revenge on you. Leopold, what have you done?"

What *had* he done? "Uncle, I don't know. Is everyone safe? Those that are hurt, are they all right?"

"Yes, thank the good Lord. He was like a demon, this man. I told you no good would come of your father's dabbling."

"Please don't talk about my father," he muttered. It was an old refrain.

"Nothing like this would have happened if he hadn't meddled where he didn't belong. And you!" Suddenly, Yanko's hand was on his left wrist, pulling Leopold forward and pushing up the sleeve. "This! My God. It is even worse now. What have you done?"

He yanked his tattooed arm away from his uncle and pushed down the sleeve. "It's no business of yours. You've given me the warning. You can go now."

Yanko raised his head, fixed his thumbs in his waistcoat pockets, and spread his boots apart. "You dismiss me? Like I was a...a...*servant*? I should teach you lesson like I used to."

"You can try." Leopold stared him down. *Let the old man try to strike me. Let him.*

But Yanko did nothing. His frown was enough. He glanced around once more before stomping toward the front door, leaving a trail of mud in his wake.

Leopold took a deep breath and followed him.

"I go, then. That is what you want."

"Uncle Yanko..."

"No. You are *gadjo*, now. I should have known. I should have known this world outside the camp would change you."

"For the better, Uncle."

"So *you* say." He grabbed the door handle, but it would not budge. He whirled toward Leopold and gestured toward the door. "Your devil tricks."

He waved his hand and the magic of the lock clicked and opened the door. "They aren't devil tricks. It is simple magic."

Yanko looked pointedly to all the destruction in his foyer. "I see how well it has worked for you." The old man jerked around and stomped down the steps.

Leopold hovered in the doorway, watching him walk away, guilt gnawing at him. "Uncle! Uncle Yanko." He trotted down the steps to the pavement and started after him before Yanko stopped. He took out his coin purse and removed some sovereigns. "Uncle, take this to the others. It will help rebuild their caravans."

"You think your filthy money will solve everything." But even as he said it, he scooped it out of Leopold's palm and turned away again.

"Uncle." Leopold watched him go, when Yanko stopped again and turned.

"You have a sharp tongue these days, Leopold."

"I...I'm sorry, Uncle Yanko. I don't know why I am so short with you. Please. Extend my condolences to the family of the one who died."

Yanko came back with a smile and wrapped his big, calloused hand around the back of Leopold's neck. "You're a rich man. Rich men are used to yelling at underlings."

"You're not an underling. And I do worry about you."

"You worry about me, I worry about you. It is all equal, then." He patted the back of Leopold's head and let his hand fall away. "Be careful, Nephew," he said over his shoulder.

"Take care, Uncle," he whispered, watching the old man shuffle away.

With a deep sigh, he climbed his steps again, locked his door, and warded it once more, fingers dancing in patterns that glowed and meandered up the door posts and over the lintel. He was certain he had set the wards when he left this morning. They should have kept everything out, especially the supernatural. Who was this mechanical man? He knew that Leopold came from the Romani camp. Why was he following him? What vengeance did he need?

He stood in the foyer and closed his eyes, breathing deeply. No. He hadn't enough magic to clean this up. He had no choice.

He took off his coat and pushed up his sleeve. Taking the switchblade from his waistcoat pocket, he poised with the gleaming blade over his smooth, pale skin, just above the tattoo. He dreaded the cut, for he'd had to cut deeper again these days. When he first got the second tattoo, his magical strength had been renewed, and the slashes required to draw blood were a minor inconvenience, just like they had been in the beginning. But as the days tolled on, he'd had to cut deeper and deeper, losing more blood with each summoning. Eurynomos would heal the wound, savoring the blood he consumed, but Leopold feared that one day, he wouldn't arrive in time and he would bleed out. He feared it almost as much as *Sitra Achra* itself. But no. He'd do what he needed to do. And if slashing nearly to the bone was what was needed to call Eurynomos, then so be it.

Gritting his teeth, he slashed quickly across his tattooed wrist.

Instantly, a bright flash and a doorway of pure light opened in his foyer. Out stepped a huge daemon, ten feet tall, with wide shoulders. He was naked except for a black breechclout that draped to the floor. His skin was a deep red, scaly and shiny. Two enormous, twisting horns rose up from his bald scalp, and his fingers and toes sported long sharpened talons.

He reached out and grasped Leopold's bleeding wrist, closing the talons around the human arm, and instantly healed the slash. He threw back his head and licked his lips with a forked tongue as if he had just eaten his fill of a lavish feast. And when he seemed satisfied, he suddenly glanced around with alarm. "Leo, old man. What's amiss in here?"

The West End baritone of his old friend's voice always comforted. "Someone...some*thing* has gone on a rampage looking for me, leaving destruction in his wake."

"Good grief. Are you all right?" The daemon's enormous hands roved over him, looking for broken bones, he supposed.

"I am well, Eurynomos, but he destroyed the Romani camp where my family came from, and has been following me in the fog tonight. This is what I came home to."

"Unconscionable!" he bellowed. "Leo, I hope you will allow me to fix this catastrophe."

"If…if you will, Eurynomos. I was unable to summon the magic. This other enchantment seems to have overwhelmed what little magic I had left."

"Hmm. Yes, it does taste decidedly different."

"You *taste* the magic?"

"Oh yes. All the senses come to the fore when it comes to my place in Gehenna. I am not called the Prince of Death for nothing. And I don't like the taste of this at all."

"Well, I'd be obliged if you can fix what you can."

"'Fix what I can'!" He laughed, a fine, deep sound like the lowing of a bull. He drew back his arms and brought his hands together in a single, loud clap like thunder. A whirlwind seemed to come up from the floor and swirled around the two of them, while Eurynomos grinned his shark-like teeth. When the whirlwind fell away, all was as it had been before. Not a broken shard of pottery, not a speck of glass, nor tattered curtain remained. Ceramic figurines stood intact. French-style doors were as they were, and even the strange odor of the magic, seemed to have been wiped clean.

"That was magnificent. Thank you, old friend."

"Think nothing of it. Shall I pursue this miscreant? Tell you what I find?"

"Yes. That's probably the wisest thing."

"Then I shall leave you. You'll be all right?"

"Of course. Thank you again, Eurynomos."

Instead of stepping into a line of light as he usually did when exiting to Gehenna, he simply vanished. Since he was staying on this plane, he'd naturally be traveling differently. Leopold felt better knowing Eurynomos was on the case, but he knew he would have to pick up the search when the daemon had exhausted his investigations. He didn't think this creature—whatever it was—would be very easy to find.

He walked back into the drawing room and saw that the carrying case had been placed with care on the table in the center of the room. He smiled at the tidiness of his daemon friend, and crossed the room to turn up the gas for better light. He pulled the bell jar from the case and placed it on the table. "Poor little blighter," he muttered. The faery sat in more or less the same position in which Mingli had put the newest one, but his skin, instead of being pale gray, had darkened to what those mummies in the British Museum looked like, tanned leather stretched taut over the bones beneath. The same pointed ears, nose, and delicate features as the others. Though this was male. He wore no shirt and instead was bedecked in some sort of leafy briefs over his lower half. His wings were different from the female. They seemed more like moth wings.

The eyes were shut tight and he grimaced in death, as most humans did.

Dash it. He should have shown this to Eurynomos. He almost called out to him to bring him back, but he supposed the daemon's current mission was more important.

And…by Jove! He wouldn't need to shed blood to call on his *other* minion. He clasped his right hand over the All-Seeing Eye on his left wrist, and called out, "Suchah!"

Instantly, a disgusting little imp appeared at his feet. It was red, naked, and scaly, with small bat-wings, flapping webbed feet, and a forked tongue it liked to whip around its mouth. It flapped-paced in a circle, spindly arms over its head. "Oh, dread Flesh Master! Why you torment Suchah? Suchah does not wish to smell the smells of humans and listen to their feeble woes."

"Oh, shut it, you little rotter." Leopold rolled his sleeve down again. He hated the little imp, but he had captured mastery over it, and he saw no reason not to use the creature when necessary. "I want you to tell me something."

"Horrid master. Yanking Suchah here and there. Always for stupid questions."

"If you don't shut it, I'll shut your mouth permanently."

Suchah slammed his hand over his mouth and stared up at Leopold with wide, glowing eyes.

"I want you to look at this creature and tell me all you know about it."

Suchah's eyes darted toward the bell jar and squinted. "Will do so because master ordered. But Suchah no like worldly things."

"So…faeries are part of this world…not another?"

The imp crinkled his nose. "Smells like it, too. Faeries, goblins, selkies, red caps, phooka…all of this smelly world. No like them."

"How did this one die? I thought…I thought an immortal thing couldn't die."

"Master is stupid mortal. Knows nothing."

Leopold backhanded the creature. "Answer the question."

Suchah held a hand to his cheek, though Leopold couldn't tell if he'd left a mark, since his whole body was red. The only mark that he *had* left was some six months ago; the Hebrew glyphs he'd cut into the flesh of the beast's little torso, the incantation that bound him to Leopold.

Suchah gestured petulantly toward the faery. "Obviously not. Immortals can die with right spells. Smelly Flesh Men are bad with such spells."

"Then are you saying that it wasn't men who killed this faery?"

'Not know. Not care. It is dead. Good." He spat at the jar. It sizzled on the glass. Leopold quickly wiped it away with a sweep of his magic. He didn't want the corrosive quality of Suchah's spittle to crack the jar.

"You're such a little cretin. Does nothing give you pleasure?"

"Death gives Suchah pleasure." He smiled wide. His sharp piranha teeth glistened.

Leopold pressed his fingers into the points of his weary eyes. It was too late to deal with the imp and to think more about it. "Very well," he said, without looking up. "Begone."

He didn't turn but heard the pop as Suchah hastened to leave.

Leopold sighed and peeled off his waistcoat, trousers, and shirt. He was even too tired to divest himself of his underwear. Instead, he switched off the gas and flopped into bed.

But when the chimes of his clock pealed far too early and woke him, he lay in bed blearily staring at the ceiling, wondering whether he need bother about getting up. Until he remembered he was meeting Mingli.

He sprang from bed, washed with the cold water in the jug, shaved, combed his mustache, and stood before his wardrobe, rubbing the warmth into his arms. He tried not to think of the alluring Miss Zhao, but it was impossible. He wanted so much to…to… But it was useless. Here she was, so worldly, so experienced, while he…

And then he thought about her "experience" in her uncle's brothel and gritted his teeth. Angry beyond comprehension at this uncle of hers, and her parents for selling her to him, Leopold shook in frustration, for he knew he could do nothing. Her parents were dead, this uncle was dead — killed by the very daemons or ghosts that had protected her. Now she, in turn, served the ghosts, not unlike Leopold's situation. Though, her contract seemed infinitely kinder. She did good in the world because of it. But Leopold…all he could do was cringe, waiting for the time they would call him, take his soul. There was no knowing when. There was no recourse or of working off the debt.

He *had* to study to discover what he could do to save his father while he was still able. So little time was left to him. That was all he knew. When he discovered from Suchah six months ago that his father *hadn't* died in the dreadful world of Gehenna but was instead trapped, he'd thrown himself into research. Only Eurynomos knew. Indeed, he'd been angry at the daemon, for he had known all along and hadn't told Leopold. But he had reconciled with Eurynomos. After all, the daemon had assumed there was nothing they *could* do.

Leopold refused to believe it.

He couldn't imagine the torment his father had endured all these years. Àkos Kazsmer had sacrificed himself for his son. And Leopold had so little time to figure out how to bring him back. Should he tell the others? Should he consult with Mingli? But no. There was too much at stake. He had to rely on his study, for he was now the expert on the realm of Gehenna and the dreaded pit, *Sitra Achra*. After all, he'd been there himself.

He had thought many a time of giving up his magic act to devote all his time to study, but how would he live? How could he have afforded the many books he had obtained? He supposed he could work the streets as he had done as a Romani thief, but that didn't sit well with him.

And what would Miss Zhao think if he had simply become a thief and beggar on the streets? How would he explain it?

"Ah, Mingli," he sighed, thinking of her mischievous smile, the gleam in her eye, her long slender neck, her shapely form, her...her legs when she raised her skirts to grab her ridiculous gun...

He leaned against the wardrobe. How did other men do it? They had their lovers. It needn't be a great romance. They had their fun with whores or mistresses, and the women wouldn't dream of getting in their companions' way.

But Mingli Zhao was so very different. She was not a strumpet to bed and toss away. And hadn't she had enough of that in her young life? No. He didn't want to use her and toss her away. He wanted to hold her, comfort her...love her...

"I'm a fool."

"Probably. Over who, now?"

Leopold whirled around, slamming against the wardrobe. "Spense!"

Inspector Despenser Thacker raised his bowler. "At your service." The bowler was transparent, as was his Ulster coat. And his handlebar mustache and face, when it came down to it. The man was a spirit, after all. A ghost.

"I'd appreciate not being scared half to death," said Leopold, turning back to his wardrobe and putting a hand to his thumping chest.

"Death ain't so bad. Don't knock it till you've tried it." He gave a loud guffaw and continued to chuckle for some time at his own joke.

Leopold never quite got over his guilt at Thacker's untimely demise at the hands of a demon sent to kill Leopold. And then Mingli had brought him back as a ghost, something neither Leopold nor Thacker would have wanted.

Yet, here he was.

"So, who are you being a fool over, Leo? I think I can guess."

"Can you now?" he said, bristling.

"Might it be the lovely Miss Zhao, our Special Inspector?"

Leopold felt his face blaze with heat. "I don't wish to discuss it."

"Oh. That's a 'yes', then."

"Spense!"

"Very well." The inspector glided across the room, and made as if to sit. As he had explained it, he couldn't quite feel objects in this world, but Raj had taught him how to mimic his old self and he was able to float very close to chairs. He'd practiced hard to do so. "Is she back, then?"

"Yes, she's only just returned," he said, tying his tie. He grabbed his frock coat and shrugged into it, tucking the wand in one inner pocket and his loaded Webley in another.

"And when are you going to say something to her? You're obviously within her thrall."

"'In her thrall'. Really, Thacker."

"You can deny it all you like. But it's obvious to all of us. Probably even to the lady herself. Though what you'd be doing with a Chinky…"

"I beg of you not to further use that term."

"Oh. Right. I forgot."

Leopold finished setting his cravat and reached for a hat box. "Miss Zhao and I have a working relationship, just as ours was. We investigate things. And she has brought an interesting investigation into my hands."

"Oh? Does it have to do with that damnable thing under glass in your drawing room?"

"As it happens…it does." He turned, hat fixed on his head with the slightest of fashionable tilts. "Thacker, have you ever seen the like in your travels as a…as a ghost?"

"Seen the likes of that?" He thumbed toward the other room. "I should hope not. Never heard of anything that ugly in the world. Is it a demon?"

"No. Miss Zhao says that it is a faery."

"Blimey." He burst into laughter, rocking forward with it. "That's a faery?"

"It isn't funny, Thacker. Miss Zhao has a theory of some kind that a new railway has something to do with killing them. They are, after all, immortal creatures. It seems odd that they are dying."

"Oh." Thacker stopped laughing and pushed up his bowler thoughtfully. "You mean there really are such a thing as faeries?"

"Are there such things as ghosts?"

Thacker laid a finger aside his nose. "Point. But here now. I thought if you were immortal, then you couldn't die? Ain't that the definition?"

"And I thought so too." He grabbed a walking stick which he had modified to hold his wand and headed for the door. "I must run. I'm meeting her at the theatre."

Thacker floated after Leopold and hovered in the foyer. "Shall I accompany you? I could be of help."

"Of course. Why not?" As he reached the door, the bell rang. A shape of a figure formed on the oval of frosted glass before him. It looked suspiciously like Mingli Zhao.

He pulled the door open and she turned, offering him a brilliant smile. "Mr. Kazsmer, good morning. I thought I'd catch you here."

"Miss Zhao," he said, lifting the brim of his hat without thinking, "It was my understanding that we were to meet at the theatre."

"Of course, but I thought this might be more advantageous. And we can walk there together. Oh, Inspector. How nice to see you."

Thacker had been hiding behind the curtain to the drawing room, and sheepishly drew forward. He doffed his hat. "Miss Zhao. Always a pleasure."

She moved past him into the drawing room and stood before the object in the bell jar. "Have you studied it, Mr. Kazsmer?"

"I have. Even got the opinion of my imp."

She made a face. "So distasteful a creature. What did he have to say about it?"

"Not much. I was curious as to where they came from, if from another plane like Gehenna, for instance. He confirmed that they were from *our* plane."

"I have always thought so, but confirmation is good to have. Well? Shall we be off?"

"I'll meet you there," said Thacker, and immediately vanished.

Leopold bit his lip. *Should* he tell Mingli about the mechanical man? He supposed it didn't matter. She was good at being prepared for all sorts of dangers. He only hoped he wouldn't encounter the blighter when she was around.

"I advise bringing the creature with us," she said, snapping Leopold out of his ruminations. He packed the jar back into its carrying case and grabbed the handle. Escorting Mingli to the door, he locked it—surreptitiously warding it as well—and trotted down the terraced house stairs.

They walked toward the King's Garden Theatre. Seldom were they together in the light of day and now that the fog had lifted as well, besides the usual soot and smoke in the air they had a clear view before them—and passersby had a clear view of *them*. For a moment, Leopold grew increasingly uncomfortable at the savage stares he received—just as he had garnered when he was garbed as a Romani street urchin after his father died. But he soon realized that those stares were not for him, but for his companion.

He longed to take her arm to protect her but, of course, she needed no such protection, neither from their hurtful stares nor from any other danger. She could well defend herself. And she didn't like being touched, at any rate. She'd made that painfully plain from the start.

And yet, in the next instant, he felt her satin-clad arm link with his. Her umbrella was opened behind her, framing her intriguing face and feathery hat. "I fear," she said quietly, "that the antagonistic expressions of London's citizenry forces me to hang upon your arm, Mr. Kazsmer. I hope your solicitousness will calm the more viral of onlookers."

"It is my extreme pleasure, Miss Zhao, to comply."

She turned a brief smile on him that he was loath to admit made him melt that much inside.

When they turned the corner and the theatre was in sight, he felt better. They would soon find the solace they sought within those walls. He glanced proudly at the bill posted in its gilded frame. "Leopold Kazsmer, the Great Enchanter!" it proclaimed, followed by a play about a maiden and sorcerer, and in smaller type the various acts that were included on the bill: a trained act with cats. "See Pepper's Ghost!" it screamed in exaggeratedly large type at the bottom of the bill. Pepper's Ghost was a difficult enough act to perform for any magician, but for Leopold, it was as simple as could be, having the services of his very own ghost to perform it.

He looked both ways as he unlocked the stage door, and finally opened the portal, let her through, and locked it behind him again.

"Hullo!" he called out in the echoing space. When he received no reply, he called out again, "Raj!"

There was a strange and unfamiliar sound. Clanking metal. And for a moment, he was transported to last night in the fog as he was leaving the theatre for the pub. The strange metallic sound following him...until it formed into the hissing pistons and squeaking wheels of Raj's table.

"Leopold, my friend! Oh, I have wanted to speak to you most urgently." He came around the corner and suddenly stopped. "Forgive me. I see you brought the most interesting special inspector with you, but I failed to...forgive me. Miss Zhao. Always a pleasure."

"How kind of you, Raj," she said, as they passed to the backstage area.

"I am pleased to see you again, Miss Zhao," he said with a slight bow. He was wearing the turban of gold lamé from last night, and his boiled shirt and tailcoat were crisp and clean. His accent was that of an Indian man, but neither Raj nor Leopold were ever certain of his exact origins. It could have been India as much as any other place. He was perpetually seated at his wheeled table, having only an upper torso.

Mingli took the hand he offered and gave it a shake.

Raj looked from Mingli to Leopold and seemed agitated, which was unusual for the automaton. Leopold started to ask but Raj plowed forward with. "I, er...have been reading the cards." His table turned and rolled toward the small office Leopold used for encounters with Raj, Thacker, and Eurynomos. He had requested the private office at the theatre as a discreet rehearsal space, and Barnabas Dawes, the theatre owner, had grudgingly complied. Leopold held the door open for the both of them and they went in. He then closed and locked the door.

"Oh? And what have you found?" Leopold wasn't certain of the veracity of the tarot cards Raj read, or if his mechanical mind found the layers of these predictions all on his own. Still, it was best not to discount anything his mystical friends came up with.

Raj tapped the deck neatly stacked before him. "The cards have been issuing me some interesting portents, though I little understand their nature."

"Can you tell us?" asked Mingli anxiously. She seemed to accept everything that came her way. Well, she wasn't wrong, thought Leopold. She had relied on understanding a wide variety of magical information from a staggering plethora of sources. More of which, Leopold was beginning to realize, *he* should himself be studying.

"As I understand it," Raj began, absently tapping the deck with his small porcelain hand, "there is something large approaching. Something magical and dangerous."

"I do wish your cards were more specific, old man," said Leopold.

Raj did his equivalent of a shrug with his brass cage of a body. "The cards are what they are."

"Well, I believe you didn't need your cards to predict that something was afoot with the sudden appearance of our Miss Zhao."

A loud pop of air displacement announced the arrival of Inspector Thacker. "Did I miss anything?"

Raj gestured, his gears whirring, his joints giving a soft squeak. "I believe Miss Zhao was just about to elucidate us on the current problem."

CHAPTER FIVE

"I AM AFRAID," said Mingli, walking sedately about the room, examining the various tricks and tropes of Leopold's magical career, "that I have nothing more to elucidate than I did at the start of this investigation nearly two months ago. But I hoped to get your insight on the problem, Raj. And you, of course, Inspector Thacker." She gestured to Leopold to place the carrying case on the table.

Leopold did and summarily opened it, bringing out the bell jar.

"Must you carry around that bloody thing?" said Thacker, sneering at it.

But Raj seemed mesmerized. He rolled his table closer and raised his hands in awe. "*Yaksha!*" he murmured.

"Yes," said Mingli. "We call them faeries in this country."

"How was this creature captured?"

"He wasn't captured," she said, leaning over and peering closely at it. How many times had she done so over the months, Leopold wondered, and remained intrigued by it? "He was found. Dead."

"Dead?" Raj gestured and Mingli brought the jar to his table and set it before him. He slowly turned it to examine all sides, his strange porcelain hands clinking softly on the glass. "Curious."

"And I have many more specimens just like it at home."

He looked up at her. "This is not good."

"No, it isn't. Any thoughts on the matter?"

He slowly shook his head. "Only what the cards tell me. And they warn of great and terrible events. But this…" He turned the faery several more times. "Were they all found in the same place?"

Mingli's face suddenly brightened. Leopold, enchanted, drew closer. "And now you ask the proper questions. They were all found—in various places—along the routes of the new railway, Kobold & Hob."

"And what is significant in this? Were they struck?"

"No. Not struck. I cannot find in any way that they were killed. I did an autopsy on one specimen."

"Miss Zhao!"

"Really, Mr. Kazsmer, if you are to be appalled at everything I do, I hardly think it conducive to the two of us working together."

Taken aback, Leopold straightened. When he glanced at Raj, there was a sparkle in his eye. Unnerved, he yanked at his swallowtail coat, though all was in order. "I…I merely expressed…surprise…at your taking such liberties. After all, isn't that something more suited to the likes of a physician?"

"And do you currently know of any physicians who would gladly work on the corpse of a faery and keep our secrets?"

Leopold drew silent.

She nodded. "Well then. As I said, I did not discover the cause of death. But I think it has something to do with the alignment lines."

Raj wheeled closer. "In what sense? I would suppose that the magical enhancements offered by the alignment lines would give the faeries more power."

"Yes indeed. It should. But the nature of the railway, using the pattern of the alignment lines to run their tracks along, seems to have disrupted something about the lines. Or the power itself."

Raj stared at her for a long moment. If one wasn't certain he *could* move, one might assume he *wouldn't*. But then he seemed to sigh. "Curious," he said again. "Roads have long used the path of the alignment lines to no affect. But the *iron* workings of a train…"

"Ah, yes," said Mingli thoughtfully. "I quite forgot about the iron."

"What about the iron?" asked Leopold.

Mingli rested her hand on the bell jar, studying the creature within. "Iron is one of the elements that can ward off faeries."

Leopold brooded. "While the engines themselves are made of iron, the tracks are created from steel."

"Indeed?" she said. "You are clever, aren't you, Mr. Kazsmer. The tracks themselves are steel." She gazed contemplatively into the middle distance.

Raj reached for his cards, something he was wont to do when he was perplexed. He shuffled them in a strange ballet of immovable fingers, yet did it so quickly and efficiently that one couldn't guess exactly how it *was* done.

He laid out one card and then another. "A terror is coming," he said. He laid another card above the first two. "Power and speed will lead to death." Leopold and Mingli exchanged knowing glances. "The agents of destruction know no limits. They will not stop. They will show no mercy." Card. "The City of the River will find no peace when the dead walk." Card. "It begins in the circle." Card. "The crown will fall."

Raj laid his hand upon the upturned cards and lowered his head. "I fear that is all the cards will tell me," he said.

"Power and speed are obviously the railway," said Leopold.

"The 'agents of destruction'," said Mingli, thoughtfully, tapping her lips with her finger. She paced. She wore green again, a deep emerald satin. He supposed it was her favorite color, and it seemed to suit her pale skin and dark hair.

"It could be the Otherworld," said Leopold quietly. Oh, how he had longed to communicate with the Otherworld when he was a boy, following in his father's footsteps. He had secretly watched him, learned the Kabbalah as his father had done, and learned to summon daemons, to summon Eurynomos. And they had become fast friends. But it was his own careless error that got his father caught up in the depths of Gehenna. He had not been careful. He had been full of his own pride. *Pride goeth before destruction, and a haughty spirit before a fall,* he admonished himself for the thousandth time.

If it were the Otherworld, was he strong enough to combat it?

"What is the 'City of the River'?" asked Mingli, oblivious to Leopold's sweating and fear.

"It's London, ain't it?" said Thacker with a shrug. "The Thames courses right through her."

"I'll grant you that," Mingli agreed. "But...the dead walking?" She suddenly looked up at Thacker.

"Here now," he said, holding his transparent hands forward. "I'm the only ghost I've ever met," he said, adding more "aitches" to his words the more agitated he got. "And I'm certainly not walking." He looked down at his feet as did the others. He made motions of walking but never touched the ground. Leopold conceded that such divination as tarot cards were notoriously literal, and since Thacker couldn't technically walk...

"But it does make one think," said Leopold, softly.

"Indeed," said Mingli.

"'It begins in the circle'," recited Leopold. "'The crown will fall'. The latter I take to mean the kingdom will fall. But 'it begins in the circle'..." He could not help but smooth out his mustache with his fingers as he paced against Mingli's direction.

"'Begins in the circle'..." she chanted. "A circle. It must be a henge of some sort. A circle of power. Stonehenge? Or a smaller one? Which one is closest to London?"

It clicked something in his mind. Leopold paced a few more steps before it was clear. "A circle. Or...*circus*." He stopped and turned toward her. "Piccadilly."

She stared at him intensely, but then a beatific smile spread on her lips and she marched toward him. "Leo! Yes."

Pleased that he had solved at least the first part of the problem, his mind suddenly completely shut down as her lips touched his cheek. He was enveloped in the scent of her lilac perfume and the warm spot where she'd kissed him.

"Piccadilly," she said, already marching away from him. "It's as I thought. That's where the Kobold & Hob Railway line begins. And that's where I've found the faeries. So! The next step is talking to Pratt and Sinclair."

"What shall *I* do?" asked Thacker.

Leopold shook his head and snapped out of his Mingli stupor. "Spense, I should like you to go to the records office and spy into the files. Find all the paperwork you can on the Kobold & Hob Railway: when they incorporated, who else might be the investors, and how they appropriated the lines. Can you do that?"

He tipped his bowler. "Lemon squeezy." With a pop, he was gone.

"Well then," said Raj, shaking his head as he gathered his cards again. "I suppose there is nothing left for me but to think on it. Except...Leopold. Might you have a moment? Privately." He seemed to be excited, unusually so.

"Sorry, old man," he said slowly. "But it sounds as if there's no time to waste."

"It's...it's very important I discuss this with you —"

"I'll be back for the show." He patted his friend's metallic shoulder. "And we can talk after."

"But...Leopold..."

Leopold was already making his way out of the office where he almost took Mingli's arm, stopping himself before he actually touched her so that he wouldn't find himself thrown down onto his back.

He cast a glance over his shoulder toward Raj. He'd never seen him like this. Stopping, Leopold thought to go back just then, until Mingli shouted for him outside the theatre. *Well,* he decided, *it could wait.*

"Miss Zhao," he said, once they were outside the theatre and she was already standing at the edge of the kerb, hailing a cab. "I should like us to take the elevated trolly."

"Why, whatever for? I thought you detested them."

"I do. But they do have one advantage; they are...*elevated.* It will afford us a view of the Kobold & Hob rail lines as they leave the city."

She tapped his breast — rather hard, he thought — with the handle of her umbrella. "*That's* the Leopold Kazsmer I've come to know! Welcome back."

He rubbed at his chest, slightly affronted. He led the way, striding faster than Mingli's hurried steps, and trotted up the nearest iron stairway up to the elevated tracks. The trolly station was sooty from the dirigible fallout above them. In fact, one of the dashed things hovered on its moorings just above the trolly station as passengers disembarked, while new passengers waited behind a wooden barrier.

Leopold paid the few pence for the fare, and he and Mingli got on the huffing trolly. Smaller than a railway car and open from all sides but the roof, the trolly was a smoky and louder ride than a train or dirigible, clacking and huffing along the tracks, but it was the cheapest transport in London. Leopold hadn't taken one since his rise as a magician, but he certainly took them as a child when living with his father, and after, when he was in town and out to earn his keep with the other Romani boys, picking pockets and hawking cheap trinkets.

He shook out the kerchief from his breast pocket and wiped down the wooden seat for Mingli and himself and sat, sneering in distaste. Had it been as dirty when he was a boy? Likely. Those were details one seldom dwelled on as a child, he supposed. Looking back on his life in the Romani camp, it seemed a dirty, hopeless day-to-day existence, those—thankfully—long ago days.

As the trolly filled—some sitting, some standing as the seats became occupied—it lurched once as it began chugging away from the station. Leopold rose and tapped a young woman on the shoulder, offering her his seat. He noticed none of the other rough men did so. He grasped the leather strap above his head and stood over Mingli. She gave him a grateful smile before turning her head and looking out.

The smokestack didn't seem quite tall enough *not* to spew its sooty billows across the top of the trolly and, when the wind was right, directly into the passenger cab.

Leopold coughed into his gloved hand, but twisted around to look over his shoulder and down the side of the elevated track. From where he was standing, he was looking down at the back of Mingli's head and to her slender neck. Her hair was piled up into careful ringlets which cascaded down the back of her head but still left her neck exposed, except for a thin gold chain that held the simple jade dragon pendant her protectors had told her to take from her uncle's brothel. She didn't know its significance, but like so many supernatural creatures, they seem to hold secrets away from mortals until some vaguely "proper" time to reveal their natures.

Even now, he didn't forget that she herself was part daemon. How was such a thing possible? And why didn't she know? Was that why her parents had sold her to her uncle? Did it make *her* immortal? And would this investigation put *her* in peril? He hadn't thought of that before. Maybe he was obliged to tell her of her heritage. But would such a curse crush her spirit to know? He certainly wouldn't want to know such a dread secret about himself…but no. He *would* want to know, though it would pain him to discover it. Perhaps…perhaps later, under calmer circumstances. Perhaps, he thought he should approach her on a more personal basis.

Thacker and even Raj had urged him to say something to her of his feelings. How did one…court? Invite her to tea, certainly. That would be a first step. Maybe there would be an opportunity today. They had to eat, after all.

Even with all his ruminating, he couldn't help but inhale her lilac scent and stare at that neck, so delectable in its naked elegance. He couldn't help but glance at her right shoulder, covered securely by her emerald satin jacket and bodice, by the ruffles and lace beneath. For he knew that under all those protective layers, was the tattoo, a logogram in the shape of the savior ghost/daemon that protected her. A tattoo that traveled down that shoulder and curved along her back to end just below her left hip.

He felt disgusted with himself for gawping at her and fantasizing. Didn't he have to tell her? Didn't he have to warn her of her heritage? It was better now than later. Especially if she found out that he had known for six months and hadn't said a word.

"Look," she said, coyly glancing over her shoulder at him.

He looked down below at the tracks, gleaming like flowing ribbons in the railyard. They were traveling above the Piccadilly station now. Before, it had been silent and still when they had investigated at the dead of night, but now it was a bustling place of commerce. Trains puffed and huffed, waiting patiently at the platforms like great beasts reined in until they could gallop. He could see people through the glass roof covering the platform, even as streaked with dirt, soot, and bird droppings as it was. Men in dark suits held newspapers to their faces, while women in feathered hats held the hands of small children. Women of lower station sat on roped bundles and their men smoked clay pipes or cheap cigars above them. Even dogs wandered about, begging for scraps. It was London in miniature, he supposed.

They soon passed by it as the elevated trolly tracks curved away. It afforded Leopold another view of the tracks that led north, and they seemed to stretch to infinity, lost to the haze of mist and sunshine.

When the trolly came to its first stop, they disembarked and said nothing as they trotted down the iron stairs. When they reached the pavement, Mingli turned to him. "What did you think?"

"They appear to be ordinary tracks."

"They *appear*, yes."

"I saw nothing and…" he touched his left wrist, "felt nothing."

"Interesting." She stepped to the kerb and waved her hand for a cab.

"Really, Miss Zhao. You must allow me."

"I don't see why." A hansom diverted from the main thoroughfare and halted before them.

"Where to, guv'nor?"

It suddenly occurred to Leopold that he had no idea where they were going. But as usual, Mingli knew the way. "Sixteen Grosvenor Square," she said. The cabby stared at her enhanced eye patch as they climbed up, but was quick about snapping the horse's reins once they'd sat within.

They were in no hurry as the cab clopped along and Leopold settled back and took a deep breath. "I say, Miss Zhao. After we've seen Messiers Pratt and Sinclair, would you care to partake of a little tea?"

She had been avidly searching out the window, but at the invitation — of which he was proud of not marring with a stutter — she turned to him with an impenetrable face. "I should be delighted," she said without emotion, and turned back to the window.

That didn't go as planned. He stroked his mustache with a frown. She could have greeted it with a bit more passion, he thought sullenly. He refused to admit to himself how disappointed he was with her reaction.

"Whose house is it on Grosvenor Square?"

"It is the home of Hieronymus Pratt. It was closer to our unscheduled trolly stop."

And just as she'd said it, the cabby pulled up to the kerb. Leopold paid the man through the trap door on the roof, and helped Mingli out.

They stood before the Georgian house, looking up at it and at the wide, green square behind them. Before Leopold could ask about the strategy, she had lit up the stairs and knocked smartly with the handle of her umbrella. He followed and stood beside her just as the door opened.

As wizened a man as ever there was greeted them. He was a footman in a double-breasted coat and waistcoat, with breaches and silk stockings. But he was so old as to be slightly bent forward and seemed barely able to stand. He said nothing, but eyed them with milky blue eyes and a fluff of white hair for brows.

"I am Special Inspector Mingli Zhao from Scotland Yard. Is your master at home?"

He looked her over—especially the eye patch with its lens, extending and contracting, examining him back—before he finally spoke. "My master is not at home. If you would leave a card…"

"When do you expect him back? It is urgent that we speak with him."

"I am uncertain of the time."

"Then shall we wait for him?" She stepped forward, but the little man barred her way.

"I have no expectation of the time of his return."

"Then can you tell me where he is now?"

"I do not know. My master does not always confide in me."

"Does he have a club, perhaps?"

"He is a member of the Saint Collen Club, in Covent Garden."

"Then I shall enquire there."

"Oh, but Madam. You are not allowed in the club."

She snorted her displeasure and drew a card from her jacket pocket. "Give this to your master and tell him that I am looking to speak with him."

The elven man took the card and stared at it, which he was still doing even as they descended the stairs.

"Such ridiculous rules," Mingli sneered when they'd walked up the pavement to Brook Street.

"Well—I mean a men's club, Miss Zhao, must have strict rules. No women are allowed."

She whirled on him. "Nor are Jews allowed, sir. Nor Gypsies, when it comes down to it."

He was taken aback by her sharpness as well as her words. He swallowed and adjusted his waistcoat. "Yes, you're right. I'd have little in common with the men of these clubs that would not allow me to pass through their doors. There is exclusivity throughout London, all the world, I dare say. I don't think that *everyone* is allowed just *any*where they wish."

"White men, Mr. Kazsmer. They are allowed everywhere."

"Not into a harem," he said innocently.

She stopped and turned. And then threw back her head and laughed, slapping him on the shoulder. "You are right, Leo. Thank you for that."

She hailed a second cab, and they were headed again toward Covent Garden where Eustace Sinclair resided.

But they were rebuffed there too. Yet just before they left, Leopold turned to the butler. "Does Mr. Sinclair, by any chance, belong to the Saint Collen Club?"

The butler—a rather pig-faced sort of fellow—cleared his throat and said in a grunt, "Yes, he does."

"Miss Zhao," said Leopold once the butler had closed the door, "might we venture to this club to see if our quarries are there?"

"But I cannot enter, and neither can you."

"My dear Miss Zhao. Do you think I go about with banners across my chest declaring my Jewish-Romani heritage? Certainly not! I'll simply …lie."

She smiled. It was of the wicked sort. The kind that made him shiver with an unnamed pleasure.

CHAPTER SIX

THE SAINT COLLEN Club stood alone on a Covent Garden street, a Georgian building with tall columns holding up a pediment with a frieze of dignitaries on horseback and wearing long gowns. But on closer inspection, instead of the staid nobility he expected, all of the figures on the frieze seemed to sport insect-type wings and pointed ears. Leopold gestured toward it so that Mingli would take note. She nodded studiously, and proceeded forward, but paused at the bottom of the step.

"Perhaps you had best go on alone, Mr. Kazsmer. I shall meet you for tea. Will Covington's Dining and Refreshment Room on Floral Street accommodate you?"

"That will do very well."

She nodded, the feather on her hat flicking once at him, before she raised her chin and marched forward along the avenue.

Leopold looked up at the structure again before climbing the steps. He turned the doorbell key and waited. A small peep door opened in the larger door, and a man whose face was obscured by the ornate iron grille, eyed him. "What business have you?"

"I am here to see Messiers Hieronymus Pratt and Eustace Sinclair."

"Who are you, sir? Do you have an appointment?"

Leopold doffed his hat. "I am...Damien Marsh, solicitor."

The eyes searched him suspiciously. "Have you a card?"

He made the merest of smiles. "Of course." He reached into his pocket, mumbling an incantation, and when he retrieved one of his calling cards, the words "Leopold Kazsmer, the Great Enchanter" had magically changed to "Damien Marsh, Solicitor, Farringdon Street". He slipped it through the grille where the man took it and closed the little door.

Leopold leaned on his cane and glanced about on the street, whistling the tune the orchestra played before the sketch of the sorcerer and the maiden at the top of his show last night.

He knew no one would take him for a Jew or a Gypsy if they didn't know. He was just a fellow with dark eyes and nearly black hair. He could have been Welsh for all they knew.

Presently, he heard the little peep door open again. The dark eyes stared at him. "They are not taking visitors at this time."

"Oh, but—"

The peep door slammed shut.

"I see," he muttered. "But they *are* here."

He scrambled down the steps and spied the servant's entrance below ground level. He depressed a button on the side of his cane and the top flipped back on a hinge. At the same time, a spring-loaded catapult ejected the wand a foot into the air, where he caught it. Closing his eyes, he felt about for the magic. There was always some magic present, more when he had just summoned Eurynomos. Most of the time the underlying buzz of Otherworld magic wasn't accessible, but for some reason, some sort of magic seemed to hum all around this building. He sensed it in the prickles in his fingertips, as well as his tattoo. He used the wand to transform his clothes from his morning suit to a servant's white shirt, dark waistcoat, and serviceable trousers, including a long white apron hanging nearly to his ankles. He transformed the cane into a wooden tray of chipped ice and oysters. Hoisting it to his shoulders, he tucked the wand away, trotted down the stairs, and knocked on the door. The door opened and a pinched-faced butler peered out at him. "What is this?"

"It's just some monks and cloisters for Mister Pratt and Mister Sinclair," he said in his thickest Cockney. "Let a bloke in, guv."

"Keep your shirt on." The man opened the door, and Leopold kept his face hidden behind his now crumpled topper and the tray as he slipped in.

"Where do I take 'em?"

"You? You take them to the kitchen, shuck them, and a proper footman will take them up."

"The fishmonger said not to let them outta me sight."

"No tradesman is going to enter into the inner sanctum of the Saint Collen Club, my man. Fishmonger or no fishmonger."

"Bloody hell. I'll get a kick, I will."

"You'll get a kick if you don't leave those and get out."

"All right, all right. Where's me bread and honey?"

"Your fishmonger will be paid at the end of the month like always."

Leopold grumbled appropriately as he set down the tray, and when the butler was distracted, he darted to a doorway, grabbed his wand, and transformed his clothes again to that of a footman. His wand magically shucked each oyster and laid them out neatly, just as the footman came through.

"Oh good," he said. "Place these on a decent platter and take them to the top floor, Goodfellow Room."

Leopold bowed with a muffled, "Yes, sir." He took the wooden tray and made as if to slip into the tiled kitchen. Instead, he hid in the shadows of the doorway and transformed the wooden tray to an ornate platter.

He settled his posture, holding the platter high to hide his face again, and set off up the long, darkened staircase.

He walked carefully up to the tiled floor and hesitated near the foyer so as to go unnoticed by the club residents. He could see them through the glass-paned doors to an inner room with dark wood on the walls, Persian rugs, leather chairs, and deep buttoned, quilted leather Chesterfields.

"What are you standing there for?" said a footman in a striped waistcoat.

"Oh. I…I was sent to the Goodfellow Room."

"Then be smart about it and don't loiter here. Quickly. Up those stairs. Top floor."

"Thank'e, guv." Leopold stepped up the hidden servant's stair and went up two floors before he reached the top. He made his way into a corridor.

Over each closed solid oak door, fanciful carvings of faery-like creatures frolicked. Above a double door was a faery lad with pan pipes and goat legs. Next to the doors, a brass plate was set into the wall with engraved letters that said, "Goodfellow Room." Leopold took a breath, knocked, and waited with his hand behind his back and his platter held near his shoulder.

At length, the door opened, and a wizened butler looked him up and down. "Yes?"

"I have brought the oysters as requested, sir."

"Oysters?" He glanced back into the room and then back to Leopold. He looked as if he was going to take the heavy platter but thought better of it. Leopold couldn't imagine those thin arms and weak shoulders being able to hold such a platter. In the end, the butler flicked his head for Leopold to enter, which he did with a bow to the butler.

"Put them there," he said, pointing to a table with a decanter of sherry and two crystal glasses. Leopold made a show of placing the platter down, and the serviette beside it that was draped over his arm.

But the butler had already disappeared through a hidden door in the wood paneling.

Two men sat in deep tufted chairs before an enormous multi-paned window with a view of Covent Garden and the skyline beyond.

Leopold glanced back at the oyster platter. He took out his wand from his jacket and transformed his clothes and then the oysters back into his cane. He retrieved it and made his way before the two gentlemen in their chairs. The one on the left wore a beard, and his brown hair was parted in the middle. The other wore a mustache similar to that of Leopold's. Both were about his own age, at thirty or so, and both wore boiled shirts, short collars, bow ties, and swallowtail coats. And neither of them bothered to move or speak.

"Gentlemen," said Leopold, tipping his topper to them with a slight bow. "Forgive this intrusion. I am Leopold Kazsmer, and I am working with Scotland Yard on a special investigation. I wonder if you can spare the time to talk to me about your unusual railway company and its construction. There seems to be some…irregularities…where the tracks are concerned."

He waited, watching their faces. But their rigid expressions never changed, nor did their gaze out the window.

Leopold moved a little closer. He turned to the bearded fellow. "Do I have the pleasure of meeting Mister Sinclair or Mister Pratt?"

He waited again, but there was no change of expression in either of them. He moved closer still.

"Er...gentlemen?"

Nothing.

He removed his spectacles from his coat pocket and fixed them upon his nose, flipping different lenses into place. After moving one lens forward, he detected a strange aura about both men. It glowed and fluttered and blurred them as if they were encased in some sort of flowing magic.

He whipped the spectacles off his face and stepped forward with an extended index finger and gently jabbed the mustachioed gentlemen to his left. He rocked back and righted, but his appearance never changed. Neither of them blinked, even when he waved his hand directly before their faces.

Leaning close and with the spectacles back on his nose, Leopold eyed the left-hand man. "Still alive," he muttered, "but quite insensate. Curious."

"What are you doing!"

Leopold startled and shot straight up.

The butler had returned. But with the spectacles on his nose, he saw a completely different figure. He was far more wizened than the old butler had been. He wasn't wearing the suit of a butler, but instead, sported leather trousers with braces over a dirty and moth-eaten chemise. He was bald except for extreme tufts of white hair spraying from his long, pointed ears. His nose was likewise long and pointed and his teeth were in sharp little rows.

As the creature approached, Leopold backed away, eyes wide.

The being stopped. He smiled a dreadful curving of flat lips, and narrowed his eyes. "You can see me, can't you, Mortal?" Even his voice had changed to something harsh and raspy.

Leopold brandished his wand, and as he reached about him for magic, he suddenly realized there was little to be had.

"A wand!" cried the little man with delight. "You understand magic. How interesting... and how bad for you."

He wound back his arm, but Leopold didn't wait to find out what he intended to hurl. He dove out of the way and zig-zagged about the room. Something burst with a muffled explosion upon the carpet where he had stood. He smelled the burning threads and singed wood floor. He flicked a glance back once before fleeing toward the hidden door in the paneled wall.

The creature cackled and threw another magical bomb that exploded near the door. Leopold caught a glimpse of the two men still sitting sedately in their chairs before he dashed through the entry and ran full pelt down the narrow staircase.

With the spectacles still on his face, he saw the corridors as no human would ever look upon them. They were not ornate carved panels, but stone carved out crudely like a cave or mining tunnel. The air was thick with some unnamed odor and he hurried through, looking for another stair.

Something shot past him and he smelled burnt cloth. He looked down and realized it was him! His coat tails were singed and smoking. When he looked up, the creature was at the top of the staircase. "You won't escape, Mortal," he cried in a strange melodious voice.

Leopold hurled himself down the cavern corridor. He saw a door and grabbed for it, throwing it open. It was a nightmare den of more creatures like the butler, and he couldn't imagine that they were anything but goblins. Before them was a furnace which blasted hot air. They busily shoveled coal into its fiery depths, one after the other. Their egg-shaped bodies were naked from the waist up, with hair sprouting in all the wrong places. They sheened with sweat and coal-dust. They also wore the same leather trousers and their feet were impossibly long in pointed shoes.

They didn't look up from their labors, which Leopold thought was a good thing, but beyond them was a window. Leopold shot past them and tried to open it. It was nailed shut.

The door opened behind him, and the butler stood in the doorway. Face lit by the fiery furnace he looked like a devil himself, straight out of *Sitra Achra*. "There you are," he said with a chuckle. "You shall be a tasty dish indeed. I haven't eaten human flesh in some time. Come here, me lad."

Leopold stared at the horrific goblin coming toward him, looked back at the shut window, and decided.

With an incantation he hoped would work, he hurled himself toward the mullioned window, crashed through it in a cascade of splintered wood and sparkling glass, and cast himself over the side into the unknown.

CHAPTER SEVEN

THE SPELL BROKE the window and caught his fall, slowing him considerably. He was able to study at his leisure the building's façade on his sluggish way down, the many windows each with pediments, the long columns, the statues on ornate plinths on the side of the building, and the glittering cascade of glass that followed his slow progress.

When he saw the pavement growing closer, he tightened the hold on his wand and his cane, using his wand hand to keep his hat on as well, and twisted his body to land feet first. When he descended enough to land, he bent his legs like a spring to take the brunt of the fall and straightened with a flourish. Glass tinkled to the pavement all around him. Astonished onlookers stopped and stared with mouth agape.

Leopold took them all in and bowed. "You can see me—Leopold Kazsmer, the Great Enchanter—perform at the King's Garden Theatre in Piccadilly tonight!" He reached into his jacket, took out a handful of calling cards, and tossed them to the crowd. They started to applaud. He bowed again, and ran toward Bedford Street, looking back at the Saint Collen Club building. And even as he looked up to the topmost floor, he could detect no broken windows at all.

———•———

HE FOUND THE sign Covington's Dining and Refreshment Room between the many flower warehouses and shops, and hurried through the door. Searching, he found Mingli sitting at a table in the bay window just as the hostess approached him. "No, thank you, I found my party."

He sat opposite Mingli after tipping his hat to her.

"Mr. Kazsmer!" she said. "Look at the state of you."

He did, and realized he had coal dust, dirt, bits of glass clinging to his coat, and a singed lapel. "Oh." He noticed people looking at him, but they might have been just as curious to see who would be the companion to the Chinese woman with a telescoping lens for an eye.

"We are quite a pair," he said, trying to brush off the bigger bits.

"Indeed, we are," she agreed. She lifted a gloved hand and signaled to the server.

They waited to speak until after the server—a young woman in a starched apron and cuffed sleeves—served their tea and food.

"I'm famished," said Mingli. "May I serve you, Leopold?"

"Please, serve yourself. You've been waiting too long."

She did, but then poured Leopold his tea the way he liked it with a splash of milk and two sugars.

He tucked into his cold boiled beef, pickles, bread and butter, and almost moaned. He hadn't realized how hungry he *was*.

"I take it that all did not go well," said Mingli after she bit into her bloaters on a slice of bread, and dabbed delicately with a serviette to her lips.

"That club, Miss Zhao, seems to be teeming with...well...goblins, for lack of a better word."

"Interesting," she said, cutting a saveloy into bite-sized pieces. "Did you see them?"

"Not only saw them but talked to them. The fellow who pursued me said that he intended to eat me. I must say, that was a trifle disconcerting."

"Then they *were* goblins. Did you see them with your spectacles on or without?"

"With. But I wonder since I saw through their glamour with the spectacles that I wouldn't need to wear them further. At least, that's the legend."

"It's true. Once seen, they can't be unseen. Did you speak to Messiers Pratt and Sinclair?"

Leopold wolfed down another bite of beef and chewed. "I saw them, but I daresay, they didn't see me. They were under a spell. A fairly powerful one. God knows how long they have been there under enchantment."

"That isn't good news, is it. I do hope Inspector Thacker brings us useful tidings."

He slurped his tea, wiping his mustache with the serviette, and speared another pickle with his fork. "I can't imagine what's behind this affair. I'm glad you discovered what you found out initially. It would have been dashed difficult to have let this thing go on longer and try to sort it out later."

"I have always been observant," she said without a shred of the self-importance. "I suppose it's a curse as much as any sort of gift."

"Look here." He finished his food, wiped his mouth again with the serviette, drank his tea for courage, and settled in. "Miss Zhao, I…well, I have wanted us to share a meal for some time."

"Oh?" She sipped delicately at her tea, holding the cup handle with elegant grace.

"Yes. Er…it has been my fondest wish to, er…to, er…get to know you better. And for you to get to know me better. I hope to share many more meals with you. Teas, suppers. The like."

She gave him a brief smile. "Certainly. I have no objection to that."

"No objection," he muttered. "That is…good. But what I was hoping for was…a certain level of enthusiasm for the occasions."

He waited expectantly; hands folded on the table.

She set the teacup down in its saucer, primly dabbed her mouth again, and raised her face. "A…'level of enthusiasm'? Should I be leaping about in joy?"

His shoulders sank. "Of course not. I was merely looking to see…trying to ascertain…if…if…"

"Mr. Kazsmer, what, may I ask, are your intentions?"

"Quite honorable, I assure you!"

She smiled and shook her head. "I had no other expectations, Mr. Kazsmer. I know you are an honorable man. But what I meant to say was—let me see if I am surmising this correctly—is it your desire to *court* me?"

He scooted closer to the table. Breathlessly, he answered, "It is my fondest desire to do so."

"I see."

She sat for a long time, neither moving nor speaking. Leopold's heart stuttered. "Oh. I...have mistaken your interest. Forgive me. I can see that you merely see me as a colleague. Well that's...that's enough, then." He wadded the serviette in his hands, folded it, unfolded it, left it on the table. He reached for his coin purse.

Mingli leaned over the table and put out her hand to stop him. "Wait." She sat back again and glanced off to the side with her good eye. The other, with its telescope, seemed to have calmed and stopped moving. "Mr. Kazsmer...I am deeply flattered and honored..."

"Dear me." He felt his face flush with heat. "There's really no need for you to go on." He started to rise.

"Please sit down, Leo."

He thumped back into his seat and stared forlornly at the crumbs and grease on his plate.

"It is only polite to allow me to finish." She took her serviette from her lap, folded it neatly, and laid it gently across her plate. "As I said, I am deeply flattered and honored by your attention. And...you must know how very attractive I find you."

Leopold looked up, his face flushing with a different kind of heat.

"But...I have no time to cultivate what one might consider an intimate relationship of the kind you are no doubt expecting. I am a busy woman, with great ambition. Most men do not find that conducive to forming ties." He tilted forward to speak but she held up her gloved hand. "Please, allow me to finish first." She laid her hand back into her lap. "Because of this drag on my time, I find it impossible to do the usual courting. On the other hand, I realize that we are mutually attracted to one another, so an occasional sexual encounter might be more to the point. I would agree to that."

Blinking stupidly, Leopold sank back against his seat. "W-what?"

She leaned in, speaking softly, and resting her chin on her hand. "I would agree to sexual trysts. Sexual *intercourse*, Leo, if that isn't clear enough."

He realized his jaw fell open, but he was unable to do anything about it. "Muh-Miss Zhao!" he breathed. His face blazed with heat and he turned his head this way and that, certain that everyone was staring at them, could hear everything that was said.

"Leo." She took his hand and captured it on the table. He could not tear it away, nor did he want to. "What's wrong with relieving a little sexual tension? I know you want it. And you must surely realize by now through all my teasing banter that *I* want it…with you…"

It took great strength on his part, but he slowly withdrew his hand and stared at it in his lap, cold and suddenly devoid of her presence. "It pains me to say this, Miss Zhao, about your very…" He swallowed. "Very kind offer, but I'm afraid…I must refuse. You see…my interest in you is far more than mere physical l-lust. My *feelings* for you…go far deeper than that. And so—even as tempting as the prospect might be— I can accept nothing less than to court you, and, after an acceptable interval, the inevitable joining of our houses." He swallowed again. Even after all that tea, his mouth was surprisingly dry.

He'd said it. He'd actually said it. And had refused her offer. *Oh God, her offer!* "Erm…please accept my apologies," he went on. But when he finally had the courage to raise his eyes to hers, fully expecting to see an expression of annoyance—or worse!—contempt, she instead offered a look of wonder, her one eye glittering with moisture.

"Mr. Kazsmer…I am…" She blinked and shook her head. "I am, frankly, shocked. But no. I should not have been, knowing your character. And I am deeply, deeply touched by your heartfelt words. I can honestly say—"

He did not know what her next words would be. For the window in which they sat suddenly exploded, and a great weight landed upon him while the patrons screamed and cried out amid the tinkling of shattered glass.

And the only thing that next filled his ears were the sounds of pistons and gears.

CHAPTER EIGHT

SOMETHING CLAMPED AROUND his neck and squeezed. His breath was gone. He snapped opened his eyes and looked into the face of a man…a man with brass goggles over his eyes. But deep in the irises, he saw metal gears turning.

"I have you at last!" came the voice like something in a tin speaker, like a bad connection on a telephone device.

The grip on his neck tightened and Leopold was in real fear of his eyes popping out. But more immediately, he realized that breathing was the priority. He clamped his hands to the man's wrists but they, too, were made of metal.

He tried to kick the man but each area that caught the toe of his boot proved also to be of some kind of metal.

"Who are you?" he managed to croak.

Amazingly, the grip on his throat slackened and he inhaled great gobs of air.

"You…you don't even know me?"

As the mechanical man said it, Leopold thought he just might recognize the man. There was something unaccountably familiar about him. And the more he looked him over — the colorfully embroidered waistcoat, the tattered and gaudily patched overcoat, the dented topper — he seemed to be dressed as a Romani.

His hair was unusual: shaved on one side of his head, and the other side sporting long plaits braided together like rope. He wore an earring in one ear, and trinkets…no…*charms*, fastened to leather cords that hung here and there from his waistcoat. His *aspect* wasn't like any

Romani man he'd ever seen, but his voice, with its Hungarian lilt, chimed something deep in Leopold's memory.

And all the while, Leopold detected the constant *tick, tick* from a coiled spring and gears. His head was filled with the sound. Like clockwork. Like a giant clock.

The man drew back, grabbed a rather medieval-looking axe with a curved blade, and sneered at Leopold's obvious confusion. "It's no good if you don't know me," said that hollow voice. "Think back, *didicoy...*" And then the man pulled up short, as Mingli's rapier, unsheathed from her umbrella, pressed against his neck.

"I don't think you should make another move, my good sir," she said.

He paused and then shot an arm out and wound it around the blade. Any normal man would have cut himself to ribbons — and indeed, the coat sleeve fell away in strips — but the arm was quite solid and shone in golden brass and rivets.

He yanked the blade from her hand and tossed it away.

There was the sound of policemen's whistles and the pounding of many feet approaching. The mechanical man gave a roar of rage. Leopold still heard the *tick, tick* of clockwork before the man pushed away, leapt to his feet with a hard clang, and flew out the ruined window whilst brandishing the axe, the metal feet resounding on the pavement. The cobblestones rang with it far into the distance at terrific speed.

Leopold levered himself up, but he was captured in the strong grip of Mingli Zhao. "Leo, are you all right?"

Leopold had wanted her passion and it looked as if he'd gotten it at last. Her face was earnest in its concern, and her arms held him in a decidedly protective embrace.

He smiled up at her. "Tip top," he croaked.

The police arrived, and the rozzers helped Leopold to his feet. He explained, as best he could, what had transpired. The police were not inclined to believe him, until Mingli showed them her badge and told them that all was under control.

They concluded that the man was the sort to use the new-fangled enhancements sold in the shops that boasted of allowing a chap to run faster, etc. Such things were sold as steam-powered and seemed all the rage. Leopold rather thought they were shams.

The man had not had those particular sham enhancements, as far as he could tell. Not with the memory of gears spinning in his irises and the distinct sound of clockwork.

The police left reluctantly, though they did help to clean up the glass and other debris.

Leopold paid for their meal and took Mingli's arm to steer her away from the broken glass and wood. She leaned into him—without complaining of his hand on her arm—and asked, "Do you know who—or *what*—that was?"

"I'm afraid I do not. However..." They were safely away and standing near a park. He rubbed at his bruised neck. "I feel that I somehow...know him. He's Romani."

"Well, he certainly knew you."

"I wasn't treated the best when I was a boy in the camp. I'm a half breed, a *didicoy*. My Jewish heritage did not endear me to them."

"I gathered as much from what you've told me before."

"But obviously, there was no mechanical man when I lived in the camp. And my uncle paid me a visit, early this morning. He warned me that this man had come to their camp and caused destruction, and that he'd killed a man when looking for me. Indeed, he found my flat and rumbled it."

"I saw nothing of that."

"Well, magic is very handy. Especially when performed by a helpful daemon."

"Eurynomos," she breathed, eye glittering.

"Yes. I summoned him after my uncle's warning."

"You shouldn't return home if he knows where you live."

"It is warded...but then again, it had been warded when he broke in. At least I thought it was. I sensed him. Malevolent magic."

"Could someone have done this to him? Some great evil?"

"Unquestionably. But whom?"

"Well..." She looked around, her eye patch lens spinning and adjusting. "My offer still stands."

"Off...offer?" he rasped. His mind filled with images of her smooth skin, the bare shoulder she showed him when revealing her own tattoo; the offer of...sex...

"My guest room. It is available to you. And it is a very safe place."

Guest room. He brought himself back from all the images. Guest room.

"I couldn't impose."

"Don't be ridiculous. It could end up being the safest place in all London." She tapped her umbrella on the pavement. The mechanical man had broken her sword...but maybe she had repaired it. She had her own brand of magic about her, one he couldn't easily identify.

Perhaps it was her daemon side.

"We'll discuss it later. I'm afraid..." He pulled out his pocket watch. "I must get to the theatre. I still have a show to perform tonight."

"Come to Scotland Yard first."

"Very well. I'll just hail a —"

But she had already stepped to the kerb and whistled for a cabby.

———◆———

AT SCOTLAND YARD in Thacker's old office, Leopold paced. Who was the mechanical man? He knew Leopold, so perhaps he'd met him before, but not remade as he was. It was damnable not remembering.

He was particularly troubled by the clockwork of the man. He was some sort of hybrid of human and mechanism, some horrific melding of living flesh and cold clockwork. Who could have done this? Was a Romani capable? It would have required a deep understanding of the cross between human biology and mechanics. Leopold was most expert, having studied the intricacies of Raj's clockwork, but he never imagined himself capable of creating an automaton on his own, let alone a living one. Someone had done this magic, and a beastly person it must have been, for it to have been done with malevolent magic. He still felt it on him like a stench, like something he couldn't quite shake off. Not even with a long bath.

He looked up suddenly, recalling where he was amid his musings. Here was the familiar office that his friend Thacker had used when he was alive, and Mingli had moved into it the day of his funeral. It had been a shock, to be sure. And all the old familiar things were now long gone: the Wellington boot he had used for an umbrella stand; the sculpture of a cat made of ebony that sat on a corner of his desk; the indiscriminate piles of papers and leather boxes of files…

They were all gone, replaced by a very Mingli arrangement of books and art. There were slightly scandalous European sculptures of nymphs and satyrs in marble on the shelves next to books of research, and other tasteful English country scenes of manor houses with cows depicted in oils and hung in appropriate frames on the walls. There appeared to be only two Chinese items in the room that he could see: a long scroll of Chinese lettering, ancient, by the look of it, mounted in a simple frame on the wall opposite her desk, and, instead of the ebony cat that had been on Thacker's desk, there now sat a jade lion, its mouth agape, its eyes sizing up the room.

Mingli laid out maps and a Bradshaw's Railway Guide atop her desk. "Before you return to the theatre, Mr. Kazsmer, I thought we could go over these maps, give you something over which to ruminate."

He moved to the other side of the desk and leaned over. But when Mingli leaned too, he was bombarded with the unmistakable scent of lilac. Thankfully, she moved away from the desk and took up her pacing.

Leopold scoured the maps, seeing nothing of interest, nothing to particularly catch his eye. He compared it to the Bradshaw with its graph of timetables, but nothing clicked there either. It was no use. His head was filled with thoughts of the clockwork man, with Mingli's incredible offer, and with the magic show he was to perform in just a few hours.

"I don't…" he began, straightening, when the ghost of Thacker passed through the walls.

"I'm glad I found you here," he said, straightening his transparent Ulster, though he had no need to. "I discovered some interesting things in them files, I can tell you!" But then he seemed to notice Leopold's appearance. "What the bloody hell happened to you?" Remembering Mingli's presence, he raised his bowler with a, "Begging your pardon."

"Well…" Leopold tried vainly to brush off the debris from his coat. "First I ran for my life from a cache of goblins at the Saint Collen Club and then after that I was attacked by a clockwork Gypsy."

Thacker seemed to freeze for a moment before he brayed a loud guffaw. "Oh, you will have your jokes, won't you, Leo."

"I'm afraid, Inspector," said Mingli gravely, "that it is all quite true."

"Go on!" he said, though he didn't seem as sure. He looked to Leopold who nodded.

"It is true, Spense."

"Goblins? Leopold! I mean…bloody goblins?"

"'There are more things in heaven and earth than are dreamt of in your philosophy'," said Leopold. "And mine, come to think of it." He pushed his topper up his head and scratched his temple. "I can cite you all the Otherworld daemons and demons you like, but I never knew that faeries and goblins existed in our world."

"Cor!" said Thacker, his own bowler pushed back off his forehead as well. "You say you saw them at the Saint Collen Club? What were you doing there?"

"I was trying to get an interview with Hieronymus Pratt and Eustace Sinclair. But they are under an enchantment and held captive by goblins wearing glamours. And I'll be damned if I can figure out why. I barely escaped with my life. The damnable things were going to eat me."

"Then where does this clockwork Gypsy come into it?"

"I don't know. He attacked me and Miss Zhao when we were taking tea in Covent Garden."

"Was he made by them goblins?"

"I…I never considered it, but…that might be worth bearing in mind. It had to take a great deal of magic to create such a hybrid." He knew nothing of goblins except some faery stories from his childhood. Did they have the magical capacity for such a thing? And why? Why should they want to do it? And why should they wish to control a railroad?

"At any rate," Leopold went on, "he's been after me for some time, according to what my Uncle Yanko reported to me and the fact that he rumbled my flat. It's against me personally. I think he's a Romani. Or was."

"You do find them, don't you, Leo. Sounds like you had all the fun while I had me head stuck in some dusty old files."

"Don't keep us in suspense. What did you find out?"

Thacker's pacing was different from Leopold's and Mingli's. For one, his feet never actually touched the carpet, but floated above it by inches. Instead, he glided back and forth, his legs moving in memory of what he used to do in life. It was almost good to see, Leopold thought, but after a while of watching it, it became more upsetting. For he would never be able to walk as a man again. He was a spirit, and that was not going to change.

"Well, it looks like there are other investors, but I can't for the life of me — or the death of me — discover who they are. They don't exist. And I'll tell you something else, old son," he said, pointing at Leopold's face, "I got curious about the name of their railway, so I looked up them names, too. There's no Kobold and no bloody Hob city, town, or park named that. But I did find the names. Did either of you know that a 'kobold' is the name of a sprite from German folklore? A most mischievous little devil." He rocked on his heels when he added, "It's very similar to the *kobalos* of the Greek isles. I looked that up too."

Leopold exchanged a glance with Mingli. The lens covering her right eye spun and lengthened.

"And that 'Hob' is a very old word for goblin, as in hobgoblin. That seems to fit in with your goblins at the Saint Collen Club."

"By Jove it does! What can this mean? Our railway tycoons were quite insensate and held captive by goblins. Why do goblins want to control a railway?"

"A railway," reminded Mingli, "that runs along alignment lines, lines of power."

"Yes," said Leopold.

Thacker glided toward them. "But that ain't all. I also discovered that their consortium bought out the Necropolis Railway."

"What in blazes is that?" said Leopold.

"The Necropolis Railway?" said Thacker, somewhat surprised. "It takes dead bodies out of London to cemeteries outside the city, that's what. Haven't you ever heard of it?"

"Ah!" said Mingli. She moved toward the desk and pushed maps and pamphlets aside until she found the one she wanted. "Look here." Leopold came around the desk to stand beside Mingli, while Thacker moved through it to stand on the other side of her.

"The Necropolis Railway," she began, "was designed to relieve the overcrowding in the churchyards of London. The medieval people of this city never imagined there would be so many souls here that graveyard space would eventually be used up. And so the railway not only takes the bodies of our deceased from the city to outlying graveyards, but many of the mourners as well. Now look here." She pointed to the map. "This is the Necropolis Railway line. It follows exactly the same line as the Kobold & Hob Railway. It isn't just the alignment lines, but this railway. Now why should these...well, goblins...wish to utilize the Necropolis Railway *and* the alignment lines?"

Leopold shook his head. "I don't know. But whatever it is, it certainly can't be innocent."

Her dome clock chimed, and Leopold glanced down at his own pocket watch. "I'm very much afraid that Inspector Thacker and I must go."

Without looking up from her maps, Mingli said over her shoulder, "Meet me later after your show. You can have supper with me at my flat."

Leopold stumbled and stared at her. Thacker moued.

"You're invited too, Inspector. I'm sorry you can't eat."

"So am I, miss." He touched the rim of his bowler. "Even sorrier I can't drink."

"And Leopold," she said, smoothing out the maps and holding them in place with various objects on her desk. "If it isn't too much trouble, perhaps you could summon Eurynomos. He should also attend."

Well, that certainly put the kibosh on it being an intimate supper. He straightened his coat, gave a nod to Thacker, and hurried from the room.

CHAPTER NINE

HE WAS LATE getting to the theatre. Agnes Templeton, one of his twin assistants, horse-laughed as he rushed about backstage. She was already in make-up and costume, a dress whose hem was well above her ankles in their spats and boots. She put a fist to her hip. "I was scared I'd have to do your routines by m'self."

"I hardly think that would have been appropriate," he said, tearing off his coat and desperately searching for his tailcoat in his wardrobe. She calmly pushed him aside and slipped it off its hanger, handing him the boiled shirt as well. "Don't you worry about a thing, Mr. Kazsmer. I had Aimee go and tell the house manager to hold the curtain. Can't have a show at all without the star attraction."

"Thanks, Agnes. That's very enterprising of you."

"Ta." She gently patted the curled locks at the back of her head. "I'm always telling Aimee we have to take care of the star attraction. You, sir, if you get my meaning. Where would we be without you?"

"Indeed." He struggled into his shirt, dismissing switching his trousers since she would not seem to leave the dressing room, and was startled into submission again when she grabbed him and began tying his tie.

"You do present a good face to the act, Mr. Kazsmer, if you don't mind my saying. Your boiled shirt and tailcoat. It's a crowd-pleaser, it is. I said that to Aimee just the other day. A crowd-pleaser. A handsome young man with the air of a far older gentleman. It's a crowd-pleaser."

She stepped away while he adjusted the tie in the mirror, and there she was again, holding his coat out for him to slip his arms into. No sooner had he done so, she was handing him his topper.

"There you are. The Great Enchanter indeed."

"Thank you. Where's your sister…"

And just then Aimee poked her head in. She never said much. It was Agnes that did the talking for the three of them.

"Are we ready for our show, me chickens?" said Agnes cheerfully.

Even though there was much on his mind, Leopold was cheered by her constant merry talk. He offered her a grateful smile. "This chicken is ready to crow."

She horse-laughed again. "I think you mean *cock*." She elbowed him hard, but he was able to recover, rubbing at his sore ribs.

The orchestra got the cue to begin its vamp, and the house lights dimmed so that the footlights were the only illumination on the red curtain.

He glanced over his shoulder and caught a glimpse of the faintly glowing Inspector Thacker. His would be the finale of the entire show. But the opening act was just as interesting.

A glint of light on gold, and Leopold snatched a glance at Raj. Though he could not speak while the Templeton sisters were nearby, his porcelain face had an apprehensive look about it and Leopold only then remembered that Raj had been anxious to speak to him. No matter. He'd do so after the show.

The magician music began and the curtain rose. Leopold moved forward with his Proteus Cabinet, having Agnes wheel it on stage as he crossed to the center of the footlights. The applause rose at his appearance, and soon died down. As much as he enjoyed performing true magic, he was just as satisfied with his illusions, for the mixture of real magic and illusion had made him a growing star amongst the greatest of magicians. Yes, some of his audience thought that he was *always* performing real magic. These were already the superstitious sort. Still others simply loved to marvel at the cleverness at his illusions, shaking their heads and doing their damnedest to figure it out. And still others, true skeptics, felt he was manipulating the crowds, like a confidence man, tricking them out of the coin they paid. There was no satisfying the latter, although sometimes he could sway them with a bit of real magic.

The Proteus Cabinet was a simple illusion, and there was no tingle of real magic or the slicing of his arm to do it. An illusion, plain and simple, done with mirrored walls and a hiding place within. The cabinet was up on legs with wheels, so that the audience could be assured that no one could climb in from beneath or behind. Of course, there were many similar cabinets where a mirror was placed at the back of the wheeled legs to hide just such an entry and exit. But this one was the simple kind with the angled mirrored wall in the back. Two mirrors, situated at a steep angle from one another, showed to the audience the walls of the cabinet and not the audience members themselves. The angled mirrors were on a pivot post in the center of the cabinet holding a lantern, allowing the magician or assistant to pull the mirror away enough to slip into the cavity the angled mirrors provided behind them. Simple.

Leopold made a great show of opening the cabinet doors, his arms moving with the elegance of a ballet dancer. He slipped his wand into his hand from his sleeve and tapped the walls, showing that nothing was within but the lantern.

He extended his hand to the silent but smiling Agnes who took it and stepped up into the cabinet. As quickly as he closed the cabinet doors, he opened them again, and she had — amazingly — disappeared!

The audience gasped and applauded. Leopold stood for a moment, a smirk on his face and his topper tilted forward over one eye. He closed the doors again, and just as quickly opened it to show that she had returned, unharmed. Agnes raised her arms in a flourish, and the people applauded louder.

Leopold stood at the footlights, and pronounced, "Perhaps someone from the audience wishes to come up and prove that my magic is real."

Several brave or skeptical men raised their hands, and Leopold pretended to look them over, when he seemed to spy the perfect candidate. "You there! Madam! Do you dare to step into my Proteus Cabinet?"

It was Aimee, disguised as an old woman, with shawl and feathered hat, whose brim and netting shaded her face. She nodded and did a fine acting performance of moving with the aches and pains of the elderly: slightly bent and using a cane to make her way through the row of the audience. Ushers helped her up the steps to the stage, and she shied away from the footlights. After all, make-up and a net face veil could only do so much.

Leopold bowed and took her gloved hand, kissing it. The female members of the audience gushed with approval. "Thank you for accommodating me," said Leopold softly, but projecting enough that the house could hear him. "If I may help you…" The assistant brought forth a step stool and helped the woman up. "Now, you promise not to be afraid? I am fairly certain I can bring you back."

The lady seemed to pause, but in the end, after his cajoling and kissing her hand again, the flattery seemed to convince her. She was looking all around inside the cabinet and even behind her when Leopold suddenly closed the doors. He instructed his assistant to turn the cabinet three hundred and sixty degrees — proving there was no escape — while he postured with his hands in an expression of conjuring, and as soon as the cabinet was returned to the careful marks on the stage floor that meant it would be facing the audience straight on, he threw wide the doors and … no one was there!

The audience gasped and applauded. Leopold offered a wicked smile and closed the doors behind his back. He made a flourishing gesture, and the assistant again turned the cabinet. When he cast open the doors, the old woman was there, looking flustered and just a little frightened. He graciously helped her down the stool and to the stage floor, took both her hands and kissed them, pulled a bouquet of real flowers — carefully folded and compressed in a secret pocket from within his jacket — and presented it to her with much blushing and grateful thanks on her part. He watched her depart, shuffling carefully with her cane, across downstage and to the steps into the arms of waiting ushers to the thunderous applause of the audience.

He bowed, and began his exit from the stage as the curtain came down and the stagehands prepared for the next act with trained cats.

After that was a female singer, doing a brief aria with some expertise, though Leopold wasn't enamored of the higher pitched notes that seemed to drag out too long. And then he vaguely wondered if Mingli could sing and just what she *would* sing — English or some dissonant Chinese tune — and then he thought about her seeming agreement to his courting her…and supper tonight…though it wouldn't be alone. Ah well. Small steps.

It cheered him considerably. He adjusted his white waistcoat. He was going to be courting her. That was the important part. He would try not to think about her *other* offer. By Jove, she was a tempting woman! How would it be to…to marry such a person? He couldn't imagine it. He couldn't imagine her keeping a house for him or making a meal. But of course, she wouldn't! There would be servants for that. Servants they could trust who wouldn't speak of the magic that would abound in their household. And just like that, he decided that she should continue to do whatever it is she did. Of course she would! She must continue her important work as a Special Inspector. He couldn't imagine Mingli wishing to be like any woman, running a house and having… "Oh." Having children.

He swallowed hard. Children. Should he raise children in the life he was beginning to create around him? With sagging shoulders and furiously blinking his eyes, had he the right to even think of it with this sword of Damocles hanging over him? He couldn't help but push up his sleeve and stare at the All-Seeing eye stamped upon his inner wrist. He stared at it with the hatred he'd come to harbor for it…and then it blinked and looked back and forth.

Startled into a sound of dismay, he didn't know whether to hide the beastly thing under his sleeve or expose more of the tattoo, dreading what this movement of it revealed. He was abruptly blasted with sharp pain from the thing, and heat like a flame burst over his skin. He gasped, bit his lip, and stumbled back, falling against a piece of scenery stored in the wings. Holding his arm forth, the eye slowly turned toward him and stared.

He did cover it then, trembling and clasping his hand over his cuff as if to keep the tattoo from crawling forth and wreaking its destruction.

He braced himself against the painted canvas, breathing in short gasps, waiting for the pain to subside…when it finally did. All that remained was an unpleasant tingle, and the sensation on his body of pins and needles.

How could he perform? But more importantly, what was this portent his mark had tried to warn him of?

Stealthily, he peeked through the edge of the curtain. He saw nothing unusual.

No. Wait. About three rows back from the orchestra, the entire row of men sat with blank faces. Yes, he noticed them when he was on the stage, but didn't think much of it. But now that the comic play was being performed, and while the rest of the audience smiled and laughed and applauded, these men did nothing. Not anything at all. They didn't smile, they didn't clap. They didn't move. As if they were under an enchantment…

The curtain came down and the orchestra vamped the magician music again. He couldn't seem to pull himself away from the side of the proscenium until the curtain rose…on a blank stage. He'd missed his cue!

The maestro in the orchestra pit moved his baton to stop the musicians to begin the vamp again.

Leopold straightened his hat, met Agnes' wide eyes of surprise and took the box she shoved toward him—it was a table on wheels—and pushed it forth to the stage, centering it.

He faced the audience and accepted their applause by bowing and tipping his hat to them. He showed the inside of the hat, proving nothing was there and placed it upon the box.

"Ladies and gentlemen," he said, always flourishing his hands in their white gloves. It served as a distraction, to keep their eyes busy on him and not on the routine he was about to perform. It was his dove act, but he was also keeping his eyes on the stoic row of unmoving men.

"You will note, there is nothing in my hands." He took but a moment to unbutton the tailcoat and strip it off his shoulders. "And nothing up my sleeves." He spread his arms in their tailored shirt. For indeed, there *was* nothing up his shirt sleeves. It was all in the table.

He raised his empty hand and the wand suddenly appeared. And yes, that was a spot of real magic. There was enough of it present to use a small amount, though he felt far too drained after performing it than he should have. It gave him pause, but he continued on, stepping behind the table and positioning his hat—with its hidden flap—over the special trap door on the table's surface.

Doves were small-boned creatures and could be squeezed into the tightest of places. This was why they were often used in such routines. A vast amount of doves secured in one's coat or in a table was astounding to the eye of the punter, but the magician knew just how many he could secure in the secret pockets of shirt or jacket and how many could be entombed, no matter how temporarily, within a table.

Raj favored feeding the doves and they took to him like a…well…like a pigeon to a statue, he supposed. They were sweet things, really, and Leopold admitted he liked their soft cooing.

His eyes swept over the third row of men and he suppressed a shudder. Something was definitely amiss. And he felt the sensation of malevolent magic drifting toward him like a stench.

Leopold realized he'd stopped. The audience moved uncomfortably in their seats. He felt the lights shining in his face, the heat from both the gas and electric lights; the strange distance and yet an intimacy between where he stood on the stage, and where the audience sat before him in the gloom of cigar and pipe smoke and darkness. They were close enough to see his tricks and routines, but far enough away that they couldn't touch him. The orchestra pit and the apron of the stage assured that. And yet…he was filled with an unexplainable uneasiness.

He cast his glance to the third row even as he slowly reached into the hat through its trick opening and into the trapdoor of the table. His gloved fingers closed on a dove. He felt its warmth, its vitality even through his cotton gloves. It wasn't afraid. He knew that. It had been handled hundreds of times by him. It would fly into the arch of the ceiling, around the theatre, and thence to the backstage where they'd return to their perches or to their roosts on the roof of the theatre. They knew the way. People in the theatre always said that animal acts were unpredictable, but not birds. They always returned.

He slowly pulled it out and set it on his shoulder. He reached in again and pulled out another, placing it on the other shoulder. The more he pulled out, the more the audience reacted. "There simply couldn't be any more," they'd think, as doves perched on his shoulders, all the way down his arms, his head, until there was no more room. This was a trick that would fascinate, not frighten. The doves were beautiful and white, and glanced about as if waiting for a cue…which, of course, they were. At last, he lifted his arms sharply, and this was their signal to fly. And just as their wings began to flap with a gentle brush of feathers across his cheeks, the glamour fell from the third-row men like a rainfall.

Gone was the veneer of mustachioed gentlemen with bowler and top hats, leaving behind the grizzled and bent figures…of goblins.

They scrambled from their seats, climbing over the chair backs, stepping on the shoulders of the men and women in front of them, denting hats and bending feathers. It wasn't just Leopold who had seen their glamours fall, but the audience. Their screams rang out as they rushed out of the way.

The goblins jumped, some snatching doves out of the air and clamping down on their sleek, white bodies with sharp teeth. Blood spattered their faces *and* the horrified audience they climbed upon.

The audience ran for the exits. Those that reached the righthand doors first were bowled over as the doors burst open. Screams renewed and grew louder as they spied the figure silhouetted in the doorway, blocking their escape, a long two-headed axe at his side.

The figure moved forward with a whoosh of pistons and a clang of metal feet.

Leopold drew out his wand and pointed it at the Clockwork Gypsy. "Stay back!" he warned.

The Romani man threw back his head and laughed, his long plait whipping behind him. His goggled eyes suddenly projected a beam of light that strafed the crowd and landed once again on Leopold like a spot light. "Your feeble stick will not stop me. Not now."

Men grasped crying women and dragged them away to any available exit as the clockwork man stepped forward, each of his heavy steps ringing down the aisle.

Leopold made the decision in a split second. He dropped his wand and drew out his dagger instead, slicing his arm in quick order. "*Tishmor!*"

The downstage floor erupted in scorching flame and the smell of brimstone. Eurynomos burst up through the floor, twisting horns shooting upward, followed by bald head and grimacing mouth full of pointed teeth, then finally the broad chest and loin cloth made their appearance.

"Who dares?" he bellowed, his voice reverberating on the rafters. He turned his eyes immediately to the clockwork man and then scanned the scrambling goblins.

As Leopold watched, the goblins did not seem to move in concert with the Clockwork Gypsy. Instead, they seemed as surprised as the audience at his appearance. They had been moving toward Leopold, toward the stage, but now they seemed startled to immobility. Suddenly, they awoke, scrambling over the seats to escape the theatre.

Interesting, he had time to ponder, before the clockwork man rushed forward, swinging his axe at the theatre seats, splintering them beyond repair.

But Eurynomos launched himself toward the man, and when they clashed, there came a burst of bright light. Leopold turned away. He could see the painful light even with his eyes firmly shut, even with his arm thrown over his face. Amazingly, he could see the bone of his arm through his closed eyes, and through his skin and muscle.

The man roared his frustration. "Get out of my way, daemon! I must kill him!"

Eurynomos grunted as he clutched both metal wrists, pushing back against the man and keeping that axe from swinging toward him. Their struggle dented and scorched the floor in the aisle. Sparks flew and magic clashed in billows of smoke and a shower of ash. "I'm afraid I can't let you do that, old man," Eurynomos grunted. "And what, if I may ask, *are* you?"

The Clockwork Gypsy shoved Eurynomos back and freed himself, brandishing his axe. The smoke settled around him. He panted and glared at the daemon, only now getting his footing under him. "I'm not afraid of you, *Eurynomos*." He said the name with great distaste. "One of his many devils, no doubt," he said, pointing at Leopold with his weapon he scarcely needed. "I knew you were a fiend, Kazsmer. I saw you with this…this *creature* at the camp. I knew you were the devil's own."

Leopold grasped his bleeding wrist. It dripped a trail of blood upon the stage floor, for Eurynomos had had no time to heal him. He staggered to the edge of the stage. *The camp?* "Why are you trying to kill me? What have I ever done to you? Who are you?"

The Clockwork Gypsy looked aghast for a moment before he renewed his scowl. "I am Midnight. I am the Last Breath. I am Death. Do you hear the ticking of my mechanical heart? It ticks down to the final beat of your own." He lunged forward, feinting one way and fooling Eurynomos, before he launched himself the other way. His brass legs must have been part coiled springs, for he leapt the span of ten rows and over the orchestra pit before landing just short of the apron, where the brass fingers of one hand dug into the wooden stage so deeply the floor cracked.

He used his axe to pull himself up and Leopold tottered back. In one swift, swinging leap, the Clockwork Gypsy was on the stage, marching toward Leopold.

Leopold slipped on his own blood and fell backwards. He tried to skid away from the fiend, but he could get no purchase from his feet or his hands.

And his sight was fading. Too much blood. He'd lost too much. His eyes could no longer focus, and his mind began to diminish. If he fainted now, he'd be dead.

He raised his bloody hand to the unrelenting man and intoned a spell to stop him. His lips moved and he breathed the words, but nothing happened.

Eurynomos appeared beside him with a decided pop. He clamped his taloned fingers around Leopold's wrist and instantly the pain, the hollow sounds, the dizziness ceased. He realized the daemon healed him and, remarkably, restored the blood lost. Leopold jumped to his feet and this time, with both hands poised, his spell caught.

The clockwork man froze in place, and even as he tried to move forward, his feet slid on the floor. But his anger seemed to flood him with purpose. He raised his fists and roared out his rage, and suddenly, Leopold slammed back as the spell broke, like a cut rope.

The Clockwork Gypsy closed the space between him and nearly touched Leopold's lapel when Eurynomos stepped in front of him. The daemon seemed to have grown. No, he *had* grown, and was growing still. His shoulders widened and his head slowly rose into the fly space above the stage where the ropes and catwalks resided.

The Romani merely watched him, a perpetual sneer on his lips. "You need your devils to fight your fights, eh, *gadjo?*"

"Who the blazes *are* you?" cried Leopold, picking himself up a second time.

The clockwork man wound up—gears and coils ticking—and with all his might, snapped back with his brass fist curled, sending the twelve-foot-tall Eurynomos crashing into the stage-right set pieces. "Ha!" he laughed. "You can do me no harm," he said. "The old fortune telling vampyre told me so. His last prediction." He tossed his axe into the air, letting it spin around the long handle before he deftly caught it. "And then I beheaded him. His predictions are no more. As you will be, Kazsmer."

But the daemon was quick to recover and in an eyeblink, he was there again, arm curled around the man's neck, his muscles bulging as he tightened his grip. "You are a very troublesome metal man, aren't you? I little care for the prophecies of the undead. My friend has asked you a question. I think we'd both like to hear the answer."

The man struggled to get at Leopold, who had nothing with which to protect himself but the magic unwinding from the movements of his hands in glowing tendrils. It slowed the man's struggle, but Leopold could tell that Eurynomos—even as big and as strong as he was—fought to hold the man in place.

The Clockwork Gypsy appeared to have more brass on his face and on his neck than the last time he saw him. The shaved part of his head had riveted plates now where before was bald skin.

"I am Miklos Antalek!" he cried, pulling, straining from Eurynomos' grasp. "Do. You. *Know*. Me?"

Leopold froze. Memories flooded back. No. This couldn't be he. The Miklos Antalek he knew was a gangly boy, a ruffian who, though he belonged to the Romani camp where Leopold grew up, often went his own way: ignoring his elders, disrespecting their counsel, thieving and whoring. The elders decided on their own to banish him from their camp, which was no slight thing. He had vowed revenge and—some say accidentally, some say deliberately—killed one of the elders who had banished him. There had been a manhunt. And then… and then… Leopold's memory failed him. He couldn't remember what happened to the horrifying Miklos after that.

"Miklos," he breathed. "In all likelihood, you brought this on yourself." It had been the wrong thing to say.

Miklos roared again. The governors and pistons within him whirred faster. "You don't remember? YOU DON'T REMEMBER?"

"I remember the foul boy you were. I remember you stealing from me, beating me. I remember…how much I loathed you."

"And do you not remember casting this spell upon me, cursing me?"

"Me?"

"Yes. *You! You* made me. *You* cursed me. It was *you*, Leopold Kazsmer. And now…*you* die!"

CHAPTER TEN

SUDDENLY, MIKLOS BROKE free from the daemon with a clash of sparks and smoke. Eurynomos shrank, seemed to bend from the exertion. Indeed, he was breathing harshly, his eyes wide in shock.

Leopold doubled his efforts of weaving a magic cage around himself, and he backed away as Miklos approached. The mechanical arm swatted at the magical barrier, and with a grimacing effort, he seemed to break through it.

Leopold fell back and could not get to his feet before Miklos loured over him. "You've gotten rich, Kazsmer, while I...I became...*this*! A monster."

"I didn't do it, Miklos. I never would have done it."

"You said you hated me."

"That's different from truly getting revenge. I learned from my father to forgive."

Miklos hesitated. And in that moment, Eurynomos appeared there in an instant, ready to grab him. But Leopold saw something different on Miklos' face, in his eyes through the strange goggles his eyes had become.

"Your Jewish father."

"Yes. A man you never knew. A man you ridiculed. A man who would have had pity on you, helped you. As...as *I* will help you now."

"Leopold, no!" cried Eurynomos. "He is a creature now. He has nothing left but his vengeance."

"I don't believe that," said Leopold. He slowly got to his feet, keeping his eyes on the Romani man, but his hands were at the ready to hurl magical weapons and defensive spells, just in case. "I don't think he would even have remembered his name if he were that far gone."

Miklos leaned on his axe and raised one hand to his head, the side that still had skin. "It…it is getting harder to remember. Harder…to be who I was. The gears. They are taking over my mind. There will be nothing left of me. I sought you. I killed to get to you. I traveled the world looking for a cure. But there was nothing and no one to help me."

"I didn't do this, Miklos."

The ferocity was back in Miklos' eyes. His frown hardened. "I will not listen to you. I will return, Kazsmer. When you least expect it. When you are alone."

He whirled suddenly and raced off the stage in a giant leap, crashing onto the house floor, cracking the wood. Rushing up the aisle he burst through the doors, loosening one from its hinges and hurling it away.

Eurynomos flew off the stage in pursuit, but Leopold called out to him. "NO! Eurynomos, don't."

The daemon's talons dug into the floor as he skidded to a stop, mere inches from the broken house doors. He looked back at Leopold with eyes and mouth wide. "But Leo! He'll be back. He'll kill you."

"No. I don't think he will."

"But…" He turned toward the doorway where the clanking steps of the clockwork man were disappearing into the noise of the London street. "You don't know that for certain."

"I think I do. And what if I *had* done it, Eurynomos? What if by some chance, some strange circumstance, that I *had* done it?"

"What if you had? Do you think you deserve the fate he would mete out to you?"

Leopold sagged. "I don't know. What's happened to him, it's…it's abominable. And if it *were* me…then maybe I do deserve to die."

The daemon stepped toward him. "Leo."

Leopold waved him off and staggered toward the wings. "I…I have to study. I have to prepare myself to go to Gehenna to fetch my father." He grabbed at his aching wrist and held it. "I've dallied too long. There's no time left."

The daemon had shrunk down to the size of an average man. He gripped the apron of the stage, his head barely reaching over it. "Leo," he said softly.

But Leopold had already gone.

———◆———

HE HURRIED HOME. He had not wanted to look Raj in the face, nor his assistants, who surely had questions now that they had seen the real magic he had performed. Had seen Eurynomos. And goblins. And...*good grief.* How was he to tell them? It didn't matter. The feeling of malevolent magic flowing off of the mechanical man created a new fear in him. A fear that he *might* have actually done it. In those early wild days, when he started to experiment with magic — forbidden in the Gypsy camp, but he had practiced it anyway — he *could* have done it. Surely by accident, but he could have. Yet it was no excuse. That man had lived like that for thirteen years! The terror. The inconsolable horror of it. He couldn't blame the man.

It made it all the more urgent that he find a way to free his father. If he couldn't help the clockwork man, then he had to at least rescue another innocent from a life of abomination.

He hadn't any idea how long he was at it. His fingers were stained with ink. Papers covered his desk in the drawing room. Notebooks with pages of notes he'd made surrounded him. Books of Jewish mysticism lay open, layered one upon the other. There were no examples of how to get a human out of Gehenna, only various ways of drawing out daemons from it.

And all the while, the dead faery in the bell jar sat mute on a table, overlooking his paperwork.

The doorbell chimed.

Lost for a moment as to where he was, he raised his head blearily. He cast a glance to his mantel clock. It read near midnight.

The bell chimed again, and he levered himself up from his chair and trudged forward. The foyer was dark. He hadn't lit the lights. But when he reached the door, he could see a female figure through the frosted glass.

When he opened the door, an angry Mingli Zhao stood at his entry, her gloved hand tight on her umbrella handle. "Oh," she said. "So you aren't dead, lying in a ditch somewhere."

He smacked his forehead. "My dear Miss Zhao. I completely forgot. Can you ever forgive me?"

She pushed through the door and marched across his foyer, heading toward his drawing room. "And what, pray, has kept you so preoccupied that you neglected our supper this evening?"

Leopold passed a mirror and pulled up short. His hair was in a disarray and his tie was completely missing. He was in his shirt sleeves and the tails of his shirt were untucked. Stuffing them back into his trousers, he stumbled along as he hurried to catch up to her.

He found her standing over his desk and sneering at the books and papers she could easily read. She ticked her head.

"I encountered the Clockwork Gypsy at my theatre this evening," he blurted.

She snapped her head up with eyes wide. "What happened?"

"Well..." He raked his fingers through his hair, trying to smooth it down. "At first, I thought it was the goblins I would have to contend with. They were glamoured and sitting in the third row, ready to attack me while I performed — which they tried to do."

"With the audience present? Were you able to repel them?"

"No. The clockwork man appeared and he frightened them off."

"Hmm. Then perhaps they are *not* in league."

"This I already know. The mechanical man — one Miklos Antalek — was a man I knew from the Romani camp when I was a boy there. He...he blames me for his current condition."

"But of course, it wasn't you."

He sat heavily into his seat, all decorum set aside, for Mingli still stood over his desk and he hadn't offered her a chair. "I don't honestly know. When I was young, I practiced magic in secret. My uncle forbade my use of it. My spells were sometimes wild and ill-conceived. It was only when I could secretly summon Eurynomos that he was able to properly teach me. I *could* have done it, Miss Zhao. I could have condemned him to the life he's been living these past thirteen years."

She did sit then, in a chair across from his desk. "But you never did it intentionally."

He shook his head. "That's just the thing. I might have. He was my tormenter. He humiliated and beat me incessantly. My anger could easily have manifested into magical mischief, even without my knowing it. It could be my fault. He'd be in his rights to kill me."

"Nonsense. Anything you might have done, you could surely correct. Did you tell him that?"

"Yes. I don't know if he believed me. He ran off. Even Eurynomos had a difficult time fighting against him. And I have so little time." He dropped his head into his hand, rubbing his forehead.

"So little time? Whatever do you mean?"

He dropped his hands to the books and papers before him. "I have to study. I have to discover…" He shook his head. "I have to study."

Mingli snapped to her feet, punching the end of her umbrella into the rug. "This obsession with the Kabbalah has closed you off from far more important magics, Mr. Kazsmer. I fail to understand your fixation."

He leaned his head heavily on his hand. The words and symbols all seemed to run together in his mind, and he didn't even realize when he said, "I'm obsessed with the study of the Kabbalah because I'm trying to discover a way to save my father."

"But your father is dead. You said so your—"

"He's not." His voice trembled, and tears blurred his vision. "He's trapped in *Sitra Achra*. And that's my fault too."

Mingli gasped. "Leo…"

"I'm sorry for that outburst." He wiped the wet from his eyes and licked his lips, trying to master himself. "I never meant to say. I had thought that my father sacrificed his life to save me. But…recently, I discovered that this wasn't true. That he is trapped there. Trapped for nearly seventeen years. And I have so little time. You will recall when I received the second tattoo." He pushed up his sleeve and stared at the stark black mark on his pale arm.

"Saving the life of your daemon friend."

"Yes." He turned his arm over to glare at the All-Seeing Eye, the Eye of Providence. "Though this first mark protected me from enslavement from those of the Otherworld and aligned me with Eurynomos, the second, done in desperation, indebted me to the Unholy Hosts. They are the ones holding my father. They could call in their debt at any time. They could force me to work some great evil. Or they could swallow my soul as they have done to so many. So now…perhaps you understand my obsession."

"But Leo," she said softly, and much closer than he expected. He looked up and she was standing beside him. "Why didn't you tell me? You know I would have dropped everything to help you."

"I…well…I didn't want to burden you. And I didn't know where you were for the last six months." He hadn't meant for the last to come out as harshly as it did.

She knelt beside him and laid a hand on his arm. "I would have come to you had I known. I would have moved Heaven and Earth to come to you."

He turned to her and her one eye was filled with such tenderness…and then she leaned in.

He should have protested. He hadn't been prepared, but when her lips closed over his—so warm, so sweet—he could utter nothing but a groan from deep in the core of him. Those soft lips moved over his, pressing, skimming, until he felt the strange intrusion of a tongue force open his mouth and plunge in.

He made a squeak of protest for only a second before he discovered the brilliance of such a move. Sheer. Utter. Brilliance! He rose, still joined by their kiss, and reached up to encircle her with his arms. He felt the stiffness of the corset beneath his fingers—*oh God, corset!*—the smooth satin of her dress, the layers of petticoats crushing against his groin. And all around him like a gentle cloud was the scent of her, the taste of her, the feel of her fingers curling into his chest, digging deep.

Overwhelmed with emotion—and an undeniable physical response—he gently pushed her back—gasping—and leaned back against the table. He slowly opened his eyes.

"Miss…Miss Zhao…"

She chuckled softly. "Mingli. Can't you call me Mingli?"

"Miss Zhao, I…I…"

"You are a delight," she said, still smiling, cupping his jaw affectionately.

I am…untried, he couldn't help thinking and hating it. Some man of the world *he* was! But then it all came crashing back into his consciousness; the Clockwork Gypsy, his father. He turned away. "I'm sorry…"

"Leo…"

The tinkle of glass breaking.

Leopold looked up, startled. He glanced at his window, but the heavy drapery covered it. Would it not have moved had the window been broken?

He stepped away from Mingli to look at the floor beneath the window. No glass shards. Perhaps it was a mirror? He turned toward the fireplace but the glass above the mantel was unharmed. Then what—?

"Leopold!"

With her voice unnaturally distressed, Leopold whipped toward Mingli. "What is it?"

In answer, she raised her arm and pointed. His eyes followed.

The faery's bell jar had cracked open and lay in pieces on the table. And the faery was gone.

"What the devil…?"

Something on the rug beneath the table…moved.

He crouched to look.

It had been a mistake.

It flew at him, tangling at his shirt. Claws and teeth snapped and scraped his skin. He slapped wildly at the creature. A squirrel? A cat? He punched it hard, dislodging it. The small thing rolled toward the hearth and thudded against the brass fireplace fender.

"My God, Leo!"

He couldn't believe what he was seeing. The dark brown thing unfurled itself and stood. It was the faery.

"It's alive after all," he gasped.

Mingli drew the sword from her umbrella. "No, Mr. Kazsmer. It most assuredly is not."

"What? But it attacked me. It's moving. It's…it's coming toward us again…" But even as he looked at it, its tanned skin hadn't changed or bloomed with life. The skin was still thin and stretched taut over a fine-boned skeleton. Its mouth was still grimaced with sharp teeth, though now they were wet with Leopold's blood. But the eyes… The eyes were still shut tight, desiccated, absent. It moved stiffly, as any long-dead and suddenly animated *corpse* would surely do…

CHAPTER ELEVEN

"WHAT IN THE name of Heaven is this?" said Leopold.

"I don't know how it happened," said Mingli, backing up with Leopold, "but it seems to have reanimated."

"But it's dead. I mean...*look* at it!" He wiped his neck and looked at the blood on his hand.

"That doesn't seem to change the fact that it is moving with every intent to do us harm."

"Are...are faeries known to resurrect from the dead?"

"None that I know of. And it has nothing to do with their immortal nature. At least I don't think so."

They found themselves backed up against the desk.

The faery's grimace turned to a smile with the cracking of the dried skin at the corners of its mouth.

"Oh damn," said Leopold. He girded himself and, before he could properly gather his magic, the thing leapt again.

Its battered wings were able to send it toward his face, but he caught it by the neck and struggled with its immense strength. He yawed and swayed with the blasted thing, wings beating furiously against his arms. He couldn't help but look directly at the mummified face. *It's dead! I know it's dead*, he thought furiously. *How is it attacking me?*

"Leopold! Hold it away from you."

Mingli's cry made little sense as he was working his damnedest to do that very thing. He managed to straighten his arms, and it was only then that he flicked a glance toward her. Her umbrella had been reassembled and she held it at the point like a cricket bat.

"Wait!" he cried, thinking of his hands, but the umbrella swung.

It caught the faery in the stomach with such a loud thwack that it flew from his fingers. The tiny creature arced into the air for only a moment before it landed squarely into the flames of the fireplace. A scream and a stench arose as the thing struggled on the pyre, flailing arms and legs. Its wings went first in a puff of black smoke before the flames quickly consumed the body in a whoosh of bright green fire. Black, greasy smoke arose, and the creature stilled at last. The charred remains crumbled in the coals and soon there was nothing left at all.

They both stood before the hearth, watching the gray ash tumble over the glowing embers and disperse.

Mingli collapsed into a chair, her hat flopping over her forehead. "*Tiānshàng de shén!*" she breathed.

"You can say that again," he muttered, falling into his own chair.

They both said nothing for a long time, glancing now and again into the hearth to make certain the faery was not going to arise again.

Mingli sat forward first, adjusting her hat. "Well. That was...interesting, to say the least."

"Interesting? That thing nearly tore out my throat."

"I'm awfully glad it didn't."

He touched his neck. "So am I."

She reached up to her hat again and pulled out a long hat pin. She removed the charming hat—like a miniature topper, with bows and netting—and laid it into her lap while she patted her curls. And then she began unbuttoning her tight jacket.

"M-Miss Zhao—"

She removed it, stood, and laid it on the back on the chair. "I'm just getting comfortable. We are in for a long night of research." She stepped toward the table, just as if a resurrected faery had not attacked them, ready and able to help Leopold save his father amid everything else.

He gazed at her then with unfettered affection. "I should have known you would selflessly put aside your own work to help me," he said softly.

"Of course! How did you ever doubt it?"

But before she could get around him to the desk, he reached out and grabbed her hand. He was fairly certain at this juncture that she would not throw him over her shoulder to the floor in indignation. "Miss

Zhao... Er, Mingli," he said softly. "We can't put aside what just happened. Why did that faery suddenly come alive? What is the meaning of it all?"

"Yes. I'm suddenly thinking about my cache of similar faeries at my flat. Did *they* come alive, I wonder?"

Just as he got comfortable holding her petite hand, they both became aware at the same time of distant screaming. They needed only to exchange one glance before they were running for the front door. Leopold got there first and threw it open. They stood on the threshold, straining their ears. The mist had risen and it was impossible to see deeply into the dense fog. But there was the distinct sound of several cries of distress coming from many directions, though nearly swallowed up by the vast gray.

"Do you see anything?" he whispered.

"No. But I hear...something nearby."

A shuffling step.

It came from Leopold's left and he turned, squinting in that direction. His own breathing was loud as he strained to hear, and then Mingli's breath was suddenly at his ear. He couldn't help himself and, when he turned to her, he indulged in gazing at her from close proximity. Her skin was flawless...no. Not entirely so. There were the minutest of freckles running over the bridge of her nose, hidden by a light powder.

She noticed his staring and it seemed she could read his thoughts. She offered an impish smile.

He moved his gaze to her lips, so full and plump. And he had kissed them. And now—despite the strange happenings around them—he could think of little else...until she frowned and suddenly and roughly shoved him out of the way. She whipped her gun out from under her skirts and aimed past Leopold's head. He tried to duck but the explosion blasted his hearing, ringing loudly in his head.

When he looked past her outstretched arm, he saw a man lying in the road.

"Why did you shoot him?" he shouted. He couldn't hear himself any other way.

She ran down the steps to stand over the dead man, his head in the gutter, his body lying awkwardly on the pavement. His forehead had a large hole in it from her strange pistol, but there was no blood.

"What sort of bullet is that?" he asked, bending over to study the man. Was the bullet able to cauterize as it pierced? But then he observed the man himself; an old man wearing a suit caked with dirt.

He stared at her gun, a bulb of liquid where the barrel should be. He couldn't even see a place where a bullet could be stored.

"A specialized blast that can do a great deal of harm," she said. "But it doesn't seem to have done him that much damage."

"Well, he's dead. But there's no blood that I can see."

"He *is* dead, Leo, but not from my gun."

Turning to her, he asked, "What do you mean?"

He let out a shout when a hand clasped his wrist. Snapping his head back toward the dead man, he saw that his eyes had flicked open and he was rising from the street.

Leopold pushed hard at the iron clasp on his wrist, trying his mightiest to dislodge him.

Mingli raised her pistol and fired again. The man soared backwards, releasing Leopold's wrist.

"He...he..." Leopold stuttered.

"He was already dead when I shot him. He was still dead whilst I shot him a second time. And when he rises again, he will also still be dead."

"What are you saying?" he asked, examining the bruising on his wrist, and taking care to keep an eye on the man lying flat on the street. But even as he watched, those eyes opened again, even when one of them had been shot out. He sat up and turned toward Leopold.

Leopold leapt up, grabbed Mingli, and rushed her back into the house. He bolted the door and warded it with magic, backing away from the entry. He expected the walking corpse to beat upon the door, but nothing happened. Leopold crept to the side lights and cautiously pushed the lacy curtains aside.

There was the dead man, shuffling down the street, not bothering to even glance back at Leopold's door.

But to Leopold's horror, right on his heels, a full skeleton — from the skull head to the tiniest of toe bones — head cocked to the side, and with the remnants of ancient and ragged clothes dangling from the more protruding parts of his joints, walked.

"That's impossible!" he cried. "What in great Heaven is happening? Why are the dead walking?"

"It's very peculiar."

He glanced at Mingli then. There was no fear on her face, just bafflement at trying to figure out a puzzle. He suddenly blurted a hysterical laugh. "You are the most undaunted woman I have ever met."

"There's no sense in screaming and crying over it."

"But, my dear Miss Zhao. Dead men, skeletons, dead *faeries*, coming to life? Surely that is something worth screaming over. I must confess. I am doing all I can to stop myself from screaming."

She rested a gloved hand to his cheek and he immediately fell lost in her single eye. "That's because you are a sensitive man, sympathetic to the plight of others. I have long ago trained myself to look at all problems with logic and detachment."

He lay his hand over hers on his face. "It's only one of the many reasons...I...I love you."

Her composure cracked then. Her eye widened in astonishment, and her alluring lips parted. "Why Leo..."

He dared it. He leaned in, paused, then leaned in the rest of the way to press a kiss to her mouth. He felt her fall toward him, and he was able to engage in the lesson she had taught him earlier, by opening his mouth and thoroughly kissing *her*, this time.

Magic. Bliss. Glory.

He pulled back unwillingly and was surprised to see a glazed expression on her face. "You're a fast learner," she breathed.

He smiled. "I like doing research."

She chuckled and patted him on the chest, pushing him further back. "I'm afraid we can't indulge right now. We have a puzzle to figure out."

They turned back toward the door when they heard more shouting in the streets. The clanging bell of a fire wagon whizzed by the house and disappeared around a corner. Leopold hurried to his front window and cast open the drapery. Slow-moving figures—both corpse and bones—made their way from every direction in the fog. They simply wandered the streets, not going in any particular direction.

Out of the fog, a man with a tall custodian helmet, a copper, appeared, waving about his baton. He seemed to be trying to admonish one of the shuffling men...when all at once, the strange man reared up and clamped his mouth to the policeman's throat.

Leopold threw open the sash...but it was too late. The rozzer fell, and the shuffling man—a dead man, Leopold decided with a sickening stomach—simply shuffled on.

Leopold wrestled with himself. Should he go out and help the man? But the decision was taken from him when he saw the policeman slowly rise, leave behind his baton, and shuffle forward.

"My God," said Leopold. "Something quite fiendish is afoot."

"The dead attack the living and once they are dead, they rise and attack *more* of the living."

Leopold shivered. "It's diabolical."

"'The City of the River will find no peace when the dead walk'," said Mingli. She yanked him back and shut the window, pulling the drapes closed. "Remember Raj's tarot cards? 'The City of the River will find no peace when the dead walk.' Someone is creating this enchantment."

He stared at her. "The dead would leave their graves to *kill*?"

She cocked her head, looking at him with an amused expression. "I review all available evidence and make a logical conclusion based on that evidence. Certainly, *you've* seen far worse and stranger things in your travels, Mr. Kazsmer."

He had to admit that he had.

"Therefore, I've concluded that whatever enchantment this is—and I've no doubt that it *is* an enchantment—then even my dead faery collection is not immune."

"Anything dead..." It *was* diabolical. Horrific. He was coming to the conclusion that he couldn't let it lie. "We...we can't rescue my father just now."

"But Leopold..."

"No. Everyone in London is in danger. He'd never allow me to abandon *them* to save *him*. It wasn't his way. We must discover who is doing this."

Mingli moved to his desk and sat, looking over the assembled papers and books, before she leaned forward on her elbows. "Very well, Leopold. Let us look at this logically. Tell me again everything you saw at the Saint Collen Club."

CHAPTER TWELVE

THEY TALKED FOR hours, exchanging ideas, even as cries rose up out of the streets. Mingli was certain it had something to do with whatever the goblins were planning with the Necropolis Railway, but couldn't seem to fathom the intent or how it was accomplished.

But when she had to be prodded for the second time to answer a question of Leopold's, he realized that they had been awake far too long.

"Look, Miss Zhao, it's very late. And it isn't safe for you to go home. Why don't you stay here for the rest of the night? I'll sleep here in the drawing room, and you can have my bedchamber."

She raised a sleepy smile to him. "We could share the bed."

Breathlessly, he nodded and turned away. "Yes, I suppose we could. But...I still feel..."

"You're right," she said, waving him off. "I'm much too tired to argue. To bed, then." She levered herself up from her chair, stretched sinuously, and trudged toward the bedroom.

Leopold watched her and felt a little disappointed as she closed the door. He took himself to the sideboard and poured a glass of brandy from a crystal decanter. He tipped back the glass and drank the small amount, delighting in the burn and warmth it offered. It was only then he realized the fire wasn't lit in the bedroom.

He strode to the door and knocked gently.

"Come in," came the muffled reply.

He opened the door softly and stuck only his head in. "I'm so sorry, but I didn't realize the fire wasn't lit..." But when he glanced toward the hearth, it was burning merrily.

She sat at his dressing table and was unbuckling her eye patch-telescope from its strap on the back of her head. "You know, I do possess a modicum of magic myself, Leo. I can start a wee fire when I need to."

"Oh. Forgive me…"

She pulled off the patch and laid it aside. She unpinned her bountiful hair and let it cascade downward, before turning around.

He braced himself. He was afraid of what horrors would lay beneath the patch. A scar, the ragged remains of an eye? But as a proper gentleman and as the man courting her, he felt obliged to confront it without revealing his true feelings on the matter.

He sucked up his courage and looked…but it wasn't at all what he expected.

She rose and approached him. The topmost buttons of her blouse were already undone, leaving her throat bare.

To his great relief, the eye remained intact, only there was no white or iris. Instead, the entire eye was a polished black, like a marble or a billiard ball.

No, that wasn't quite true, for the closer she came, the clearer he could see it.

"Mingli," he gasped. "It's…it's…*amazing*…"

As he gazed, he seemed to be pulled deep within its depths, for it looked for all the world like galaxies, like a field of stars in a night sky that pressed on into the infinity of the universe.

"Interesting, isn't it?" she breathed, her face close to his. "I cover it because…well. It's not that I can't see from it, but that I see far too much. It was an enchanted sword that that devil struck me with, and though the eye no longer has the usual ability to conventionally see, I can '*see*' well beyond this realm. I can see auras, and multiple layers of dimensions…all at the same time. It was driving me quite mad. Until I made the patch with its filters."

"*You* made it?" he said in wonder. "But of course you did. You are so very clever."

"And then I couldn't resist enhancing it like your spectacles."

"It's beautiful." He couldn't stop staring and knew that he must, so he turned slightly away. "It reminds me of — do forgive me for the comparison—but of a marble I once had as a child. It was a great prize of mine. Until another boy stole it from me." He frowned, remembering the incident so long ago. "Come to think of it, it had been Miklos who stole it from me."

Mingli's fingers were on his chin, turning his face toward her again.

"Well, I can assure you, no *boy* will steal *me* from you." Before he could speak again, her lips brushed his in a quick kiss that ended far too soon.

She studied his face with a gentle smile.

"Do you…" He felt his cheeks flush with heat, but he had to know. "Do you *really*…I mean…Oh dash it! Mingli, do you truly have feelings for me?"

She smiled that mischievous smile and kissed him quickly again. "What do *you* think?"

"I know what I'd *like* to think. But I need to know the truth. Because, I don't think I could quite bear it if you were only toying with me."

She moved closer, reaching for the open neck of his shirt—spattered as it was with his own blood from the faery's teeth—and hauled him in. She kissed him soundly again, and his hands found her waist, bringing her closer as their mouths moved over one another's. And he couldn't stop himself from thinking what an extraordinary thing it was, this kissing business.

When she moved away this time, she bit her lip.

"I care for you a great deal," she said. "More than I really should. More than I feel comfortable feeling. Do you understand now, Leo? Do I love you? Of course I do. Very much so."

"Oh." His throat was thick and his heart hammered in his chest. He licked his lips, tasting her there. "Oh. Jolly good, then. Well." He gave a little bow. "Then I'll say good night."

There was tenderness is her one good eye. "Good night, Leo."

"Good night." He hung on the edge of the door unmoving, before he roused himself, blushed again, and closed the door. He rested his forehead on it, letting the feeling of genuine happiness wash over him. He realized with a pang, that he hadn't felt such an emotion since he was a child, at home with his family.

But now, here it was again. This woman. This remarkable, amazing, frustratingly beautiful woman loved him. And he simply couldn't believe his good fortune…even as the screams and cries outside rose up into the night.

———— ◆ ————

HE IMAGINED HE slept. He didn't quite know how he possibly could have with all of his thoughts whirring about, shooting over one another. Mostly, he had woolgathered over Mingli Zhao, but he must have drifted off, dreaming of her perhaps, and awakened in a blissful awareness of her presence, for he could hear her in the next room, moving about, washing, brushing out her clothes, humming a tune.

Clothes! He jumped up from the settee and looked down at himself. Wrinkled, disheveled, spatters of blood and dirt on his shirt. Where was his tie? His collar!

Then the bedroom door suddenly burst opened, and he froze.

"Good morning, Mr. Kazsmer. I trust you slept well."

"I hope *you* slept well… Miss Zhao…"

"You have a very comfortable bed." She winked.

He froze again until she laughed. "I'm sure you'd like a change of clothes," she said, buttoning the last of her cuffed sleeves. "I'll ring for your landlady to bring us some coffee and muffins, shall I? Or would you prefer eggs? Yes, I'm rather hungry this morning. Eggs, ham, and sprats, yes?"

She reached for the speaking tube and pulled the lever that rang the bell on the other end. She fit the brass earpiece to her ear and listened for his landlady. Leopold suddenly gathered himself and rushed into the bedroom, slamming the door after him. But standing in the middle of the room, he was suddenly struck blank. He didn't know what to do. All he knew—when he suddenly became aware of it—was that the room, somehow, smelled like her. Surely…surely she didn't carry her lilac perfume with her. But maybe she did. He knew so little of the habits of women.

He snapped a glance at the bed. The dented pillow. *She* had used it last night. He hurried over, picked it up, and pressed it to his face. *Oh God, it smelled like her!* How was he to ever sleep in this room again?

He pulled up short. "Get ahold of yourself, man," he muttered, placing the pillow — a little sheepishly — back where it belonged.

And then he thought of the dreadful events of last night. He flung the curtains aside to glance out the window, expecting more mayhem…but there was none to be found. No shuffling corpses, no gutters running with blood. There were, however, bodies here and there covered in sheets, with perplexed policemen standing over them, but the resurrected seeming to have ended the nightmare once the sun rose. That meant that he and Mingli had some precious time to do their investigations.

But first, a wash.

He divested himself of his shirt, chemise, and trousers, poured more water into the bowl on his washstand, and scrubbed his face, neck, and arm-pits with plenty of soap. He stropped his razor and made himself slow down to shave his face around his carefully coiffed mustache. Shaking off the razor, he peered at himself in the looking glass and nodded in approval.

He doffed his underwear and plunged into his chest of drawers for fresh ones, both sleeveless chemise and drawers. He dressed quickly, reaching for a clean shirt, collar, and tie. He combed his hair — adding a touch of lavender water—and then donned his frock coat. Even his shoes had clean spats.

When he emerged from his bedchamber, he felt himself again: confident, complete, and ready to do battle.

The landlady—looking understandably frazzled from last night's doings—was laying out the breakfast on the drawing room table, and scowling at Leopold the whole time. "Thank you, Mrs. Granville," he said with a flourish of praise for how good it all smelled, and how convenient it was to start the day with a hearty breakfast with his Scotland Yard colleague who had happened to stop by quite early this morning. He walked Mrs. Granville to the servant's door, gave her a little bow, and watched as her scowl turned to a skeptical eyeroll.

"Oh dear," he said. "I wonder if she believed that."

"What difference does it make if she does or doesn't, Leopold? You're a grown man, after all. Now come, sit down. I've poured you coffee. Do you take it with milk?"

He walked over and sat as she offered the small milk jug. "Just a splash."

As she poured, she smiled. "My, you look dashing today."

He pulled at the lapels of his coat. "Oh. Thank you very much. And you look...fresh and lovely as always."

Under the brim of her hat that was tilted low, her good eye seemed to glitter with delight.

Their mission was urgent, and they felt no need to stand on ceremony as they devoured their food, forks and knives clacking on their plates with little conversation in between. There was no telling when they would have time to eat another meal.

A pop, and the shade of Inspector Thacker passed suddenly through their table.

"Oh! Blimey. Sorry about that, Kazsmer." And then he turned his head. "Why...Miss Zhao? A...pleasure to find you here. This morning. So early." He lifted his bowler, and then slid a sly eye toward Leopold. "This is...very interesting," he muttered out of the side of his mouth.

"It's...it's nothing of the kind," Leopold stuttered. "Miss Zhao came by early and we simply —"

"I arrived last night," she interjected. Leopold felt his blushing face flush all the way down his body. "I stayed because of quite unexpected events."

"Well, well," said Thacker, pushing the bowler back from his forehead and resting his hands at his hips. "I'll wager they were."

"Spense!" warned Leopold.

"Do you not recall, Inspector," said Mingli, sipping her coffee, "that last night the dead rose from their graves and walked the streets of London?"

Thacker guffawed. "Pull the other one."

She set her cup down in her saucer. "I assure you, Inspector, that I am not engaging in any foolery." She gestured toward the window.

Thacker flew toward the window with its drapes thrown wide and shivered as he looked on at the shrouded bodies and police milling. "Well. Now that you mention it, last night, I felt...something. Like, a shudder in the universe. Like something odd was going on. And you say the dead were walking? Like, corpses? Not like…" He gestured to himself.

"Yes," said Leopold. "And attacking the living, killing them. Making more walking dead."

"No wonder the Yard was all alight with activity. I was in the secret archives in the undercrofts, trying to ferret out what Kobold & Hob had to do with the Necropolis Railway… Cor blimey!" He smacked his forehead. "The *Necropolis* Railway!"

"Yes," said Mingli, using her fork to cut away a piece of her fish. "I've certainly made that connection, too, but we have as of yet to understand the whys and wherefores."

Thacker grew silent, thinking. When the spirit glanced at Leopold again with widened eyes and a ticking his head toward Mingli, he seemed to be asking the silent question.

Leopold cleared his throat. "That blasted dead faery came alive," he began, cutting his food carefully. "We fought it off and sent the little blighter into the fire. But then we began to hear screaming outside and I was attacked by a dead man. Then a policeman was killed and…well, it simply wasn't safe out there. I couldn't very well send Miss Zhao home in all of that."

"Oh, of course not." Thacker wagged his head.

"No, and then, er, we got to researching it all, and it got late, and…there you are."

"There we are." Thacker broke into a smile. "And there we are," he said to Mingli.

"Really, Inspector." She shook her head, laid her utensils on her plate, and pressed a hand to her stomach. "That was just what was needed. But I fear I will burst my corset."

Leopold nearly spit out his coffee, but swallowed and coughed at the last second.

"Are you all right?" she said.

"Quite." He wiped his mustache with his serviette and stood. "Shall we begin our investigation?"

"Yes. I'm ready." Her clothes were as wrinkle-free and as fresh as when she arrived the night before. He wondered if she used magic for her toilet.

He headed toward the door and grabbed his walking stick with the wand, and his Webley from the foyer's cabinet, checking to see that it was loaded, before tucking it away inside his coat.

Thacker floated toward him.

Leopold paused. "Er...where exactly are we going?"

"To the Saint Collen Club, of course. I hope, Inspector, you will accompany us. It's time we exact some answers from those blasted goblins, don't you think?"

CHAPTER THIRTEEN

IT WAS LITERAL Hell on the streets. There was weeping from all quarters, coppers everywhere, and the disinfectant men with their white suits and their handcarts seemed to be at every corner…along with funeral carriages. There didn't appear to be any dead walking during the day. "I'm hoping," Leopold wondered aloud, "that they only stalk at night."

"Yes, that seems to be the case," said Mingli, meditatively as she looked out the window of their hansom cab. "At least there will be relief and a reburial during the day. Though it would be wiser to simply burn the bodies. I shall have to send that dictum to Scotland Yard as soon as I might. God knows what will happen at nightfall."

They were quiet until the hansom brought them to their destination.

The Georgian-style building seemed to reach up to the clouds, and proudly proclaimed the "Saint Collen Club" in bold, Roman letters incised with gold leaf. The pediment, sitting on columns over the entry, with its carved bas relief with the trooping of the faery court, fascinated Leopold.

"I never had no call to come to this club," said Thacker, looking it over.

Startled at his pronouncement, Leopold had somehow forgotten Thacker was with them. "Why faeries, I wonder?"

"Don't you know?" said Mingli. "Saint Collen was said to have defeated the king of the faeries, Gwyn ap Nudd. But all he truly did was insult him and his court. The king wasn't defeated. He just disappeared. Monks can be unaccountably rude where their religion is concerned."

Leopold exchanged looks with Thacker. "I'm afraid I don't know that story."

"Well, you see, Saint Collen was invited to meet the faery king—whom he insulted by calling him a demon and a devil. Saint Collen was to come to the top of a certain hill at noon to meet the king himself. He arrived and found a splendid white castle, shining in the sun, and promptly entered. All of Gwyn ap Nudd's court was there, resplendent in glittering gowns of blue cloth. There were faeries dancing on the tails of will-o-the-wisps, a feast laid out for all, music to calm and entice, and the king himself on a golden throne. The king graciously opened his hands and told Collen that this feast was given in his honor and that he could partake of anything he desired. And what did Collen do? Instead of accepting the invitation with the same grace that it was offered, he pulled out a bottle of holy water and sprayed it all over the crowd. What were they to do? Instead of immediately killing him, they promptly vanished at his insult. The court, the feast, the king, and even the castle, were no more. Of course, in Saint Collen's defense, one is never to consume food or drink from the faeries, or you shall never escape them. But still. I find his tale is about rudeness, not holiness."

Leopold stroked his mustache with a finger. "I take your point. Er...did it actually happen?"

She shrugged. "Who can say? I'm certain in one version or another, something very like it must have happened."

Leopold shuddered. Trapped with the faeries for all eternity? Though it did sound a great deal more pleasant than being trapped in Gehenna.

"But I daresay," she went on. "I doubt Saint Collen had a moment of peace afterwards for the rest of his life. Faeries can be very unforgiving."

"So," he took in both of his companions, "what are we to do? I can glamour myself and probably you too, Miss Zhao. I think the Inspector can fend for himself."

"Right, then," said Thacker, pulling on his transparent Ulster's lapels. "Shall I reconnoiter the place?"

"I am curious, Spense, as to whether or not you can see through a glamour as a spirit. Do let me know."

Thacker tapped the rim of his bowler. "The supernatural. It's a corker, ain't it?" He laughed and instantly vanished.

He turned to Mingli. "Well, then. Time to glamour ourselves. What would suit you? An old man with mutton chops?"

"I should be delighted," she said with a sinful smile.

He gathered the magic that seemed to swirl around the building, rolling it in his hands like a fiery ball. Looking both ways down the street and, seeing no one approaching on the pavement, he tossed it underhand toward her. Her figure began to pull and prod and reconfigure into that of an older gentleman in a frock coat and topper, with gray hair and muttonchops that joined to a mustache.

"How do I look?" said Mingli with a rumbling old man's voice. It was most disconcerting.

"Capital. Truth be told, you mostly resemble the physician with Scotland Yard, Dr. Woodbine. And now, me." He gathered the magic again into a ball, slapped it into his face, and magicked himself into the form of a popular Italian baritone. "And me?" he said with an Italian accent.

Old Man Mingli laughed. "By Jove!"

"Then let us get to it." He moved up the steps and rapped on the door with his cane. The small peeping door opened and a face glared out under dark, bushy brows. "Good morning, gentlemen. Who's calling?"

Leopold demurred to Old Man Mingli. She stepped up to the peep door and scowled. "Don't you know who I am, man? I'm Dr. Woodbine with Scotland Yard! And this is my companion, an opera singer of some renown. We are the guests of Sir Wilfrid of Wilmington."

The man seemed flustered and he immediately opened the door. "I beg your pardon, doctor. And Signore Giraldoni. I can scarce say I did not recognize *you*, signore."

Leopold made a grand gesture with his hand but said nothing. He glanced around the foyer—a place he had been denied access before—with its white marble floors, rubber plants, fluted columns, and carved niches with bronze sculptures of various visions of faeries…none of which resembled the real thing, he mused.

The footman asked, "Dr. Woodbine, are you a member of this club, sir?"

"Of course not!" He waved his umbrella about. "I'm here to see Sir Wilfrid. Oh, get out of my way. I'll find the man."

Under the onslaught of the renowned doctor and his celebrity companion, the footman could do nothing, and Leopold, as always, followed Mingli in her Dr. Woodbine guise.

They moved throughout the large foyer, where above was a glass dome that lit the entire marbled rotunda. They came to some double doors and pushed through. The room was on a more comfortable scale, with a lower coffered ceiling and walls lined in dark wainscoting and deep green foliate wallpaper.

Young mustachioed gentlemen sat in leather wingback chairs, reading newspapers, while others—some older men with white muttonchops and balding heads—sat on Chesterfields, smoking cigars or pipes, and talking in low tones with one another in small klatches. Leopold overheard them, and they were discussing the goings on last night. Indeed, the newspaper headlines that he could see as he passed the men in their chairs spoke of the killing spree of the resurrected. Leopold grabbed a paper from an empty seat and took it up.

"Look here," he said in the Italian accent he couldn't get used to. Mingli/Dr. Woodbine approached and glanced over his shoulder. "It says that those killed by the resurrected, themselves soon rose to kill others. And so on. It's ghastly."

"We were safe last night, but who knows if that will last?" she said in Woodbine's gruff voice.

Leopold read on. "As we thought. They dispersed at sunrise. So they begin their haunt at sunset. We've got a day, then."

"We must stop this." She edged closer to him. "Since you saw the goblins without their glamour, do you see any of them now?"

Leopold scanned the room and shook his head. "The servant's stair…" But even as he said it, a butler appeared from around the corner, carrying a tray of crystal glasses and a decanter of liquor. As Leopold watched, the butler's image flickered. Leopold shook out his head and looked again. A goblin! Shorter than the butler, and far uglier.

He tapped Mingli's shoulder and pointed. She must have been focusing her enhanced eye as she tilted Woodbine's head until she suddenly straightened with shock. "He's a right ugly fellow, isn't he?"

A footman followed the butler, but he wasn't a footman either.

Mingli elbowed Leopold. "Those men over there are talking and smoking, but those over there with the newspapers. Have you seen any of them move?"

Leopold watched. Surely one of them would have turned the page by now. They'd have to be exceptionally slow readers, or reading every article, every advertisement and *still* dally over each page. "By Jove," he muttered.

She fastened her stare at them with the sound of her enhanced eye shuttling in and out. "Ah. Their auras. They are under an enchantment. All of them."

Leopold longed to take out his multi-dimensional spectacles, but he dared not, lest it drop *his* glamour.

And then, as if in some sort of assigned choreography, all the men with newspapers in their wingback chairs suddenly folded their papers all in synchronous motions. They folded them together, folded them again, and rising in concert, dropped their papers on their chairs. They turned like automata, and marched toward Leopold and Mingli.

"The jig is up," said Leopold and grabbed Mingli's arm to back away.

"We've got to get to that stair."

"I can't run with this Italian fellow's body. Drop the glamours?"

She nodded. He snapped his fingers and both their glamours fell.

The cigar smoking men on the Chesterfields made sounds of surprise, and some got to their feet. "There's a woman in the club!"

"Damme, it's a Chinky!"

Leopold grasped her hand and ran with her along the edge of the room. The goblins saw them and sneered, raising their hands to hurl spells. Meanwhile, the enchanted men turned and marched toward them again.

Leopold watched the goblins as a bright light of power left the erstwhile butler's fingertips and speared toward them. He yanked Mingli down to bend at the waist and reached the door just as the bookcase behind them exploded.

As they passed through the servant's door and shut it, Leopold heard one of the men say, "What are these damned ugly creatures doing in here?" before his voice was cut off by the sound of a whistling spell rushing by.

"We've done it now," he said to his companion, glad that she was back to looking like the woman he loved rather than the old doctor.

They slowed as they peered around the corridor that looked to be a cave. "What *is* this place?" asked Mingli.

"We have to assume the entire building is glamoured. When I fell out the window yesterday, there was no sign of any sort of broken glass." He touched the stone walls. "I wonder if it has always been glamoured. If this club really exists at all."

Mingli eyed the tunnel with her telescoping eye. "Perhaps there was something of a club here at one time, but it was glamoured to make it more enticing. And the memories of those older members were enhanced. Surely the goblins would need funds to make their plots work. And a club such as this would lure the wealthiest of patrons."

"Like Sinclair and Pratt."

"Precisely. This plan—whatever it is—must have been arranged a very long time ago. Possibly decades."

They came to end of the tunnel with a sheer drop-off. But the outer cavern expanded into an enormous cavity, reaching far higher than their low tunnel. A sludgy river churned far below. But beside that river lay two shiny rails. "I say," said Leopold, pointing. "That looks like railroad tracks."

"You're right. We've got to get down there."

"You have returned," said a voice behind them.

They whirled. It was that ugly goblin Leopold had encountered the first time.

"And now you brought another tasty dish." He licked his lips. "It's about time for elevenses, is it not?"

"I'm afraid I'll have to disappoint you again," said Leopold. "Who is in charge of this operation? May I speak with them?"

The goblin laughed, a terrible, disgusting sound, like a gurgling strangulation. "You will never get in to see Gilpin Horner."

"And who is Gilpin Horner?" he asked.

"A goblin leader," said Mingli. "A very powerful individual. I'm afraid I've met him before."

The goblin rubbed his hands one over the other. "Oh ho! You must be the Special Inspector from Scotland Yard." He clapped and hopped about. "If that is the case, then perhaps I *should* take you to him at once."

"Maybe that's not such a good idea, old man," said Leopold, pulling out his Webley.

"What's that?" said the goblin.

Leopold aimed, closed one eye to draw a bead, and fired.

The explosion startled the goblin, and so did the impact of the bullet to the chest. The creature looked down at it, poked it. But he failed to fall or die.

"You're not acquainted with faery folk, are you, Mortal?"

Leopold frowned. "Immortal, are you?"

"Very." He plucked the flattened bullet from his chest, examined it for a moment, and then flicked it away. It arced over the side of the ledge and disappeared somewhere below. "Now don't be a pest, and come along. Master Horner will be very excited to see you two." The goblin gestured behind him toward a door they had not noticed before. Possibly it had been doubly glamoured. Leopold reluctantly led the way.

The door was warm when he touched the knob. And when he opened it, a torch stood close to the door in a sconce. It led to an impossibly rickety stairway, zigzagging downward into a shadowy shaft.

Leopold hesitated. It seemed nothing more than sticks and questionable pegs holding the thing together.

"Go on," said the goblin.

"I say, old man, I don't think it will hold our weight."

The goblin jerked forward and shoved Leopold onto the first step. "Don't test me, Mortal!"

Leopold straightened his hat. "No need for that," he muttered, and grabbed hold of the railing to carefully reach the step below.

Once Mingli was on it and then the goblin, the whole thing began to sway. Leopold couldn't tell if the entire rig was attached to anything other than its own enchantments and those didn't seem to be holding it together all that well.

Leopold looked down once they had descended quite a way. "Who made this stairway? Doesn't seem to be very safe."

"Made by goblins, the best!" chortled the creature, who kept pushing Mingli. Leopold wanted to clout the little blighter. "By goblins, *for* goblins. Might fall with weighty mortals on it." He continued to grin.

"Then…it would take you down too," Leopold pointed out.

The goblin laughed. "Remember. I'm immortal."

Leopold scowled.

They kept descending far below the original building. The walls of the shafts were shot through with coiling roots thick as Leopold's body, as if some great, ancient oak of magical origins grew directly above it. The roots even wound round the stairs and handrails, twisting so tight they seemed to squeeze wherever they touched. It followed them down in its own twisting path, seeming to lead the way to their doom.

Finally, there was a landing of solid stone and Leopold was relieved to step down onto it. He took Mingli's hand to help her cross from the rickety structure and used it as an excuse to hold her close, though he suspected she knew the truth of it.

This time it wasn't a tunnel, but a narrow ledge with torches in sconces every few yards. Leopold tried not to think of the sheer plunge downward should he slip on the narrow and sometimes slick ledge carved deep in the bowels below London's streets. How far down did these tunnels go? To Hades itself? Except that Gehenna—or Hell or whatever name one prescribed to it—didn't exist on their world. One had to perform some elaborate spells to be able to step through a gateway to Gehenna.

He didn't want to contemplate that now. He needed to stay sharp. Despite what the goblin said, immortals *could* die. He'd seen the evidence of the dead faeries. He just needed a spell or some other way to accomplish it.

An incongruously grand door stood at the end of the ledge's passage. It was medieval in appearance, arched and made of hewn oak, with elaborate scrollwork of black metal hinges crawling across its exterior.

But it couldn't be iron, Leopold mused, for iron was one of the materials elementals, such as faery and goblin, could not abide. He started to remember other stories that his Romani godfathers and godmothers told him about faery folk: the use of salt as a barrier (as one would do for protection against demons), turning one's coat inside out, sticks made of rowan, ash, and gorse; running water—good, clear water, not like that running sludge they saw before—and hag-stones, stones that had a hole in them made by natural means of erosion or water.

But he didn't have any of those things. Neither did he have the religious faith his aunts and godmothers always admonished him to have, thrusting crosses and rosaries at him as a direct insult to his Jewish heritage. It was a wonder he had come to like any of them at all.

The goblin took out a key made of bone and plunged it into the lock. When he opened the door and shoved them through, the passage appeared to be made of black stone, smoothed and gleaming. They walked down it to another door, whereupon the goblin knocked. Leopold heard no reply, but the goblin opened it anyway.

Inside was very like the interior rooms of the Saint Collen Club, with wood wainscoting, wooden bookcases, plush carpets, swagged draperies, and carved furniture. It looked like any proper drawing room to Leopold...except that when he looked closer, the wainscoting had wooden pillars every few feet, and they were carved into the fearsome shapes of beasts—trolls, he suspected—with wide sloping shoulders, bulging eyes, and heavy jaws with tusks protruding from lower lips. He shouldn't want to meet their like in person.

There was a perfectly serviceable table with a carved dog-like beast as its pedestal.

A wooden chandelier was made up of grimacing wooden pixies with angry faces.

Such was fashionable design, goblin-style.

On a raised dais in the middle of the room sat a magnificent chair. More like a throne, the chair was elaborately carved with a high back and enormous arms. A wizened creature sat atop it, legs not long enough to reach the footstool sitting in front of it. He was partially hidden behind a massive ledger, with puffs of smoke—presumably from a pipe—rippling above.

"Master Horner," said the goblin, "I bring you guests."

One big puff emerged from behind the ledger, and slowly the book lowered. A goblin, older but no less ugly than the others, looked them over. He had a long nose, twisted like a carrot and just as sharp at the end. His ears were long, pointed, and stood out perpendicular to his head, with tufts of white hair over his ears, *in* his ears, and one at the top of his head like a cluster of grass. His sharp teeth clenched down on a long-stemmed clay pipe filled with foul-smelling tobacco.

Unlike the other goblins who wore dirty, moth-eaten shirts with leather trousers and braces, he wore a proper shirt with a checkered waistcoat and a large gold fob chain draping across his big belly. His trousers were still made of some sort of utilitarian leather, but they seemed to be tailored better. And he had the same peculiar long, pointed feet as his compatriots, only they were clad in shiny leather shoes with spats. If it weren't for the odd proportions, strange garb, and the face that belonged to a Punch cartoon, he would have seemed like any prosperous gentleman.

"What is this? What have you brought me, Phinneas? Ahhhh." He leaned forward and looked Mingli over. "The inimitable and dangerous Miss Zhao. I can't say it's a pleasure to look upon you again."

"*My* feelings exactly," she said, with a flick of her head.

Leopold expected the dry tones of a king, but instead, heard the gruff accent of a merchant counting his pennies and dropping "aitches" left and right.

"But who is this other?" said Horner.

Leopold stepped forward. "I am Leopold Kazsmer, the Great Enchanter."

"Enchanter? Enchanter of what? *Mortal* magic. Tut, tut."

With a sigh, Leopold made a show of straightening his cuffs. He noticed the dirt on his sleeves and tried in vain to brush them off. "Oh, I am a passing fair magician."

"He escaped me before," offered Phinneas. "He leapt out the window and slowed his fall."

"Pedestrian," snorted Horner. And then he looked up sharply at the goblin. "Are *you* still here?"

The goblin lost his smug expression at last. He frowned, bowed, and backed out of the room, closing the door behind him.

"I'd offer you refreshment…"

"But we aren't fool enough to accept it," said Mingli.

"As I thought." He snapped the ledger closed and set it on the angry dog-beast table beside him. "So, it was you who discovered us," he said to Leopold.

Leopold nodded, grasping his lapel with a sense of pride. "Yes. We were looking into something curious. It seems that Hieronymus Pratt and Eustace Sinclair, two railway barons, hadn't been seen in public for months, and they with an unusual partnership. One would think they would be making all sorts of public appearances: on the steps of the Parliament building, at their own railway stations to cut ribbons and so forth. And yet…none of that was happening. Imagine my surprise to find them *both* at the club and quite stupefied with an enchantment."

Gilpin Horner pulled the long-stemmed clay pipe from his mouth, opened the side of his lips, and puffed perfect rings of smoke, not unlike Mingli with her own brass pipe. He fitted the fingers of his other hand into his waistcoat pocket. "Yes, I *can* imagine. Foolish not to allow them to make some of them appearances. I took advice—poorly reasoned, as it turns out—that it would be safer to keep them here. I see that that little ruse was no good under *your* scrutiny, Mr. Kazsmer. I often underestimate mortals…much to my regret."

"Don't fret yourself, Horner. Better men, er…creatures than you have always underestimated me."

"You are the perfect companion to our Miss Zhao, I see." He turned his attention to her, with bulging eyes, glowing somewhat yellow. "I thought she had been killed the last time I saw her. How very disappointing."

She smiled. "Well, that's the thing with underestimating humans, Master Horner. You never know when you've met your match."

He grunted and shifted on his throne. Leopold noticed a strange pillow that seemed to be embroidered with the face of a goblin, though squashed flat under Gilpin's posterior. "And mortals never realize when their enemies have the upper hand." He sniffed long and luxuriantly. "Ah! Mortals smell wonderful and taste magnificent, and I haven't indulged in many a day. It isn't wise to simply walk into my parlor and present yourselves as my feast. Like a fly walking right into the spider's web." He laughed at his own joke.

"There won't be any of that!" Leopold pressed the button that sprang open his cane, shooting his wand up into the air, where he promptly snatched it and aimed it at Horner. But there was something wrong. He suddenly felt no magic. Not in his body, not in his wand.

"You must be wondering about now where you magic is, Mortal. These walls are warded. Do you think I'd let just anyone come in here, brandishing a wand or a broom and threatening me? I'm Gilpin-bloody-Horner! I didn't get rich and powerful by being a punter."

The goblin raised his hand, and Leopold's wand slipped out of his fingers and slapped into Horner's grip. He glared at Leopold as he snapped it in half and let the pieces fall.

Leopold gasped and stared at it on the Persian carpet. Gritting his teeth for a moment, he suddenly lifted his face, and with a supreme effort, raised the edges of his mouth and formed a smile. "Well. You have to admit, it was a good try."

Horner leaned forward and stared hard at Leopold. He suddenly threw back his head and laughed. "You, my friend—what was it? Kazsmer?—are an unusual mortal. As unusual as your partner here from Scotland Yard. Go on. Ask your questions that are burning a hole in your heart. It won't really matter in a few minutes."

He flicked a glance at Mingli before settling himself before Horner again. "Since you had…kidnapped?. . .Pratt and Sinclair for an unspecified length of time, one had to assume that *they* did not plot this scheme to build a 'Kobold & Hob' railway, but that *you* did, to build them along the lines of power. And further, that your shadow consortium purchased the Necropolis Railway as well, and that it has to do with the most unfortunate events of last night involving resurrected corpses. Am I getting warm?"

"You're red hot, me lad. Keep going."

"That was all Miss Zhao's supposition. But there you have us stymied. As Miss Zhao observed, it has something to do with killing faeries, but beyond that, we are lost."

Horner turned to Mingli and bowed. "Had I known you were still alive, Miss Zhao, I would have taken better care to hide the dead faeries. Well! You've sussed out a great deal. I shall be forced to confess that I did indeed steal away with Pratt and Sinclair and force them to sign papers that poured their considerable wealth into this venture. And you are right, Miss Zhao that it was built specifically to take advantage of the alignment lines—the lines of power. It enhances our own, you see, and has the added benefit of sticking it to the faery kingdom. Goblins and faeries, you know. We don't mix. Like oil and water, we are. They're so…" He gestured vaguely, airily with his long-fingered hands. "And goblins are so down to earth. You get me, Kazsmer? We appreciate the value of coin." He rubbed two fingers together. "Coin of the realm. Of almost *every* realm. Gold." He winked. "You know it, don't you, Kazsmer? I can recognize a fellow traveler, a poor man who wanted to better himself. That's all *I'm* doing. Betterin' m'self. And, with the addition of the Necropolis Railway, well… We're letting nature—and a bit of magic— take its course."

Mingli put a gloved finger to her chin in thought. "The alignment lines, coupled with the Necropolis Railway—a train simply filled up with souls and the lingering milieu of the Otherworld—mixed with goblin magic, created a concatenation whereby the dead along the lines would rise and kill those in its path. And the more dead that were made, the more that would rise and kill others, until…" She shook her head in disbelief, at the horror of it. "Until all of London were killed. None left alive. Diabolical."

He chortled and slapped his knee, pointing at Mingli. "She's got it in one! They'll all be dead. And not just London. It would spread to all of England,

Scotland, Wales, and Ireland. We'll have the whole kit and caboodle. Because, you see, none of the goblins would be affected. Only mortals…and faeries. We'd have it all. All the banks with all the gold and the whole bloody island. Who knows what we couldn't do from there?"

"You're insane!" cried Leopold.

The goblin turned to him and lost his jovial expression. "*I'm* insane?" He rose from his throne and started down the dais toward him. "You just think for a second, old son, what your lot has done to this here island. It used to be the domain of me and my folk, and all the other creatures of the woodlands. And where are those woodlands now? You cut down our ancient oaks. You cleared the marshes of peat. You built your roads and fought your wars. You mined tin, coal, and gold where you didn't belong, into the caverns of *our* folk, and then you built these blasted railways with your stinking, choking smoke, and you filled the clear skies with more foul smoke from them dirigibles." He stood at the edge of the platform, now eye to eye with Leopold. "There is no place that you haven't touched and desecrated. And now to come to me to complain that we've finally risen up to wipe you out? You've got your bloody nerve." He wound back his arm and slapped Leopold hard across the face. Leopold staggered back, holding the hot cheek that radiated pain.

"Enough of this," Horner grumbled, jumping off the last step and ambling toward the door in a strange rolling gait. "The two of you are invited for supper." He grabbed the doorknob and turned back to them with a sneer. "On a platter!" He opened his lips and bared his sharp teeth as he laughed, and that rolling laughter followed him out the door and into the passage, even once the door was shut.

Leopold looked sorrowfully toward Mingli. "I'm afraid that didn't go very well."

She rushed to him and grasped his arm. "Do you feel any magic at all?"

He shook his head. "I don't. It's blocked. I can feel the wards."

"Can you summon Eurynomos?"

He hesitated. "If I try and can't bring him, I'll…I'll bleed to death and that wouldn't help you at all."

She made a sound of frustration and fisted her hands. "This is untenable."

"Maybe we can find a way out of here by more mundane means. Let's try the door."

They both marched to the entry. Leopold grabbed the doorknob...but of course it didn't budge. There was no use in hurling himself against it. They had both seen how substantial it was.

He turned around and cast his gaze about the room. A heavy fire iron sat by the arched fireplace. He hurried toward it, but when he reached out to grab it his hand passed through. "Dash it! A glamour. Of course a goblin wouldn't have an *iron*. I don't suppose the fire is real either." He waved his hand into the flames and felt nothing. He spun away from the hearth and searched around the room. "There must be something..."

There was a pop.

Glancing at Mingli, he raised his brows. "I say, did you hear something?"

Before she could answer there was a loud crack and another pop. Mingli whirled around, looking. "I certainly heard that."

"What do you suppose..."

The pillow on the throne stirred. It seemed to inflate, and the squashed face of the embroidered goblin filled out. But it wasn't an embroidery at all, but a *real* face. The enchanted goblin rose up in the chair, shaking his head out. His ears popped out first, then his carrot nose. He blinked several times, glancing once at Leopold before ignoring him and instead addressed the side table, the one that looked like a horrific carved dog.

The table shuddered and a carved leg stretched suddenly away from the tabletop, and then another, until it all unfolded into some sort of grimacing beast.

The pillars of twisted trolls lining the wainscoting tore away from the walls with another loud report, stretched, and rearranged themselves on two feet or dragging long massive arms down to the ground and balanced on their knuckles. Their skin was still lined with woodgrain. Either they were enchanted alive, or they were some sort of wood nymph variant.

Then the chandelier's pixies untangled themselves and used each other as a chain to climb down from the ceiling, brandishing lit candles.

The strange menagerie collected together on the Persian rug, checking each other and taking stock.

Until they all suddenly turned and faced Leopold and Mingli.

"Oh bother," Leopold muttered under his breath.

CHAPTER FOURTEEN

HE DREW HIS Webley and aimed it at the nearest creature, the goblin pillow. He fired. The goblin jerked back with the shot, and just as Phinneas had done, plucked the spent bullet from the dent. He grinned and took another step.

Leopold took aim at one of the troll pillars, walking stiffly as if truly made of wood. When he fired, the bullet struck the woodgrain skin, chipping off a piece, but it didn't slow the fellow down.

Looking at the gun as if to blame it, he reckoned he could use the Webley as a cudgel, but the two of them wouldn't last long amongst *all* those creatures. Especially with those pixies waving around their lit candles as weapons.

And then the pixies suddenly ran forward, screaming in high-pitched tones and jabbing forth with the flaming tapers. Mingli reacted first, lifting her skirts and kicking the little blighters with her pointed boots. They flew over and into one another, landing on the carpet, angrier than before.

Leopold grabbed a chair and swiped it at them, taking out a whole pixie line. He drew back his arm again to strike at more when the chair was stopped cold and was yanked out of his hand by a wood troll.

"Are these things quite alive?" he asked out of the side of his mouth.

"They're alive enough," she said, a little out of breath.

The troll wound back and heaved the chair at Leopold, who ducked as it flew over his head. "Definitely not a glamour." The gun seemed useless, and he stuffed it away inside his coat again.

Mingli snatched a floor chandler and brandished it. The next troll that moved got a swat in the face and staggered back. "Leo, grab a candle from a pixie."

He reckoned her meaning and crouched low, facing off with a pixie grinding its teeth. He lunged, stepped on its face, and yanked the candle from its hand. He then kicked the creature away from him, grabbed a fringed tablecloth from a gate-leg side table, and lit the cloth. He took careful aim and tossed it in the face of the nearest troll.

The flaming cloth wrapped around its face and it screamed as it caught fire. The other trolls stared at their companion but only moved away from it, not wishing to be caught in the inferno. The troll keeled over and was down, smoldering on the carpet.

"We can't keep this up," Leopold admitted. Then an idea sparked in his mind. He pushed up his left sleeve and turned his wrist over, staring at the All-Seeing Eye staring back at him and pressed his finger to the tattoo. "Suchah!" he shouted.

Instantly, the little red imp popped into existence. "Flesh Master wants Suchah?" he said wearily. Then the imp turned. "Oh shit!"

Leopold found himself and Mingli backed against the far wall with nowhere else to go. "Suchah, get rid of these."

Suchah glanced back over his shoulder. "Me?"

"That's why I summoned you, you little carbuncle. *Do* something! That's a command!"

Suchah rubbed his little webbed hands together and licked his thin lips with a forked tongue. "No like this world," he muttered. He raised his hand and snapped his fingers.

The trolls, goblins, and pixies froze, but just barely. They seemed to be moving but in exaggerated slowness.

Leopold breathed again. "Well done, Suchah!"

"Won't last. Must leave."

"Then get us out of here. I can't perform any magic. The place is warded."

"Weak Flesh Man," he muttered again. His webbed feet flapped on the wood floor as he waddled forward. He edged around the wooden pillar trolls, the dog creature that had been a table, the goblin pillow, and the warring pixies as Leopold and Mingli carefully followed.

Leopold looked the troll pillar in the eye no more than a few inches away as he slid by it, holding his breath as it blinked ever so slowly at him. He held tight to Mingli's hand as he maneuvered by each creature, stepping over the pixies as the still melting wax dribbled down the candles and over their spikey hands; shuffled around the dog/table and waited anxiously for her to catch up. He feared that to touch any one of them, even a slight brush, might make Suchah's spell fall.

They made it to the door unscathed while the imp tried to open the passage. "Spells are strange," Suchah muttered.

"Well, strange they may be, but we need to defeat them." He looked back at the slow-moving trolls and creatures. It looked to Leopold that they were beginning to move faster. And they were minutely turning to where he and Mingli now stood. "Hurry up, Suchah."

"Suchah trying, dread Flesh Master. But this magic is strange."

"Strange? How?"

Suchah gave Leopold a filthy look over his shoulder. "Different. Complicated. Tangled."

"Well, *un*tangle it!"

"*Untangle it,*" Suchah mocked under his breath. His fingers were flapping, his hands moving in unusual patterns. "Nothing works," he grunted.

In frustration, Leopold hurled himself at the door, trying to crack the lock, the jamb, anything.

Suchah stepped back with a sigh. "Are you done showing stupidity of humans?"

Leopold straightened his coat. "At least I was *doing* something."

"Something stupid," said Suchah, not so under his breath. The imp tried again, using different configurations of his hands. It seemed that his textured lizard skin was sweating.

"Leo," said Mingli with urgency in her voice.

He turned and noticed that the trolls and beasts were beginning to unfreeze.

"Suchah. Hurry. Or freeze the beasties again."

"Can't freeze again. Must open door."

"Then bloody open it!"

"Trying…"

One of the pixies seemed to free itself. It was moving at a normal pace and marching forward with its candle, using it like a sword. And then the pillow goblin broke free of the enchantment and sneered, cracking its knuckles.

"Running out of time, Suchah," said Leopold urgently. He attempted to push Mingli behind him, but she looked at him as if he'd lost his mind and stood her ground. He pulled the Webley from his coat again and Mingli reached down, pulling up her skirts to grab her own gun from the holster lashed to her thigh.

Leopold searched for anything of use, anything they could use in defense. When his eyes scanned the vaulted ceiling, he spotted another chandelier not made of pixies. It was fashioned of heavy wood with a rope keeping it aloft.

He elbowed Mingli and used his eyes to show her. She looked and slowly nodded.

"Are you close, Suchah?" said Leopold.

"Trying…"

"But are you close?"

"Not know. Still trying. Need more time."

"Then I'll give you time." He nodded to Mingli and said, "On the count of three. One…two…THREE!" They raised their guns together and pulled the triggers.

One bullet and a separate volley of power struck the rope and sliced through the strands of hemp at the same time the four wooden troll pillars freed themselves of the enchantment.

They pivoted, snarling.

"Still trying…" growled Suchah.

The chandelier seemed to hang suspended by its own mysterious means for long seconds…before it finally began to make its descent. Leopold backed up, desperately grabbing for Mingli's arm to drag her with him.

"Trying…" said Suchah, breathlessly.

It crashed. The heavy wheel broke the necks of the trolls, crushed the pixies, and flattened the dog/table. The pillow goblin was nowhere to be seen amid the crush.

Suchah looked up mildly, and returned to his spellwork. The door suddenly slipped open a crack.

Leopold grabbed hold of the edge and tried to pry it. "More, Suchah!" he grunted.

"Not working!" cried the imp.

Mingli jostled Leopold aside and did her best to pull the door, shoving Leopold up against a bookcase. He was about to try again when the nearby sconce stretched and wrapped its arm around his neck, yanking him back. His hat tipped over his eyes while he struggled. The lamp's arm squeezed tighter as he yelped.

Mingli glanced back and made her own sound of surprise. She bashed the lamp with the butt of her gun, smashing the lampshade into flattened fabric.

"Is every bloody thing alive in this room?" he wheezed.

"That appears to be so," she said, struggling to pry it from the wall. "Suchah," she said to the imp, "help your master!"

"Master always needs help." He didn't bother turning to snap his fingers. The lamp seemed to go limp and Leopold shoved it away from his neck. He rubbed at his collar and retrieved his hat and gun from the floor. He tucked the gun away and fastened his topper again.

"The door," he croaked, and moved with Mingli to grab it and pull.

All at once, it simply released and all three—humans and imp—fell backwards to their backsides.

"Did it," said Suchah, picking himself up. "I go now?"

"No," said Leopold, offering Mingli a hand. "We need you to help us get out of the building."

"Maybe magic returns to you."

Leopold rushed out onto the ledge. Yes, there was some magic, but not enough for even a humble transporting exit. "Let's go," he said, moving forward, wary about his lack of magic and using every opportunity to snatch some from the air.

They got to the second door, but this time Suchah needed only to snap his fingers for the lock to turn and for the door to whine open.

The ledge opened up to a rock bridge with a view below of the sludgy river and the railway tracks.

A figure suddenly popped through the rock wall in front of Leopold. "What the bloody hell happened to you, Kazsmer? I've been looking all over for you."

"Spense," he said, heart pounding. "We were trapped in a warded chamber. Could you not detect us through the wards?"

But Thacker was already glaring at the imp. "What the hell is that?"

"That's my servant demon. Suchah."

"Blimey, Leo. If I'd've only known about all this before I croaked…"

"You would have been Mr. Kazsmer's friend anyway," supplied Mingli with a sly smile.

"Well." He pushed his bowler up his forehead. "I reckon so. Oi. Suchah. So you're Kazsmer's mate, then?"

Suchah sneered and spit where Thacker's feet would have been. The spittle bubbled and burned the stone.

"Crikey!" said Thacker, pulling away from the smoldering acid. "A simple 'no' would have sufficed." He elbowed toward Leopold. "Not the same as Eurynomos, then."

"Not in the least. But look here, Spense. We're trying to find a way out. If you have a path to follow…"

"Right. I've been all over this place. It's like a warren; all ferret passages and a maze of rooms and tunnels. I suppose it makes sense to them goblins. I even found a treasury room."

"A treasury room?" asked Mingli. "Do you mean gold coins and such?"

"And such indeed! Gold statues — and I would have arrested the lot for having such filth as them statues, posed and naked as they were. When I was alive, that is. And all manner of other things, like plates and goblets, all of gold."

Leopold shook his head. "What in blazes does a goblin need with gold?"

"It's in their natures," she said. "They covet it. They…perhaps rely on it to do their dastardly plans in our world. Glamouring themselves as human. To purchase railway stocks, for instance."

"I'll be blowed," said Thacker. "Imagine them goblins disguising themselves. Going about London just as they please and no one knowing. 'Course, *I* can see them. Their glamours don't get past me."

"Spense! You can see them as they are?"

"'Course I can. I'm a spirit. Part of another world beyond the veil. I can see a lot." He said the last with a pall in his eyes.

Leopold stretched out his hand to comfort the man...but his hand passed right through. "You can always talk to me about it, old friend. I'll listen."

"I reckon." He seemed to realize what he sounded like and straightened his transparent hat and coat. "Enough of that now. I've got to get you out of here."

"Wait," said Mingli. "I should like to see that 'treasury room'."

Before Leopold could object, the imp stepped forward.

"You have ghost friend now. Then Suchah go?"

Leopold sighed. "Look, Suchah. I can use your help. If you wouldn't mind staying."

The creature gave him a questing look.

Leopold shrugged. "The thing of it is, I regret ordering you about. And...striking you. I should have just asked nicely."

Thacker made a sound of distaste and Leopold rounded on him. "There's no use in treating him badly. There's already enough poor treatment in this country of the under classes. Of whom I am one, I might add. So treating this imp no better than a bootblack doesn't sit well with me. I...I was simply following tradition. But some traditions need to end."

The imp set his hands at his hips...or where hips would generally be found. It was difficult to tell just where they were due to the roundness of the creature's midden like a ripe melon that sported the Hebrew glyphs Leopold himself had incised there in order to capture him. "Suchah not understand."

Leopold crouched low to be at eye level. "I'm apologizing. For treating you badly. You helped us immensely and I appreciate it."

Suchah looked at him sideways, a frown pulling down his face. "Now what trick?"

"No trick," he said straightening and surveying the open cavern below. "I have found that if we work together, we can get more accomplished. And I'd simply like it if we could. Without my ordering you to."

The imp narrowed his eyes. "So...Suchah can go if Suchah wants?"

Trust goes both ways, Leopold, he told himself, but he couldn't quite bring himself to have enough confidence in the imp's eyes. "Well...for now, I want you to stay."

Suchah threw up his hands in exasperation and grumbled in demon language.

He felt Mingli's hand pressed to his arm. "The point is," she said softly, "you tried. You must keep trying." She gave him a smile of reassurance. "Now then. Inspector. We need to see that treasury room."

CHAPTER FIFTEEN

"THERE'S A SHAFT a few yards that way," said Thacker. "It starts with a ladder and then I suppose you'd have to crawl the rest of the way. Miss Zhao, I know it ain't convenient, you being a woman and all…"

"I'll do what I must to survive, Inspector."

"So you would," he muttered. "Well then. I'll lead the way. But quiet like, because there was a group of them goblins nearby coming this way."

They followed Thacker. "It's a fair sight easier to navigate when you're walking through the walls," Thacker said, conversationally, "but I suppose that ain't no option for the rest of you. I think the turn should be around here somewhere." He floated slowly forward, peering strangely with an elongated neck, until he seemed to spy what he was looking for. "Down here."

Leopold heard Mingli's enhanced eye scope swivel and lengthen. He wondered what it was she could see, almost envied it.

Leopold himself hadn't noticed the rift in the wall when they had traveled this way before. It was most cleverly hidden in the texture of the rock. The imp went first, followed by Mingli, while Leopold took up the rear guard. The passage itself was dark, but the slight glowing from his ghostly friend was enough illumination for them to see their way through. The path led downward and soon they came to an area that opened into a shaft. And just as Thacker had said, there was a ladder that descended into darkness.

"I'll go first, shall I?" offered Leopold.

Mingli sighed. "I suppose those wearing skirts should go first."

"Why?" He was affronted by her pushing him aside…until he caught up to what she said. "Oh! Well…yes, of course! You…you should definitely go first. It's just that I…"

"You wanted to protect me. I understand, Mr. Kazsmer." She smiled mischievously and grabbed hold of the top of the ladder before she began her descent.

Leopold quickly turned to Thacker and in a hushed whisper, said, "She understood what I meant, didn't she?"

Thacker chuckled. "Oh, you're hooked good, aren't you?" He nodded to the ladder. "Best catch up."

Mingli had disappeared down the ladder and Leopold scrambled to climb down with the imp above him, giving him a most distasteful view. Had Mingli been above him… Oh, yes. It would have been far better, but likely more dangerous to his concentration.

Down they went, lit faintly again by the ghost's illumination, until he heard Mingli say, "Is this it, Inspector?"

Leopold met them all again on another narrow ledge where there was a short tunnel hewn from the rock. "Suchah, I think you should go first. Can you make some light for us?"

"Flesh Master's magic has not returned?"

"I'm afraid not. Not enough to do us any good. So…in you go."

The imp, just as insolent as before but with a question glittering in his eyes, snapped his fingers to create a glowing orb that gave off considerably more light than the ghost of Inspector Thacker, and ducked down into the tunnel.

"Perhaps you will allow me to go ahead of you now, Miss Zhao."

"Be my guest, Mr. Kazsmer."

Just as Leopold was about to get to his hands and knees, there came a loud explosion from deep in the depths of the walls and caverns. Suchah poked his head out again. "Goblins know what you did," he said with a smirk.

"Dash it. And they'll be looking for us."

Mingli was at his elbow. "Which is why I wanted to get to the treasury room so we will have leverage."

"If you could explain that…"

"As you go," said Thacker, looking worriedly behind him. "Talk as you go. Quick march, now."

Leopold ducked down into the tunnel, following Suchah once more. He looked over his shoulder to make sure Mingli was there and they all crawled forward. The bobbing light Suchah had conjured gave them only a brief view. It seemed like an endless cave of darkness passing into the distance. And the rock itself felt warm all around them, like the very bowels of Gehenna itself. Of course, that was ridiculous. They had passed through no gateway, no barrier that would lead them to the Otherworld, but in that pitch blackness, that constricting tube like some horrific throat of a demon, he couldn't help but feel a helpless anxiety as they crawled and crawled. His knees felt as if they were wearing away, and his hands bloodied from the uneven floor.

"Don't give up hope, Leopold." Mingli's voice was like an angel's prayer, echoing in the tight space. "It isn't your imagination that it is hot, constricting, and anxiety-inducing. It is designed for goblins, after all, not humans. The very walls are imbued with their suspicions and hatred of us. It has left its mark. And we, unfortunately, can feel it."

"You are wise, Miss Zhao. I almost gave myself up to the interminable despair."

"Don't. I should hate to lose you now."

Thacker's face emerged through the wall and paced with Leopold. "Is there something you wish to mention to me, Leo?" His mustache twitched.

"Nothing at the moment," Leopold mumbled.

Thacker snatched a glance back at Mingli. "I see. Mum's the word, eh?"

"Spense, there's no time for that now. Er...Miss Zhao," he said louder, "you said you would explain..."

"And so I shall," said her echoing voice. "A goblin's treasure is important to their entire society. It's written into their blood. Without it, they lose their trust of their hierarchy, their leaders. We are simply going to eliminate it and cause disarray."

"Oh. I see. And how do you suggest we do that?"

"I have a bomb with me."

He skidded to a halt and turned as best he could to face her. "Miss Zhao, why do you always find it necessary to carry a bomb with you?"

She gave him her prettiest smile. "Because it comes in so awfully useful."

Thinking about it, he nodded, and proceeded forward. "I suppose it has so far," he admitted reluctantly.

The tunnel ahead seemed to have no outlet as they continued in their tortuous crawling forward. "Does this damned tunnel ever end?" Leopold lamented aloud.

"End now," said Suchah ahead of him. Leopold hurried forward, popped up through the arch of the tunnel, and stood.

"Thank goodness for that," he said, and leaned down to offer Mingli his hand.

She brushed off her skirts with a despairing sigh at the sight of them. "Where to now, Inspector?"

"Down this way." He floated onward and they followed…until the ghost pulled up sharply. He sent a look of distress toward Leopold. "They're coming," he said.

CHAPTER SIXTEEN

LEOPOLD SEARCHED WITH his senses as his father had taught him to do, to reach for magical tendrils that might be near.

"It's important, my boy," Àkos had said all those years ago in his faint Hungarian accent, *"to empty your mind. Close your eyes."*

"But what if you're in trouble, Papa?" he had asked in his newly breaking voice. *"How do you empty your mind when you're full of fear?"*

"You think of sheep. Think of all those dusty wooly bodies huddling together, baaing and mumbling to each other. Think of them flank to flank, protecting each other out on a green pasture. Sheep and green for miles and miles. Think of sheep."

Think of sheep, he told himself, forcing his lungs to breathe deep and evenly. *Sheep, as far as the eye could see.* His heart slowed, his breathing eased. He reached out...reached out...and the magic, like a moth hovering in the wind, fluttered before him. He grasped it with his senses...and caught it!

Drawing it in, it reached his nose first, the smell and then the taste of earth and moss filling the back of his throat. It began to surge through his limbs like a wash of a rushing stream, stronger and faster. Yes! He had found it, found the breach, the place where it flowed through to this world from...he didn't know where. Because *this* magic was different. It hadn't the acrid taste of the Otherworld of Gehenna and *Sitra Achra*. Instead, it was pungent and alive and full of a different kind of strength. Perhaps it came from the center of the Earth, from all things *of* the Earth. Earth magic. It intoxicated like nothing he'd ever known. How could it be that he had not *known*, not *felt*, not *tasted* this before?

When he opened his eyes again, he felt as if they glowed in the dark, and perhaps they did, in a sense, because Mingli was looking at him with awe. "Do you feel that?" he asked her. He nearly choked on his voice, feeling the magic wind around his vocal cords. "You must be feeling it."

Her eyes grew wider as she, too, pulled in the magic. He didn't know quite how her magic worked. And perhaps she didn't understand it either, but he knew that she could do the same, that she was drawing it to her core as well.

She slowly nodded. "I do," she rasped.

The goblins were coming. And now he had the power to blast them to kingdom come…but he paused. No, now was not the time to show his power. Or to waste this precious gift he had found in the very stones of the Earth. He glanced at Mingli, willing her to understand when he put a finger to his lips to quiet them all.

He closed his eyes again and swept the air in the slow pattern of a sigil that he suddenly knew the sign for, painting it in the air in hot sparks of light. And suddenly, even as the goblins turned the corner from a different passage, the four of them simply…vanished.

The goblins arrived and stopped, the ones in front getting butted by the ones behind.

"Why have you stopped?" some even grumbled aloud.

"They were here," said a greasy-looking fellow with a disgusting shirt full of holes and smeared swathes of oil. "And then they weren't. I can smell what was left of them."

Now all the goblins were sniffing the air, their long noses turned upward.

Leopold, standing next to Mingli, wanted very much to grasp her hand, but he remained as still as possible, even as the greasy goblin neared him, looked him right in the eye no more than a few inches away without seeing him, and made a loud, long sniff…

Others came close, even brushing the hem of his frock coat, but they, too, didn't see Leopold's company.

Even Thacker, looking horrified at Leopold and glowing against the rock wall, was invisible to the goblins' scrutiny. He could have vanished himself through the stone, but he somehow understood that to move was to break the enchantment. Thacker and Suchah exchanged looks with bulging eyes but nothing more.

Leopold moved his head slowly, slightly to look upon Mingli. There was a rim of beaded sweat above the cupid's bow of her upper lip. He watched, enrapt, as her tongue snaked out and caught the perspiration, licking the saltiness away…as *he* longed to do to that mouth. It was a nervous gesture, so unlike the staid Mingli Zhao he knew. But when her gaze darted toward him, there was nothing but repressed excitement shimmering in that eye.

She liked this. She liked the notion that all could suddenly go so wrong. She lived for it, for the danger, the thrill.

He gave her a slow smile in acknowledgment. Because he realized that the danger, the unknown, was something he seemed to like too.

The goblins hunched together, sniffing the air and ambling along the path right beside them. But the creatures managed to move on along the passage, muttering and arguing. One seemed to lag behind the others and sniffed again, eyeing where they stood invisible, frozen to the spot.

Leopold kept his breathing as quiet as he could, and even though he was certain his magic would hold, it did give him pause when that ferrety-faced goblin glared just where he was standing. "There's something not right here," muttered the creature.

Just as Leopold was gathering himself to protect them from the curious goblin, the creature suddenly stiffened and fell over backwards like a hewn tree.

Startled, Leopold stared at his hands. *He* hadn't done anything. Even Mingli questioned him with a raised brow. Leopold shook his head. No, it hadn't been him.

"Stupid Flesh Master," rasped Suchah. "Suchah was tired of waiting."

"Suchah!" As soon as he spoke the enchantment fell away, and they were visible again. "Is he dead?"

Suchah narrowed his eyes. "Did Flesh Master want him to be?"

"Well…no."

Smiling, Suchah folded his arms over his chest. "Then he isn't."

"Lead us, Inspector," said Mingli urgently.

Thacker's ghost floated swiftly along the passage, turned sharply at another place that seemed deceptively solid, and then slowed when he arrived at another portal with a barred door, like a gaol cell. Mingli hurried to reach the bars first and, not touching them, peered beyond them. "Suchah, can you bring your light?" she said.

The webbed feet of the imp slapped on the stone as he approached. He made his ball of light and sent it floating beyond the bars.

The ball cast its light down and returned a golden glow. The entire space was covered in gold. Coins, goblets, statues, huge amphoras, jewelry piled as high as the eye could see.

Leopold approached and whistled. "My God. It's the treasures of antiquity." For indeed, as he got closer, he could see Egyptian sarcophagi and Egyptian animal gods shining in gold. Sumerian thrones, Minoan armor, Assyrian weapons. He moved to rest his hands on the bars when Mingli slapped his hands away.

"You mustn't touch, Leo. The bars are enchanted."

He ran his hands over them, inches away. "How can you tell?"

She tapped her cheek under her eye patch. "My enhancement."

He stepped back, conceding it. "Now what?"

She reached behind her to her bustle and pulled out a small sphere. It was made of copper, with tiny rivets holding the plates of the thing together. She held it in one hand while she dragged out her necklace with the other. At the end of the long chain that usually nestled in her bosom was the jade dragon her "Ghost with a Grievance" had told her to take from her uncle's brothel before they destroyed the place and all its inhabitants.

She fit the dragon into an oddly shaped hole in the top of the orb and turned it. A key! The orb began to tick.

"You kept that in your bustle?" he said quietly.

She merely smiled in reply. Carefully, she inched it toward the bars to pass it through…when it stuck. No matter which way she turned it, it was slightly too large to fit through the bars.

"Damn," she swore softly.

"Turn it off," said Leopold.

"I can't."

His stark expression matched her own.

Desperately, Leopold looked down at Suchah. "Can you take this through?"

"And blow myself up?"

"Well, preferably not!"

"While you argue," said Mingli, voice slightly strained, "time is literally ticking away."

"Suchah!" urged Leopold.

"Oh, very well." He snatched it none too gently from her hand and vanished with it, appearing mere seconds later on the mountains of gold. He placed it carefully on one pile, vanished, and reappeared again on their side of the bars. "Satisfied?"

Leopold nodded that he was...until the ticking sphere teetered. He watched in horror as the damned thing began rolling down the golden cache—bouncing here and there and weaving between the stacks of coins—and inevitably made its way toward them and the bars.

"Run!" he cried. He took no chances and grabbed Mingli's hand before he leapt with her around the corner of the passage. He snatched Suchah's wrist when the imp simply stood by, and pulled him to safety just as the explosion burst forth. Debris blasted toward them, raining down hot metal drops upon the floor.

Once the billows of smoke began to clear, Leopold gingerly peered around the edge. The cavern had been demolished. He let go of Suchah and Mingli to go see for himself. Yes, the roof had collapsed, not only flattening the bars but most likely the precious objects within. But there was enough gold debris around them that he feared it had been a useless exercise...before the gold began to melt into the very stones. Some bubbled and wisped into the air as smoke, until every last bit of it had disintegrated.

"A very effective bomb," he breathed.

Mingli emerged, pushing her stray locks into the carefully coifed curls. "Yes. I try to have the right tool for the right job."

He squared with her. "You couldn't possibly have known that you were to encounter goblin gold today."

"Didn't I?"

Before he could offer a retort, Suchah had stepped in front of him. "Flesh Master," he said, shaking his head in wonder. "Flesh Master...saved Suchah."

"Well...yes."

"But...why?"

Leopold leaned down and rested his hands on his thighs to face him. "That's what I've been trying to tell you, you insolent carbuncle. That I consider you an ally...not a slave to throw away."

Suchah stared at him uncomprehendingly.

"Don't mind me," said Thacker, whooshing by, "but there are goblins on the way."

Leopold girded himself. "Everyone! Follow Thacker. You too, Suchah."

"Yes, Flesh Master!" he said with a grin, bulbous eyes shining.

Leopold held onto his hat and ran, making certain Mingli was ahead of him. "Thacker! Is there any way to get down to those railroad tracks at the bottom of that big cavern we saw earlier?"

The ghost glanced back at him over his transparent shoulder. "Don't you want out of here?"

"Yes, but...I think we need to see where those tracks go. We must stop this diabolical curse."

"Bloody hell, Leopold. I didn't know you were in the business of saving the whole bloody world all the time."

"Well...apparently I am!"

"All right, all right. Don't get your drawers in a twist. I'll get you down there. Do you still have that magic?"

He realized the refreshed magic he experienced had drained away or was blocked by strong goblin charms and wards. Because he could just feel—now that he was sensitive to it—the merest whisper of Earth magic along the wards' edges...like a surging sea, diked on the shoreline. If he could only breach that dike, he knew he could be flooded with the stuff again.

It was frustrating being so close to it. Yet as long as the goblins blocked it, he couldn't grab hold of it.

"I can't. It's blocked again."

Thacker shot forward and suddenly halted on the edge of precipice.

Leopold nearly went over the side himself when Mingli caught his coattails and hauled him back.

"The fastest way is not necessarily the most practical way," she said breathlessly. "Especially for mortals."

"Thank you." His stomach flipped a little as he peered over the edge.

Thacker pointed. "There's a path down there to reach the bottom, but it ain't like you can't be seen."

"Perhaps you can create a distraction elsewhere."

"You know it's hard for me to move objects on your plane."

"I know, but—"

"I can help!"

They all looked at Suchah. The imp wore an uncharacteristically animated expression as he jumped up and down, wings flapping. "I can help, Leopold Master. I can help the do-nothing ghost."

"Now look here," Thacker began.

"Wait, Spense." Leopold crouched to be at eye level with the imp. "You truly want to help?"

"Leopold Master saved Suchah. Suchah now *want* to help."

Leopold noticed that he was suddenly no longer *Flesh Master*. The moment warmed his heart. "Very well, Suchah. Please listen to Inspector Thacker's instructions."

"Suchah will. Leopold Master has strange friends."

"Yes, he does," said Mingli, with a smile curling her lips.

As ghost and imp winked out, he turned to Mingli. "Well? Shall we?"

CHAPTER SEVENTEEN

LEOPOLD AND MINGLI lay flat on their stomachs at the edge of the fall-off, waiting an interminable time for Thacker and Suchah's distraction that never seemed to appear.

"What's taking them so long?" he rasped.

"They might be arguing."

"Or Suchah might have run off and left him there to shift for himself."

"Do you truly believe that?"

He exhaled a long breath. "No. I believe the little blighter is actually on our side now."

"And all it took was a little kindness. Who would have thought?"

"The denizens of the Otherworld don't usually respond to kindness. They consider it a weakness."

"As do goblins. Experience has taught me that."

"As it has taught me in Gehenna. But...I was also proved wrong today."

"Yes," she said thoughtfully. "Things are never what they seem."

He turned his head to gaze at her. "No. Because I thought you were trying to kill me when I was attempting to destroy the Daemon Device six months ago."

"But I wasn't."

"No. And I remembered most clearly when you promised to kiss me." He grinned.

Her smile was mischievous. "And I fulfilled that promise."

He drew closer. "You certainly did. So much so that I find it difficult to get it out of my mind."

She inched closer to him. "Do you?"

He felt her breath on his mouth. "Yes," he whispered, leaned in, and took the kiss he had longed to take for hours. They lay side by side, kissing for several thundering heartbeats. The feel of her, the taste of her!

Finally—reluctantly—Leopold drew back, gazing at her again, searing the memory of her features on his mind. "You're very beautiful, you know. Even with a smudge of dirt on your nose."

Her hand immediately went to said nose and brushed it off with an equally dirty glove. "It's not polite to take advantage of a woman like that."

Leopold smiled, opened his mouth to speak, and then shut it when a sound began to groan from the depths of the caverns below.

Any goblins moving about by the tracks suddenly stopped and looked in that direction. Slowly, they clutched at their tools and walked toward the dark tunnel and out of the light of the open cavern.

"That must be Spense and Suchah," he said.

She shuffled herself to her knees. "Then let us not waste their fine distraction."

He rose and helped her the rest of the way. Then, crouching low, they hurried down the steep path that descended to the tracks. There was definitely no hiding for them. The way was narrow and slippery with loose rocks, and hewn from the side of the mountain in such a way that was unforgiving to any errors.

But the lower they went, the more magic Leopold could detect. It was that Earth magic again. And even as powerful as the magic was he could acquire from Eurynomos, there was something renewing and cleansing about Earth magic. He'd definitely have to make a study of it...if he ever got the chance.

The sludgy river was just that—sludge, from the gutters of London and it certainly smelled like it. He vowed to avoid it, and instead turned his attention to the snaking ribbons of railway tracks shooting off in opposite directions: one, into the bowels of the cavern and deep into darkness; the other, toward what he could only guess was the station at Piccadilly.

The sleek tracks strangely shone in silver lines, though light was scarce. The source of the light might have been the end of the tunnel, open to the sunlight and London itself, but he couldn't be quite sure. All he knew was that they were strangely compelling and drew him closer with the hum of magic.

As soon as Leopold stepped up onto the rails, his body stiffened. Every inch of him, every sinew and nerve pulsed with a sudden surge of power. "My God!"

When he looked toward Mingli to commiserate, he was shocked at her entirely different appearance. She looked to be lit up with golden light shining from her in every direction, and her aura, her life force, blazed all around her figure in a bright orange glow. "Just look at you!" he breathed. "You look like an angel."

"Leo, step away from the tracks."

"But it's magnificent! I can feel it. I can feel all the ancient depths of power—"

"Leo…please. Step away from the tracks."

He heard the urgency in her voice, but he couldn't understand why she would want such a thing, when it filled him with such bliss, such radiant energy. What was he now but a ball of light and power? His feet didn't even touch the tracks anymore, but hovered above them. He could do anything, go anywhere. He was…all-powerful…

Something distant was calling to him. But no, he wanted to fly up to the ceiling, experience the magic fully…and yet, the sound of that musical voice called to him, and he glanced to where the angel in all her brilliant light lifted her face to him. And her voice slowly, vaguely registered in his mind, in his ears.

"Leo, my love, come down."

Such sweet, sweet words he had never heard before. He moved toward it, wanting to be within its sphere.

When he landed back on the tracks a hand grasped his wrist and yanked him forward, and suddenly, like a curtain falling, the sensations were cut. He could still feel the magic throbbing in the background, but it no longer overtook his senses as completely as it had.

He stared back at the tracks. "What the devil happened to me?"

"You were standing on an alignment line. You were suddenly drawing all the power, the Earth magic, in enormous quantities. Oh, Leo. I was so afraid I'd lose you."

He faced her then and took both her hands. "Oh, my dear. Don't you know? It was your voice that lured me back." And he kissed her deeply then, crushing her close.

When she pulled back to breathe, she shook her head. "You looked…dear me. You looked otherworldly. You were rising up into the air. You looked like a celestial being."

He smiled. "So did you."

"But I wasn't standing on the tracks."

"But that's how you looked…to me."

She pulled away and straightened her hat for something to do. "Well, thank the gods for that. If my voice drew you back."

He was slowly coming back to himself. Yet the power was still with him, the Earth magic seemed lodged in his gut waiting for the moment to spring forth, just as it had in the tunnels when he'd made his company invisible. Only this time, he felt it couldn't be blocked. Not for a long while, at any rate. "That was an extraordinary feeling. Every part of me was transformed. I still feel it." He pressed a hand to his stomach. It seemed to be lodged in his core.

"I don't know whether it is safe for a human. You were very lucky you survived."

"It's Earth magic. It's…very different from the Gehenna magic I've grown up with. *That* I have learned to use and manipulate."

"I'm certain it was that training that saved you."

"Maybe." He pondered it. It was like a fading dream now, what he felt, what he saw. *Had* he seen it?

"Well, be that as it may, you must be careful. You are particularly sensitive and open to any sort of magic. I'm afraid it might have been your time in the Otherworld that makes you vulnerable."

"Yes." His eyes drew back to the tracks. *But it didn't feel the same as Gehenna magic*, he kept telling himself. "It's definitely powerful. How can we use this against the goblins? We can't very well destroy an alignment line."

"No. No, we can't." She laid a dirty, gloved finger to her lip and tapped it. "I'll have to think on it. In the meantime, don't you think it's time we got out of here?"

"I do. But what of the resurrected? We still don't have a way to stop that."

"Not yet. But now we know where it's coming from. We can form a plan of action. But first, we must leave this place."

"How shall we accomplish that?"

"We must follow the tracks."

He cast his glance along them as they disappeared into the distance. It was a long way to go. "We'd best hurry, then, before the goblins return."

THEY SPOKE LITTLE as they walked at a quick gait. Leopold was certain that the tunnel that seemed to have a light at the end of it, as if moving toward sunlight. But even as it opened hours later into a proper brick tunnel, they emerged, dirty and disheveled, into the platform at Piccadilly...at night.

"What the devil..." Leopold pulled out his watch. It read eight o'clock. "But that's impossible! We were never there that long. We started in the morning."

"But we were in a faery realm, and time is different there."

"Are you serious?"

"Of course." She lifted her skirts to step up to an iron stairway that led from the bottom of the tracks to the platform.

"Do you mean to tell me that twelve hours have passed since we entered the Saint Collen Club?"

"I'm afraid so."

Leopold looked around him, appalled. "That's remarkable. And I've missed my curtain. Oh. No. There *is* no performance for me. I'm certain the theatre owner will somehow blame me for the disruption of last night. And...oh dash it. I'll have to contend with my assistants who saw it all. They must have run off with the rest of them."

"It wasn't your fault."

"It doesn't much matter at this point. I'll surely be ruined. Perhaps I should become a rozzer with the Metropolitan Police. Work my way up to Scotland Yard. You'd put in a good word for me, wouldn't you?"

"Of course, but I hardly think you'd want to give up your life as a magician. You are very good at it, after all."

"Really?" He smiled, maybe blushed a little. He fiddled with his cuffs. "Thank you very much."

They made their way through the nearly empty railway station. Only the sweepers and the man at the W. H. Smith bookstall straightening the stacks of books, magazines, and pamphlets between the half-closed scissor gates seemed to remain.

The streets were dark, and the mist was falling. "We must be careful," he said, searching into the fog. "The dead will be walking now."

"I nearly forgot," she said, in a rare instance of candor.

"You will be pleased to know, however, that I am presently full of magic and can defend the both of us as well as any others, if necessary."

"I didn't doubt it," she replied.

They kept looking all around them, sometimes walking backwards to search the fog. But Leopold kept watching Mingli.

"Look, Miss Zhao...Mingli. Perhaps...perhaps it would be wise to...to stay at my lodgings tonight. This is dangerous out here. In the dark."

She ducked her head. Was she composing her face? Had she been smiling?

"Well, Leopold. If you think it best."

"Yes. You can have the bedroom again and I will take the drawing room. Again."

She made a sound of acknowledgement but somehow, it seemed more like a chuckle to him.

They moved into the dim streets, listening for those shuffling steps. Leopold noticed a body lying on the pavement. Cautiously, he approached.

It was a woman in tattered, muddy clothes. There was a gray pallor to her face, and blood on her lips. As his eyes grew accustomed to the fog, he saw more bodies lying higgledy-piggledy along the cobblestoned streets and pavement. One had even fallen over a fenced hedge.

"What's happened now?"

"It would appear," said Mingli, casting about at all the bodies, "that they began their nightly killing spree, but were suddenly...stopped."

"What could have stopped it?"

"I think *we* did."

In the distance, somewhere behind him, he heard metallic footsteps.

"Blast," he muttered. "Mingli, I think I hear the—"

"Clockwork Gypsy," she gasped.

The clanking came closer. He reached into his coat for his wand but remembered at the last moment that Gilpin Horner had broken it. The Webley? No. He had plenty of magic, and he'd need it against the man. He motioned for Mingli to take cover, but the stubborn woman would not go very far. Instead, she pulled her strange gun from under her skirts. She had told him once it was to shoot demons with, and perhaps that made more sense, under the circumstances.

The metallic steps drew closer. They sounded different in the fog, but then again, the poor wretch was becoming more machine by the moment. Who knew when he would finally succumb to the gears that haunted his sight?

Leopold braced for it, opened and closed his hands to limber up his fingers for whatever conjuring he had to do. He slowed his breathing, straining his ears to hear.

The steps got closer and suddenly stopped.

He couldn't stand it anymore. "You might as well come out!" he shouted into the gloom. "I've heard your footsteps."

The steps suddenly rushed forward. Leopold crouched at the ready.

The fog parted and a figure shot forward. The porcelain face was fixed, the boiled shirt and tailcoat came into view...and impossibly long brass legs stopped and postured.

Leopold's jaw dropped. "*Raj?*"

CHAPTER EIGHTEEN

"LEO!" CRIED THE automaton.

They stared at one another for an interminable moment. "Raj. You...you have legs."

Raj laughed and skipped in a circle before facing Leopold again. Those thin brass legs stuck out from below his flapping shirt and coat. "I've been trying to tell you, Leo!"

"But...how did this happen?"

"Are you heading for your flat? Oh, I should like to see it. I should like to see everything!"

"Come, Mr. Kazsmer," said Mingli. "I think Raj has much to tell you. As much as you may have to tell him. Let us get out of the street." She stepped forward and linked her arm with the automaton. "Welcome to walking, Raj."

"Thank you very much, Miss Zhao."

"Come along, Leo," she said, for Leopold seemed to have frozen to the spot. He shook out his head and trotted to catch up to them, stepping over the many bodies lying in the street.

He didn't bother with a key and simply waved his hand at his door once they reached it. The wards fell and the lock released its pins and in they went. He did have the presence of mind to wave his hand to lock and ward the door again. He lit the gas with a gesture, took off his hat and hung it on a peg in the foyer, and ushered them into the drawing room.

Once the fire was lit after he gestured the proper sigils toward it, Leopold took in his old friend. "Raj! Old chap!"

"I know," he said, pacing, the joint at his knees squeaking, the feet clanking. "One day I was doing my routine self-diagnostic, when I came upon a loose plate. When I explored further, the plate seemed to have been hiding an unknown switch. I know I shouldn't have done it alone, but you, my friend, have been absent of late. My curiosity got the better of me, I'm afraid, and when I pushed the lever — oh my goodness! Other connections were made, a surge of power flashed through me, and heretofore unknown plates slid back. The legs telescoped down and lifted me from the table. It was a most remarkable moment. I could not believe it. If I were capable of dreaming, I would have thought I dreamt it. You should have seen my first tentative steps. I'm grateful I never fully fell, for I do not know what would have happened if I had shattered my head."

Slowly, Leopold stepped toward him and gently took him by his narrow shoulders. Now that he was standing as tall as Leopold, he seemed to be a very thin, very long individual. "I can't believe it."

"Neither can I!" chortled the automaton.

"I have studied every inch of you, old man. I never saw those plates before."

"They were carefully incorporated into the rest of the design so as to be undetectable. My maker was a man...or woman," he said with a bow toward Mingli, who bowed back, "with a considerable sense of humor."

Leopold grinned from ear to ear. "You're no longer stuck at that blasted table."

"No I am not! Thank the gods!"

"Raj. By Jove, this is marvelous. Have a seat, old man."

Raj held up his hand. "No thank you. I've been sitting for hundreds of years. I don't mind standing."

Mingli stepped forward and embraced the mechanical man. "How can you explain it, Raj? Suddenly being aware of something so monumental?"

"I can't explain it, Miss Zhao. To be fair, I can't explain much about me at all. I do not know my origins, nor how long I've been alive nor even how it is possible. My maker must have designed me in such a way as to offer these legs as a contingency. I may not ever have been supposed to deploy them."

"Well, to hell with that and your confounded maker!" said Leopold. "This calls for a drink." He paused and turned to Raj. "You can't drink now, can you?"

Raj seemed to be grinning, even though his painted face never changed. "I shouldn't be surprised at this juncture."

Leopold went to the sideboard with his cut-glass decanters and poured two brandies. He handed one to Mingli. "A toast. To Raj and…his new conveyance!"

"Hear, hear," said Raj, slapping his metal side.

"If you're going to go walking about, Raj old chap, you're going to need trousers."

Raj looked down at his shiny legs. "Why?"

"Well…it's just not the done thing. Here, I'll loan you a pair."

"Oh, Leopold, that is not necessary…"

But Leopold had retreated into his bedroom and took a worn pair from his wardrobe and returned to the drawing room with them. "Let me help you. If, er, Miss Zhao would turn around…"

"Oh, really!" She said, but happily turned away from them.

He allowed Raj to lean on him and push a leg in one at a time. But when Raj pulled them up, they fell to his ankles again.

Leopold investigated. "Seems you're missing hips, old bean. I tell you what, when I get a chance, I'll cobble you something at the lock-up in Whitechapel."

"It's all so absurd," said Raj.

"May I turn around now?" asked Mingli.

"It's your sensibilities I'm worrying about, Miss Zhao," said Leopold with a laugh. "He'll have to go about without trousers for the meantime."

She smiled. "I think I can muddle through."

"But Leopold, what has been going on?" Raj's voice became serious. "That mechanical man! Those goblins! And what has been happening on the streets? The bodies! I have never seen the like. The theatre's been closed so I haven't been able to catch any news."

"Oh yes. What did the Templeton sisters say? Did they flee?"

"I'm afraid so. But it was for their own safety. I'm sure they'll be back." But Leopold could detect no confidence in his tone.

"Well, it doesn't matter. There are much more important events afoot. If you don't mind, I'll sit while I tell you."

Leopold unwound the story as best he knew it, with Mingli offering further explanation. Raj listened patiently, standing so still it was as if he had turned himself off. But Leopold knew better, knew his friend and his quirks. At least—looking at those brass legs—he thought he had.

"And you say the clockwork man is a fellow Romani?"

"Yes. Someone I used to know. Miklos Antalek."

"I've been thinking about your Clockwork Gypsy problem," said Mingli. She'd divested herself of her jacket and hat as she had done last night, and pressed an ungloved finger to her lips. "Tomorrow, let me take you to a consultant."

"Consultant? What does that mean?"

"You trust me, don't you, Leo?"

"Why...of course!"

"Then tomorrow. As for now, may we call upon your landlady to offer us sustenance?"

They hid Raj under their coats, and he stood as a coat rack while Mrs. Granville laid out cold meats and cheese. She barely glanced at Mingli but it was obvious she didn't approve.

They uncovered Raj as they ate and chatted, wondering about this mysterious automaton maker and what his reasons were for this or that. After they ate, Raj graciously opened his shirt for Mingli to examine his internal mechanisms, and she nodded and "hmmed" along with Leopold's explanations, which took them to a late hour.

Mingli rose and stretched her back—something that caused Leopold to freeze as he stared. "We've had a very long day," she said. "I would like to say goodnight. Raj, I am so very happy for your discovery and I can see many more adventures for you."

"Thank you," he said as he bowed.

She reached the bedroom door and turned around. "Would *you* like to say goodnight to me, Leo?"

"Oh." He rose from his seat and approached her, but kept looking back nervously at the automaton. "Well, er…goodnight, Miss Zhao." He put his hand out to shake.

She looked at it for a moment, grasped it with her own, and hauled him in. As her mouth met his, he felt her lips turn up in a smile. He would have kissed her longer, but he was already feeling his face warm with Raj watching them.

Mingli pulled away and grasped his chin. "Goodnight," she said, and disappeared behind the door.

Leopold stood facing the portal for a long moment. He cleared his throat, and turned around, letting out a nervous laugh.

"Leo!" cried Raj. "I am so very happy for you, my friend! The beautiful Miss Zhao always seemed to have an eye for you."

He adjusted his tie. "Well…"

A loud pop startled them both. Thacker and Suchah suddenly appeared in the middle of the room. "Wotcher, Leo," said Thacker. He spotted Raj, gave him a nod, and then jerked his head back. "Blimey, Raj! You've got legs!"

"Strange things in this room," said Suchah, shaking his head and completely ignoring the automaton. "Suchah no like it."

———— ◆ ————

RAJ WAS OBLIGED to tell his tale again to a gobsmacked Thacker, while Suchah went about the room, picking up objects and examining them, before tossing them aside and muttering to himself. Leopold watched his progress throughout the room and had to, once or twice, repair the ephemera he broke with a wave of his hand.

"Suchah!" he rasped. "Stop breaking my things."

The imp held a porcelain shepherdess and looked it over. "Is this a god?"

"No." He snatched it from his hand. "It is merely for display. To look at."

"It does nothing?"

"No."

"Leopold Master has useless things about."

"Yes, well. Humans like…useless things about them."

Suchah nodded sagely. "Now humans make more sense."

He ignored the imp—after taking another porcelain figurine out of the imp's hand—and turned to Thacker. "What happened when we left? We were able to get down to the tracks, and…oh, Spense—the power of the alignment lines! I was nearly overwhelmed. I have that magic still within me."

"Cor," gasped Thacker. "Well, I must say, I'm learning a lot about your magic world, Leopold. Suchah and I got ourselves into the depths of the caverns and with that fellow's help, we made noises and shook them walls. Oh, them goblins came running, all right. And still more shot through the tunnels crying about the gold that was destroyed. Your Miss Zhao was right on the mark on that one. It was like their whole world had come to an end. Then we saw some big geezer called Gilpin Horner—you know the type. Rich one, he looked like."

"Yes, we met him. He's the one who held us captive and I'm afraid we destroyed his lodgings while escaping."

"He was none too happy about *that*, I can tell you. Such language! But they're after you, Leo. And your Miss Zhao. I'd watch my step, old son."

"I expected nothing less," he said, collapsing into a chair, rubbing his forehead for the headache that was coming on.

"At any rate," Thacker continued, "you might have scotched their operation tonight. I've not seen any walking corpses."

"The walking corpses," said Raj sagely.

Leopold reckoned that the bodies in the street were all removed before Thacker could spy them.

"You look all worn out," said Thacker, looking over Leopold. "You should get to bed." He thumbed toward his bedchamber.

"I'm afraid Miss Zhao is in there. This is my bed tonight."

"Suchah can stay, if Leopold Master wants."

Leopold doffed his shoes and stretched out on the settee. He smiled sleepily. "That's good of you, Suchah. But you can go back if you'd like. I'll call you if I need you."

The imp nodded. "All you need do is call." He snapped his fingers and was gone.

"That bloke suddenly got himself a new attitude," said Thacker, scratching his head.

"Yes. It seems that kindness goes a long way." Leopold settled in, yawning. "Look, Raj, it's fine that you stay here. There's nothing to do at the theatre for the moment, and you can't be seen on the streets like that. Make yourself at home."

"I am very much obliged to you, Leo. I shall take advantage of your wonderful library, if I may."

"Of course." Leopold rolled over and didn't even mind that the gas lamp was on as he slept.

———◆———

WHEN LEOPOLD AWOKE, it was to the sight of Thacker, Suchah, and Raj playing cards. He sat up. "Suchah? What are you doing here? I didn't call you."

He shrugged and put down a card from his hand. "Was curious."

"About what?"

He grinned with his sharp teeth. "What would happen next."

"Gin," said Thacker. He had learned from Raj how to manipulate cards. It was about the most he *could* do as a ghost.

Suchah frowned as he slammed down his hand. "Ghost is playing ghost tricks. Can you see through cards?" He turned his cards this way and that.

"I told you I didn't. I've lost as much as I've won, you know."

Leopold yawned and stretched. "Have you three been here all night?"

"Suchah came later. See that Leopold Master is asleep. Ghost and...*that* were here." He gestured toward Raj who raised his chin.

"I am not a 'that', my impish friend. I am an automaton. Or mechanical man. Or simply Raj."

"Good morning, gentlemen."

The scent of lilac seemed to suddenly drift toward them, and Leopold rose to his feet. "Good morning, Miss Zhao."

"I feel as if I had missed something. Who's winning?"

Both Thacker and Suchah pointed to Raj.

"Naturally," she said with a bow.

"With Inspector Thacker a close second," said Raj. "I'm afraid our Suchah gets a little distracted by the look of the cards themselves."

The imp postured. "Distracted? Distracted? I do not!"

"I'm afraid you do." Raj ticked his head. "But it is no matter. It is simply a matter of practice."

"Shall I order breakfast?" she asked, eye focused on Leopold.

"Please do. I'll clean up." He exited to his bedroom and listened as the four of them chattered behind the door. There was a bit of scrambling when Mrs. Granville appeared, but he heard them shuffle back to their places once she'd gone.

While he washed and dressed, he worried about...oh, so many things. How was he to stop the goblins; what about the Clockwork Gypsy; and what of his father? If he got to him too late—indeed, it might be too late already—would he be little better than those poor wretches in Bedlam?

He realized he'd been sitting on the edge of his bed, contemplating it all for far too long. Mingli said they would go to a consultant, and in Mingli's world God knew what that would mean.

He finished dressing and once he emerged, found breakfast was laid out for him. He took the offered coffee with a nod of thanks and ate quietly, using the conversation of his companions as background noise to his own thoughts.

A hand landed softly on his own, and he looked up to Mingli's concerned face. "You are quiet, Leo. Tell me what concerns you."

"I'm certain you already know. The goblins have not been defeated, only delayed. And Miklos is still out there. And...my father..."

"We *will* accomplish all of these things. We are working together." She took in Thacker, Suchah, and even Raj. "And that seems an indomitable force."

He smiled for the first time that morning. "That's true. And surprisingly—gratifyingly so."

"And so, Leo," said Thacker at the small table with his card playing companions. He carefully removed a card from the deck and slid it slowly into place within the cards in his hand. Leopold knew that to move or hold objects, Thacker needed deep concentration. "Tell us about this blossoming romance between you and Miss Zhao."

His cheeks instantly bloomed into red heat. "I...I..."

Mingli rose, straightening her skirts. "Mr. Kazsmer is courting me. And at some future date, I have agreed to be his wife."

Raj shot to his feet and engulfed Leopold in an embrace. "Leo!" He ticked his head with glass eyes ablaze. "That is a wonderful thing."

"That's great news, Leo, old son," said Thacker, carefully patting him on the back, something Leopold felt as a strange cold touch. "But I must confess, I can't imagine the Inspector staying at home, keeping your house."

Before Mingli could speak, Leopold cut in. "But she won't. I can't imagine Miss Zhao as anything but a Special Inspector for Scotland Yard. Her talents are much needed there."

Mingli fixed her stare on him, mouth parted in surprise.

"I can't say that I like that," Thacker went on. "Women belong in the home, caring for their husbands and children."

He locked gazes with Mingli. "She's so much more than that. I would never demand it."

"You are a most unusual man, Mr. Kazsmer," she said at last.

He approached her and took both her hands. "As long as it's what *you* want."

"I don't understand this nonsense," grumbled Suchah. "When do we kill goblins?"

CHAPTER NINETEEN

LEOPOLD ADMONISHED HIS friends to stay where they were. Raj certainly couldn't go out during the day, and Thacker could only go so far. As a spirit, he had boundaries as to how far from Scotland Yard he could go about in London. And Suchah shouldn't be seen at all. They all argued, especially Thacker since he was invisible to the rest of the population when he wanted to be, but Leopold insisted.

"Mingli, my dear" he said quietly when they got to the street. "Would you prefer to go to your flat and change? You might be more comfortable with fresh clothes."

"Why, Leo. Are you concerned for my underthings?"

His face flushed hot again. "No! Of course not!"

"Really? What a pity." She bumped him as they walked, a coquettish smirk on her face.

"You…" He rushed to catch up to her and spoke confidentially out of the side of his mouth. "You really are a minx, aren't you?"

But she said nothing. They caught a cab and Leopold found that her lodgings were on a side street off Fleet. The building was as decrepit as he recalled, but he couldn't have been certain earlier in the fog. A dingy brick dwelling held up by other dingy multi-story houses. The cabby looked at them oddly and asked them several times if they were certain they wanted to be dropped off there. Leopold quieted his concerns with an extra coin.

Leopold headed for the house but jerked to a halt when Mingli grabbed his coattails and dragged him back. "Not by the front door, Mr. Kazsmer. Not in the daytime." She marched up the street, turned a corner, and entered a Chinese laundry.

The place billowed with steam and the clanking of the mangles and other laundry machinery. He heard the voices of the men and women, speaking in their incomprehensible tongue as he dutifully followed Mingli into the heart of the place. No one raised a brow or looked their way. It was as if they were invisible. He leaned toward her and whispered, rather urgently, "We *aren't* invisible, are we?"

"No, we aren't. They are paid on a monthly basis to ignore my comings and goings, and they do their job well."

They exited out the back to an enclosed court, squeezed between four brick buildings. Laundry from the other tenants hung crisscross above, whipping in the wind like medieval banners.

Looking up all around him at the sheets and shirts flapping in the breeze, he nearly missed it when she ducked through a metal door. When he entered and let it slam behind him, the corridor was dim, lit only by a single, lonely gas light. The floor slanted downward until they came to a singular room with a coal smoke-belching furnace. Leopold pulled his stiff collar away from his neck. It was hot as Hades in that room but Mingli was standing patiently before a scissor-gated door. He detected the merest of humming of something mechanical, until she snapped open the gates and stepped into a smaller room….ah. It was a lift.

He stepped in beside her. "I say, is all this really necessary?"

She put a finger to her lips and shushed him.

The lift jerked, nearly sending them to the floor before it began to rise, gears clicking loudly, wheels turning somewhere above.

Finally, it rose and seemed to land them to a rooftop. She opened the scissor gate and stepped out. He followed along the gravelly rooftop to a stairway bulkhead door, where they passed through and descended a staircase and ended up…opposite her front door in its dim corridor.

As she turned her key in the lock, she glanced back at him over her shoulder. "As I said before, Leo, I have many enemies."

After their visit with Gilpin Horner, he didn't doubt it.

She opened the door and walked through, already taking the hat pin from her hair and divesting herself of her hat. When some of her hair fell from its coif, Leopold couldn't resist trotting forward to embrace her from behind.

"I love your hair," he breathed to the back of her neck and dared place a kiss there. She shivered. He reached up and threaded his fingers through the lock. "It's so luxurious. It's a shame to curl it and pin it up."

"All women are slaves to fashion, I'm afraid. Otherwise, I shouldn't wear a corset."

Now it was his turn to shiver. "You…talk of this a great deal. Always mentioning your…your corset."

"Because I know just what it does to you."

He spun her around, keeping her still in his arms. "You're a wicked woman, Mingli Zhao."

"And you, sir, talk too much." She pressed forward, raised her face to him, and offered her lips for the kissing. He eagerly complied.

A low growl sounded from somewhere behind him.

He drew back slightly. "Did you hear that?"

She narrowed her eye. "Yes."

"Do you by any chance have a dog?"

"No."

He turned.

Her tiger skin rug postured, its unsupported head hanging below where its shoulders would have been. Its mouth was open with fangs bared, its glass eyes focused on the two of them. It growled again.

"Your…your rug appears to be…distressed."

"Yes," said Mingli, carefully moving out of his embrace. "It's never done that before."

"Good to know."

"I fear it is the goblin curse."

"Well damn." He swallowed. "Suggestions?"

"Er…none that come to mind…"

The tiger rug coiled to spring and, whether it had claws or not, it had a full set of teeth.

Leopold spun and furiously wove magic sigils into the air. The sigils coalesced into glowing fire and surrounded the beast before zooming in for the attack. The tiger roared and whined, rolling on the floor until the fire constricted it, consumed it, and finally there was nothing left but ashes.

Mingli barely caught her breath before she said suddenly, "The faeries!"

As one, they both glanced at the cabinet where she kept her collection. A rumble...and the doors burst open with a mass of dead and desiccated faeries like a cloud of furies, flying straight at them.

Leopold batted at them with his hands, and Mingli used her umbrella, but they were sorely outnumbered.

Leopold leapt on Mingli and shielded her with his body on the floor. Covering her and holding her tight, he couldn't maneuver as he liked, and was able to only use two index fingers to paint invisible sigils on her back, sigils that rose in shining sparks and manifested into a golden wave of power.

The wave blasted the faeries away from them, smashing them to the ground and walls. The creatures were caught up in a whirlwind of magic, swept up together, and propelled straight into the open cabinet. Once inside, the doors slammed shut and Leopold locked it and warded it with the twitching of his hands.

Leopold slowly rose and lifted his weight from Mingli. "You don't have any deer heads or anything, do you?"

She finally laughed, slightly hysterically. "No. No, thank goodness, I do not."

Still, they waited on the floor, peering about them to make sure there were no other resurrected creatures to attack them. At last, Mingli rose.

"Thank goodness you were here, Leo."

"I dread to think what might have happened. But look here. It's daytime. Why did your things come alive during the day?"

"My wards are specific and strong. I suspect that once the curse was upon them, the magic was unable to end, as if contained in a bell jar. It's the only explanation I can think of."

He brushed down his coat and waistcoat. "You'd best change before anything else comes alive. Oh! Mind your furs!"

She disappeared into her bedroom leaving Leopold alone in her drawing room. He paced, still energized from their encounters. But as he looked around the room, he slowed. He could take his leisure to learn about the things she liked to have around her. And they were all certainly unusual.

He went first to the various tribal masks covering one wall. He'd seen Zulu masks and shields in a recent exhibition, but these others were unfamiliar. Fortunately, Mingli was studious about her collections and had placed plaques on the walls. Here were masks from the Dutch East Indies, Japan, Polynesia, and various other African tribes. They were fearsome, grimacing faces that, he supposed, were designed to frighten. Much like the faces of demons he was familiar with.

He moved on to a glass case with various daggers from different cultures, all labeled carefully in her florid script. One even boasted that the blade was poisoned and one mustn't touch it.

On tables by straight-backed chairs were small skulls. Apparently, there wasn't enough left of the skulls to come alive—and he was eternally grateful for that!—but they fascinated by how small they were. They looked like...well, they looked like children. Perhaps they were...monkeys? He could only hope.

He found the incongruity of pastoral paintings like the ones in her office in Scotland Yard; green pastures of the English countryside, where sheep grazed, and tranquil cows observed the viewer. These hung in an alcove of large upholstered chairs that seemed the perfect place for reading a novel on a Sunday afternoon, enjoying a spot of tea...but he couldn't imagine her doing so. He couldn't imagine this woman—who seemed to live her life in a blur of activity—was capable of slowing down that much.

He could not help but glance back at her chamber door and wonder about this woman that he loved, who easily volunteered to his friends that she intended to become his wife. His *wife*! Was he mad? But no. She was perfect for him, just as he was perfect for her. Who else in this wide world could understand the life each had to live and the life they had lived before meeting one another? It would be mad *not* to marry.

Besides, he told himself, he burned for her. Oh yes—how he burned! She was too delectable, too lovely not to want to touch, to kiss, to make love to. And she seemed to be anxious to do the same to him. How fortunate of all men, was he.

He tried it on his tongue, saying quietly to himself, "Gentlemen, this is my wife, Special Inspector Mingli...Kazsmer."

"Oh, you think I should take your name?"

Startled, he spun to face her. "Well, I...it's customary to..."

"I don't know." She put a finger to her cheek, thinking. She was dressed again in a green suit, with a ruffle bustle and a short jacket. She seemed to favor that color and style. Her dragonfly earrings were made of jade.

"You don't want to take my name?"

"I'll have to think on it. After all, I've been known longer as Mingli Zhao. It does seem to strike fear into the hearts of my enemies."

"So it isn't that Kazsmer is a Hungarian name?"

"Look at this face, Leo. Do you think for one moment I have the luxury of prejudice?"

"I just wanted to know."

"We have time to think on it. After all, we've only just started courting. I haven't even a gimmel ring for my finger yet."

Leopold blinked. *Good God!* How had he forgotten? Of course, he never expected…when he proposed the idea, he hadn't imagined…who would have thought that she'd agree? "I have a ring, as it happens. It's back at my flat. I should be honored to give it you."

"And I should be honored to wear it."

God, she's beautiful, he thought to himself. It was the most natural thing in the world to stride up to her, take her in his arms, and soundly kiss her.

And by Jove! She kissed back, with all the fervor and sensuality of the first time. He was about to lose himself, when she must have sensed it and gently pushed him back, trailing her hand along his jaw. "I don't think we have time for that. Not the time I wish to give to it, that is."

Blimey. He swallowed. "Er, yes. You mentioned a consultant?"

"Yes." She glanced at the small watch attached to her jacket by a fob. "And we must go now. Come along."

She snatched her umbrella from the stand, and led the way out by another elaborate set of corridors, staircases, and shopfronts. He realized that she must be paying for access from all quarters of the neighborhood. Industrious was his Miss…was his *Mingli.*

———◆———

THE DISREPUTABLE STREET was much like any number of the same in London. The city had its fine mansions, decent flats like his own, and all those in between, but it did have its fair share of poverty and the sooty brick buildings and warehouses near the wharves proved that in abundance.

"Wait a moment…" Leopold glared suspiciously at the low building they were nearing. "We've been here before. That opium den!"

"Do keep your voice down, Leopold."

"But…"

"You remember the old woman? The sorceress?" She spoke quietly.

Leopold dreaded going inside. The front parlor was an opium den filled with the sickly sweet-floral scent of opium smoke, with men of all levels of society—including quite a few Chinamen—lounging in a stupor on disgusting beds stacked three high, while pipes hung from their flaccid lips. But in the back room there had been that strange enigmatic woman that Mingli had called a sorceress.

"I don't know about this."

"Leopold, there are too many dangerous situations to contend with. We must have advice from those who can see the future and the present as it truly is."

"But Raj—"

"Can read the future only in the vaguest of terms. We need a solid road to travel." When he still balked, she postured, her umbrella poised into the pavement. "Do you doubt my decision?"

How much easier had it been to argue with her when he *didn't* trust her. Now the situation was quite different. *Easy, Leopold,* he admonished himself.

"Well…I do trust you. It's simply that…I don't know if I trust that woman in there."

She shook her head, edged him aside, and plunged down the steps to the door. He could do nothing but follow.

CHAPTER TWENTY

THEY DESCENDED GRANITE stairs black with soot and grime and entered under a low lintel to a dark and smoky interior. Hazy with despair, the place was dank and gloomy. Red Chinese lanterns hung here and there. If their purpose was to cheer the inhabitants, they were doing a poor job of it.

It was one of the saddest situations he'd ever seen. Men—and a few women—who had given up the fight of their wretched states. But worse, there were men in tailcoats and evening dress who had obviously succumbed, bored with their lives of wealth. They had every advantage and squandered it all instead. He held the most disgust for them.

Thankfully, Mingli hurried through to the back of the room where they spied the old fig-faced Chinese man, puffing on a pipe filled with acrid tobacco. He wore a typical Chinese riding jacket with disc buttons, a long tunic beneath, loose trousers, and soft, quiet shoes, as well as a qing cap. He watched Mingli steadily, puffing his pipe, until she stood directly before him. She spoke in Chinese and the man nodded and answered back. He motioned for her to follow—completely ignoring Leopold—and disappeared behind a curtained entry.

The backroom was as dim as the room before, but thankfully there was no haze of burning-flower smoke, no men lying in stupors from the drug. Instead, an equally wizened Chinese woman sat at a table laying out those old, stained cards with Chinese characters on them as she had done before. It got Leopold to wondering if she did this all day, every day, at every hour.

Or had she been expecting them?

Before, when they had consulted her about the Daemon Device, she had been laying out her version of tarot cards on a cloth bearing the Chinese zodiac, and Leopold noted that, yes, beneath the scattered cards lay the old stained embroidery. But unlike the last time, she didn't sweep her cards aside to accept the coin Mingli had offered.

This time, the dried-apple face of the woman looked up and stared at Mingli and then at Leopold. Her expression seemed angry. She spoke in a raspy whisper in Chinese to Mingli, who seemed to be arguing back with her. Finally, with voices raised, Mingli whipped around with the intention of leaving…when the woman reached out with surprising speed and grabbed Mingli's wrist.

She turned back to the old woman with a frown. "This is foolish. I know you speak English now."

The old woman released her and nodded. She raised her face to Leopold. "I told your betrothed that I disapproved of her match. You are not fit to wed with her."

Leopold raised his chin and postured. "I don't think that's any of your business."

The woman twisted her wrinkled mouth. "It is all my business, young man. You have secrets you keep from her."

Leopold paused. He had scarce forgotten he had yet to tell Mingli about her daemon heritage. There just never seem to be the proper time.

And then, with a sudden jolt, he realized the old woman had said it in Hungarian.

"I will rectify it as soon as I may," he answered, also in Hungarian. The sorceress had purposely spoken in a language Mingli would not understand. She hadn't given him away. What was this old woman's scheme?

She cracked a smile on her lined lips, showing a lack of front teeth. "You may call me Madam Hui Ling."

Mingli gasped.

The old woman nodded to her. "Yes, Sensible One. I have given you my name. I wish to impart to you how serious this is, for I need no coin from you this time. It is no less than the death of the world." She took them both in under her gaze. "Though I may not approve of your match, Mr. Kazsmer is quite the only one besides yourself equipped to do the job. I know of the goblins. I am not so much a fool as to think the dead had risen on their own."

She faced away from them and poured a small quantity of some sort of golden, nearly orange liquid into tiny ceramic cups. She handed one first to Mingli—who took it with a bow—and then to Leopold. He looked into the tiny cup and sniffed the contents.

"You need not be afraid, Mr. Kazsmer. It is *huangjiu*—rice wine. This is a very ancient vintage." She raised her cup and sipped. Leopold did the same. Floral. Slightly sweet. Alcoholic.

He nodded his approval and lowered the cup from his mouth.

"Come. Let us sit and be comfortable while we discuss it." She hopped down from her stool and Leopold was not surprised to discover that she was quite short, at least a full foot shorter than Mingli. She passed through a green-painted door that opened into a comfortable parlor, dressed in the Oriental fashion. The walls were wallpapered in a design of a garden of willows, ponds, and long-legged birds. A chaise lounge alongside wooden black-lacquer chairs with small matching side tables were placed with care on sumptuous carpets. Behind the chairs stood a black painted screen with figures in Chinese imperial garb, with lanterns and hanging tassels arrayed in each corner of the lamps.

Madam Hui Ling offered them the chairs while she laid her petite body on the lounge. Beside the chair, a brass incense burner in the shape of a hippopotamus gave off a calming scent, its smoke feathering upward in a thin ribbon. "My old bones need to lie down from time to time," she explained. She continued to sip from her cup. "I don't mind saying that I have been troubled by what I see in the cards and in the crystal orbs. A reckoning is coming. From strange sources."

Leopold slid to the edge of his seat and leaned toward the old woman, clutching the little cup in his fingers. "Madam Hui Ling. I have been a student of the Kabbalah all my life, and I must humbly confess that I have been remiss in the study of other forms of magic. I welcome all your wisdom on the matter. I need to learn as much as I can."

Her wrinkled mouth smiled at last. "It is a wise man who knows his limitations…and moves to correct them." She turned toward Mingli. "Perhaps I was wrong about this *gwáilóu*. If he can learn, he is worthy."

Mingli bowed, but Leopold could tell by her stiff back that she was keeping herself in check and saying nothing.

Madam Hui Ling sipped from the cup and then held it out expectantly with a straight arm. A servant who moved on silent feet appeared out of nowhere, and filled her cup. He stood in a humble posture before Leopold, until he offered his cup forth to be refilled. The servant filled Mingli's cup last, and vanished as silently as he had arrived.

"We must talk plainly," said Madam Hui Ling. "The clockwork man."

He didn't know at this juncture that he should be surprised that she knew of that. He sipped his wine, a liquor easy to consume, and listened patiently.

"I think you know, Mr. Kazsmer, that it was you who made this man."

He sat back, stunned, hurt. "But I never would have done that."

"Ah." She raised a hand and the incense burning beside her suddenly began to smoke uncontrollably. "Watch." She waved her hand, moving the smoke into nearly a solid veil. To his shock, Leopold watched the image of his long-forgotten memory flickering on the smoke like a magic lantern show.

He appeared as a fresh-faced boy again of thirteen. His dark hair was arranged in wild curls flopping over his forehead. There was a bruise around his eye and a cut on his face. His brows were drawn down in consternation as the younger Miklos that Leopold remembered, harangued him. They could not hear the words, but Leopold recalled them well. *Didicoy*—half-breed, and other slurs for Jew that he wanted to forget.

He slid his gaze toward Mingli. He certainly didn't want her to see this, to see the weakling he had been, and his cheeks burnished with heat in the watching of it.

Miklos continued to harp on his being an orphan and every other rude thing he could call him. Young Leopold rose when he'd had enough. But Miklos wasn't done—he grabbed his arm and punched him in the face. The bruised eye, already in pain, caused more distress as the boy crumpled, his arms held over his head, trying to guard his face from more cruelty. But Miklos kicked the unprotected side, and Leopold went down. He looked to be barely conscious when an eruption of light and smoke rumbled all around his prone body. It rose, and as the suddenly terrified Miklos looked on, the power engulfed him, stiffened his limbs and shot through him with such force that it threw him to the ground. When he rose, he couldn't help but look at his hand. It had turned entirely into brass. He jumped to his feet and screamed. But even as he tried to run, one of his legs seemed unnaturally stiff. When he pulled up his trouser leg, that too, was made of brass. He ran, as the image and the fragrant smoke faded away.

Leopold's shoulders stooped. He couldn't stop his lip from trembling, nor the tears tracing down his cheek. "I didn't know," he whispered. "I didn't know."

Mingli was at his side, kneeling beside him with a reassuring hand on his. "It wasn't your fault."

"I was never capable of that sort of magic. Not then. I *couldn't* perform it without summoning a daemon."

The shriveled woman cocked her head at him. "You still do not understand, Mr. Kazsmer. That was not the magic of the Otherworld with which you had become familiar. That was Earth magic. The magic that is all around us. The magic that comes from the Earth itself. The magic…residing in your core right now."

Leopold couldn't stop himself from pressing his hand to his chest. Yes, he felt it there, pulsating in rhythm with his own heartbeat. He didn't know what it meant, that it was still with him, for the Otherworld magic always faded within eight hours or less.

"You were young. Unskilled," Madam Hui Ling went on. "It was wild, random magic. And in your distress, it came to the rescue. It seems the clockwork man slowly evolved to what you have seen today. This magic that *you* used, and used *you* as a conduit, has worked its way slowly over that wretched man. It might have been years before it had begun to accelerate."

He wiped his face. Mingli urged him to take a drink from his cup. He did, licking his lips when she took the cup out of his hand. "If I did it, then I can undo it."

"Perhaps," said Madam Hui Ling. "But there is something you should do, and it might solve two of your problems. You must find this clockwork man and take him with you to the faery realm."

"It's just that— I beg your pardon?"

"The faery realm?" said Mingli. "But how is that possible?"

"I shall supply you with an invitation. In the meantime, hadn't you better find your clockwork man?"

"But...there is so much we must know," Leopold began. "So much. My father..."

"All in good time, Mr. Kazsmer. All in its time. I am weary now. Go. Find your Clockwork Gypsy. The circle always overlaps itself. The ouroboros. Cycles returning and leaving. Certainly you must know that by now, Mr. Kazsmer."

"Madam Hui Ling..."

The incense burner smoldered again and it billowed, making the room fill with choking smoke. He began to cough. He couldn't seem to rid his lungs of the smoke, and hacked and coughed so much his eyes watered. He doubled over with it, coughing until, at last, he was able to open his eyes and fill his lungs with sweet air...and found himself and Mingli standing on the street.

"Well!" said Mingli after a long pause. "That was far more than I expected. And she told us her *name*."

If Mingli was surprised, then he felt the full import of the encounter.

"You have no idea how extraordinary that was, Leopold."

"You were very brave standing up to her."

"She said you weren't worthy of me. That's absurd."

"But she warmed to me in the end." He offered a smile he didn't quite feel.

Now he was charged with a most impossible task. How was he to find the faery kingdom? And worse. Now he had to track down the Clockwork Gypsy himself.

He could think of only one place to begin his quest: the Romani camp.

CHAPTER TWENTY-ONE

THE HANSOM CAB took them almost to the camp — they could see the smoke rising and hear the music just beyond the trees — but the driver would go no further. "It's out in the back and beyond, ain't it," he said. "I don't want no trouble with no Gypsies." He gladly took the two bob Leopold gave him for his trouble before he snapped his whip and hurried his horse back to town.

The Romani camp lay just outside London's precincts, in the countryside near Battersea. Like its own little village, it was a collection of worn caravans, sleepy horses grazing nearby, and barefoot children running out into the far fields divided by a pattern of hedgerows and ancient stone walls. Campfires burned, leaving smokey tendrils circling the meadow enclosed by forest.

The closer they came, the more their poverty was evident. The brightly colored caravans showed signs of wear, with paint peeling and general disrepair. Not only the children were barefoot, but some of the women were as well. And they argued loudly with one another both in Hungarian and brash Cockney amid the playing of instruments and a few voices raised in song.

Even though Mingli had seen the camp before, Leopold worried what she might think of him for being brought up in such a place. Would she think less of him once she witnessed it for herself? Well, there was nothing for it.

He strode boldly through. Some of the guards recognized him at once and raised their hands in greeting, though their eyes lingered on Mingli with her rotating and telescoping eye patch. She marched through holding her head high, and was not ashamed to offer cool gazes at the men in return.

Soon, the music halted, the merry chases the children played began to slow. The women doing washing in wash basins tossed down their wet clothes and shook out their hands. Men brushing horses and fixing tack stopped their chores and moved toward them.

There was now a crowd encircling them when Leopold came to Yanko's caravan. Before Leopold could get up the few steps and knock on his door, Yanko himself emerged and stood in his doorway, casually lighting his pipe. He was in shirt sleeves and his threadbare waistcoat lay open and was slightly too short for him, revealing the straps of his braces below them. His white hair was wild above his ears but balding on top. His face, as always, was in want of a shave with white stubble covering his chin and cheeks.

"Nephew," he said around the stem of his pipe, puffing as the match caught the tobacco. "So, you've come at last."

"I'm sorry for not coming sooner, Uncle." He glanced at the others, staring not at him, but at Mingli. He decided to head off the gossip. "Uncle Yanko, may I present Special Inspector from Scotland Yard, Mingli Zhao. Who is also…my fiancée."

Gasps came from the gathered. The scowls on the men proved they were none too pleased.

"Miss Zhao, my uncle, Yanko Péntek."

"Mr. Péntek," she said with a tilt of her head. "How pleased I am to meet one of Mr. Kazsmer's relations." She extended her gloved hand to shake his.

Yanko stayed leaning in the doorway, one hand on the bowl of his pipe, the other in his trouser pocket. He made no move to take her hand. Mingli soon dropped it to her side, but Leopold could detect only disappointment in her posture.

Yanko's bushy brows rose and fell. His gray eyes scanned the others, took in their faces. Finally, with a grunt, he sat down on the top step, content to conduct their interview for all ears to hear.

Furious, Leopold ground his teeth. *If that's the way you want to do it.* He cast about and saw chairs set around a fire pit. He took long, stiff strides and asked aloud, "May I?" and gestured to one of the chairs. No one naysaid him, so he grabbed it and brought it back to Yanko's caravan and plunged it roughly into the grass. He held the chair back as if it were at a fine country manor, offering it to Mingli, who graciously took it, nodding and smiling to Leopold. Leopold stood beside her and crossed his arms tightly over his chest.

The crowd moved in closer.

"I am here," he said at last, "because of the clockwork man."

The crowd murmured

"I have discovered that it is Miklos Antalek."

One woman screamed, and several others rushed to comfort her. He little doubted it was Miklos' mother.

"And so," said Yanko. He shook his head, puffing on his pipe. "You found him?"

"Two encounters. He was trying to kill me."

The crowd murmured again.

He took a breath. He used his stage voice to announce, "I...it was I who cursed him."

Now the crowd shouted and shook their fists at him. He pivoted with the elegance he had learned on the stage. "It is true. I can perform magic. *Real* magic. At the time, Miklos was tormenting me, as he often did—as most of *you* did. He had snuck back to the camp after he was banished to steal money. I discovered him but before I could tell anyone, he attacked me. The magic was random and unintentional. In fact, he had just knocked me nearly insensate when the magic reached out to protect me...and cursed him. I hadn't even known in all these years that it had happened. And for the record, I regret that it happened. And I am here to right that wrong and undo the curse. But I have to find him, first. If anyone has information about where he might be...it would be helpful to me. And..." He raised his hand, snapped his fingers, and a gold sovereign appeared between his fingers. The crowd ooed and awwed. "I'm ready to pay for that information."

At first, no one spoke. Finally, a man with trousers tucked into his boots and wearing an open waistcoat over his striped collar-less shirt, stepped forward. "Leopold," he said, inclining his head. He was Leopold's age and spoke in the same Cockney accent that was

Leopold's true dialect. He stuffed his hands into his pockets. His gaze flicked toward Mingli with disapproval.

"Vadik, is it? I remember you," he said darkly.

Vadik dragged his cap from his head and held it in both hands. "Aye. I'll wager you do. But that was a long time ago. You're *gadjo* now. I can see that."

"It no longer matters what name you put to me." He looked at the gold sovereign he still held up. "I see *this* is all you care about."

"Naw, Leo. It's high time to let bygones be bygones."

"Oh, *is* it? I don't believe that is the decision of the aggressor. It is rather the choice of the victim. But as you can see..." He gestured toward himself in his fine suit and topper. "I am hardly a victim anymore."

"Look, Leopold," said another man from the crowd, Georgios. "He don't mean naught about it no more. I mean, look at you! I can see that a sovereign here and there don't mean much to you. You've made it, m'lad. And we're proud of you."

Leopold raised his chin. "If all that is true, why has no one congratulated me on my betrothal?"

Murmuring again. Georgios scrubbed at his hair. "You bloody well know why, Leo. Not only is she a rozzer, but she's a...a..."

"Say it and I'll turn you into a goat."

Georgios took a step back, looking at his companions for support. Leopold supposed Georgios was wondering if all of them together could take him on. By the frightened looks on their faces, he reckoned not.

He threw the sovereign up in the air and caught it, closing his hand over it in a fist. "Does anyone have any information I can use?"

An older woman stepped forward. Her face was strained, and her lackluster hair was bound up in a kerchief that let the gray-brown locks fall free down her back. Her hands were held so taut at her sides that the fists shook. "What will you do with him?" she asked in a Hungarian accent.

"You're Zsófia Antalek, his mother?"

"Yes. I am his mother. He has been gone from me for thirteen years with no word in all this time. Until the day he came to our camp and destroyed our things, killed a man. And this is what you made, Leopold Kazsmer."

"I have a sovereign for information — "

"I spit on your sovereign."

He stared at the coin in his open palm before he blew on it and it disappeared. When he raised his face, he lost the proud posture, the flippant use of magic. The artifice wasn't necessary toward the grieving mother. He knew his eyes were suddenly filled with the pain she felt. "Please let me help him," he said softly. "Please."

Her mouth twisted in anguish. She had known Leopold as well as any other woman in the camp when he had come to live there after his father had disappeared. They tried to mother him, but they also tried to raise him strictly, in the harsh life awaiting traveling Romani who did not stay longer than a season in the same place.

He knew Yanko and the others would soon make their way to another location where Leopold could not find them. But, he also knew, that they would probably be back.

She edged closer to Leopold so that they could talk quietly. "You promise you will help him?" she whispered.

"I swear, Mrs. Antalek."

She swallowed. Her thin neck showed it. "He'll be here tonight, late. At the edge of the woods. I bring him food."

"Then I will await him."

She wrung her hands. "Then you and your woman are welcome to my fire, if your stubborn donkey of an uncle will not welcome you in."

Yanko rose and spread out his hands. "Oi!"

She spoke sharp words to him in Hungarian that made Leopold blush. Zsófia stepped toward Mingli and offered her hand. "You are Leopold's choice? His mother was pretty too. Come along. I make you tea."

"I'd be very pleased to do so, Mrs. Antalek."

"You must call me Zsófia."

"Then you must call me Mingli."

Zsófia linked arms with her and walked slowly, with great dignity, back to her shabby caravan.

———— ◆ ————

ZSÓFIA LAID OUT the tea and she and Mingli sat at the wobbly table inside the musty caravan. It was decorated as many of the other caravans were: like a drawing room with swags of fabric draped over the windows; a jumble of worn upholstered chairs along with stick furnishings; a bed in the back for the adults, and one above for children; a wood stove within for warmth and some cooking, though most of the cooking was communal outside over the fires.

Leopold watched his uncle for some time out of the smudged window as he paced by the campfire. Finally excusing himself from the polite conversation between Zsófia and Mingli, Leopold rose and went outside.

He'd left his topper purposely in the caravan when he went out to greet his uncle. He sauntered up to him casually, not quite looking at him or standing beside him. Yanko took up the same posture, and stood with both hands in his pockets, rocking on his heels on the wet grass.

"So, this woman," Yanko began.

"Mingli," Leopold patiently corrected.

Yanko went on heedlessly. "You would marry this woman?"

"Yes. She's...she's an amazing person."

He gestured toward his eye. "What is this contraption on her face? One of your foolish devices?"

"No. She...she was wounded in the line of duty. It is an enhancement."

"She is really a rozzer?"

"Yes. Very accomplished. She comes with the recommendation of the Prince Consort."

He made a sound of acknowledgement as he continued to look into the distance. "And you intend to marry her."

"I do, Uncle. And, whenever the wedding shall be, I would be pleased if you would attend."

"We could be far away. In Wales or Scotland."

"But if you're not..."

"She is Oriental, Leopold."

"And I'm a Jew."

"You are Catholic, like your mother."

"My mother converted to Judaism for my father."

"And what will *you* worship with this Oriental woman? Many gods?"

"I don't worship anything, as you well know."

"Bah!" Yanko's white hair ruffled in the breeze. "What will you do when you have children?"

"Raise them with love."

"But your faith, Leopold? You cannot let children grow without faith."

"*I* seemed to get on all right."

Yanko blew out a dissatisfied breath. "So you think," he rasped.

"What is this really about? Is it her race? She has two degrees from Oxford. She speaks several languages. She's an accomplished fighter."

Yanko stared at him aghast.

"Why shouldn't she be? She often comes across bigoted men like you. She has learned to defend herself. And she's an investigator extraordinaire. She's my match, Uncle. And I love her."

Yanko's brows lowered. He rubbed at his stubbled chin. "Your mother…" He stopped, rubbed his chin again, and started again more thoughtfully. "Your mother—my sister—could not be persuaded against marrying that teacher, your father. We all tried to talk her out of it: 'He was of different faith. He would not understand our ways. He would take you far from your family.' All this was true. But she told me, 'My brother, I love him.' And there was nothing anyone could say."

"She had a good life. It was far too short. But it was a good one. We laughed together, we loved together. I miss those times, Uncle. I missed them the most when both of them were gone. The two people in all the world who understood me." He ignored the scoffing sound Yanko made. "And now I have found my…my soul mate. I hope you can at least be happy for me, that I have found my peace at last."

"You weave very poetic words."

"I feel poetic when I speak of her."

He grumbled. "First you do this magic and talk to demons. You were a devil child, Leopold. Couldn't you see that? It had to be beaten out of you."

Leopold grasped his lapel and stood like a triumphant statue. "Apparently it wasn't. I have saved the world a few times with my talents."

"So you say. Then you leave your Romani cousins and uncles to go off to be a magician on the stage. The stage is very immoral, with loose women parading around half-naked."

Leopold kept silent.

"And then you come home to us with this woman…" He sighed. "Leopold, Leopold. I am an old man. Soon to die."

"You're not going to die. You're too stubborn."

"But I will. And soon." He pointed a stubby finger into Leopold's face. "You see. I die. And I have no nephew to care for me and my last wishes."

"Uncle Yanko, you know you have but to say the word and I would take care of you."

"Yes, well, I will be far away. How will you know?"

"The skies will darken, the crows will call, and the shrubbery will wither."

He gave him a sidelong look. "You mock me, but someday…"

"Uncle, I don't want to talk of your death. I want us to…I want us to be a family. I know it's my fault that I pulled away from you and everyone in the camp. I needed to get away from all this. All the pain it represented to me, to stretch my wings. And now…I'm settling down. I have a regular show in Piccadilly." *Or at least I used to*, he mulled in his mind. Aloud he said, "And I would like us to be better friends. When I came to you six months ago, I thought we had turned a corner."

"You needed me, then. You were troubled. Now you don't need me with your demon-summoning and your Oriental women."

"Woman. One woman. And the daemons I summon are good."

"No demons are good."

"Yes, *Jewish* daemons are good."

"The fantasies you weave."

"Uncle! Can we at least put this all aside and have you meet my betrothed? Please? She's…she's waiting inside. If you could properly meet her, talk to her…"

Yanko threw up his hands in surrender. "All right, all right. I will meet your Oriental woman."

"*Uncle*," he warned.

"I won't call her that to her face. What was her name again? Mingee?"

"Ming-*li*. It isn't that hard."

"All right, all right. Ming-*LEE*."

He followed Leopold back to Zsófia's caravan and grunted as he climbed the steps. "Uncle Yanko would like to meet you properly, my dear."

She turned a bright face to him. She controlled her eye patch well. In other circumstances, he knew she would telescope that lens in and out to intimidate. Now, of course, was not the time.

Yanko bowed, his hand on his heart. "It is a pleasure to meet you, my dear. Leopold speaks very highly of you. For a rozzer."

She pursed her lips, appearing to try to keep from laughing. "Well, that's very nice of you to say. I would like to add that I have never had need to arrest any Romani. And I don't see that happening in the future, just to ease your mind."

"Oh ho!" He laughed heartily. "Now I see the use of a rozzer in the family. Come! Give your Uncle Yanko a hug."

She rose tentatively, and as soon as she had gained her feet, Yanko enclosed her in a suffocating embrace.

"Be careful, Uncle," said Leopold, ready to intervene.

Finally, when it appeared Mingli was on her last breath, Yanko pulled back. He turned to Leopold. "She smells nice!"

He quite agreed.

---•---

LEOPOLD AND MINGLI strolled through the camp as the day wore on, meeting various people. Now that Yanko had acknowledged and accepted Mingli, the other men offered polite greetings when they met her and doffed their caps.

"What are you going to do when you meet Miklos again?" she asked as they strolled over worn paths in the meadow grass.

"Talk to him…and try not to get killed."

"I would most appreciate the latter."

He squeezed her hand. "My uncle isn't all that bad, is he?"

"No. I've met worse. He was trying, at least."

"Yes. That was most surprising."

"He cares about you, Leopold. I think he just aches for his sister."

"I never thought of it that way. I was mourning for both parents when he took me in. He wasn't the hugging sort. Or the kind to allow weeping and wallowing. I suppose I should be grateful for that."

"You were a boy. You were not equipped to recognize the pain in others."

He smiled, glancing down at her. "Do you know that I never imagined what it would be like having a female companion? Discussing things and such."

"I shouldn't wonder, surrounded by the decidedly male associates of yours."

"It wasn't for lack of trying. Oh, I suppose maybe it was. Women disconcerted me."

"I've broken you of the habit."

"No, you still disconcert me, but now I recognize the rewards."

She elbowed him and smiled secretly.

After a time, they stopped at the edge of the wood, staring deep into its shadowy recesses. "Look here," he said quietly, even though no one was near them. "Your sorceress Madam Hui Ling said she'd get us an invitation to the faery realm. But invitation or no, how the devil am I to find it?"

"Might your fellow Romani know? Or is it merely rumor that your people are called superstitious?"

"You may have something there. Since the old fortune teller was killed, I think there is now another. Perhaps we should see her."

———◆———

HE WAS TOLD that the new fortune teller had moved into *Nénike* Ilonka's old caravan, the one with the side painted with a crystal ball with rays of light emanating from it with a giant eye. When he beheld the side of the caravan, he scratched absently at his tattoo. It seemed to be buzzing constantly now, what with his core full of Earth magic, but he only noticed it at odd times.

He knocked on the Dutch door, and a younger woman with heavy gold earrings and layers of bauble necklaces around her neck came to the entry. He had expected an older woman, as the deceased fortune teller had been, but this one was about Leopold's age.

She raised her face in a haughty manner, moved her layered skirts aside in a swish, revealing bare feet, and gave them a nod as she bid them enter.

Because this was a working caravan where the punters could enter, the whole front half was swathed in silks and shimmering fabrics that blocked the rest of the caravan from prying eyes. A small table was situated in the center draped with a heavy tasseled cloth, and in the middle sat a crystal ball. The air was heavy with incense, reminding him too much of the opium den with its suffocating gloom of choking smoke.

"I am Jolán Palinkas," she said with a thick Hungarian accent, offering them seats around her little table. "Welcome, Leopold Kazsmer. Welcome Miss Mingli. I am humbled that you should come to me."

"Miss Palinkas," he began.

"We are family, Leopold. Call me Jolán."

"Very well. Jolán."

She didn't stand on ceremony and began laying out grease-stained tarot cards. The Tower inverted was laid out first. "Upheaval," she said. "Great change." The Wheel of Fortune was next. "Fate intervenes. All is out of your control..."

Leopold quickly stretched out his hand to cover hers. "We haven't come to have our fortunes told, but to ask for information."

She paused with another card ready to cast down. "About Miklos Antalek?" she asked suspiciously.

"No. But about...the faery realm."

She quickly set the cards down and scrambled from her chair. She went to the door and yanked it closed, pulling down the closest window's shade. "This is not something to discuss in the open. We are a religious people," she said to Mingli, crossing herself. "We pray to the Virgin."

"Oh?" said Mingli, with an innocent flick of her lashes. "Which one?"

Jolán looked at her aghast. "The *Holy* Virgin. The *only* one."

"Of course," said Mingli, sitting back with her hands demurely in her lap.

"I know all that," said Leopold, "but I also remember the stories the women would tell me about faeries and mischievous sprites and such. Do *you* know some of those stories?"

She sat back and stared at Leopold steadily. "We are religious, it is true. But the ancient ways are still passed down from Gypsy to Gypsy, from our mothers and foremothers. It is for our protection, you understand, to know the ancient ways..." She suddenly stopped, shoulders sagging, and turned to Leopold, looking him square in the eye for a long moment.

"All right," she said at last, dropping the Hungarian and slipping instead into a distinct Cockney. She sat again, gathering her cards. "There's no need to play games with you, Kazsmer. Had to be sure about you. I remember you, you know. Don't you remember me?"

He stared. "You're not this Jolán. You're Reka. What was all this Jolán business..."

"Like I said. I had to be sure. You know it, Kazsmer. You do your work on a stage, but this..." She gestured to her caravan. "This is *my* stage, get me? Now then." She leaned her arms on the table and hunched her shoulders. "All the women know the legends. It's because it's the women who go out to the streams and rivers to do the washing, right? And it's us that sees them. The little folk. They don't do us no harm and we leave them alone. It's a wise woman what leaves out a plate of milk or a biscuit on the stoop outside every night. That's to make sure your cream don't curdle and you don't wake up with tangled hair. It's a known fact."

"I see." Leopold flicked a glance at Mingli. "Are you truly saying that you, personally, have seen them?"

"Oh, aye! Seen them all the time."

"What do they look like?"

She got in close, her bangle bracelets clanking. "They don't look like what you'd think they look like. I've seen the picture books where they look like pretty naked ladies with colorful butterfly wings. But they don't look like that at all. They're more like…disfigured children. Long pointed ears and long pointed faces. And long feet too, and it just ain't their shoes, because most of them go along barefooted. The women have sheer wings, but the men have moth wings."

Leopold nodded. "That's exactly right. You *have* seen them, then."

"That's what I've been telling ya. Strange thing about them is, you can't get near them. The closer you get, the farther away they are. It's queer."

"But if I wanted to meet them…"

"You can't. They say you've got to have an invitation. And believe me, you don't want one."

"Why not?"

"Because once they get you in their banqueting halls, you'll never leave. You'll be there forever."

He swallowed hard. "But…say I *had* an invitation?"

"Cor! You don't really?"

"I do."

"Well then." She looked once at Mingli. "If that's true, I ain't saying it is or it isn't, but if true, the best place is a faery ring."

"And what is that?"

"Leopold Kazsmer! You mean to tell me you were raised by Romani and you don't know what a bleeding faery ring is?"

Mingli answered with, "*I* know what a faery ring is."

"Ah," said Reka. "Right you are, Miss. Then you take your young man to the nearest faery ring with your invitation and call out to them. That's all. They'll either take you or they won't. But if you ask me, you should pray that they don't."

"Thank you, Reka." He began to rise to leave, when Reka motioned him back down.

"If you're bound and determined, then take this." She rose, went to a shelf, and brought back an object. When she sat again, she pressed a hag-stone into his hand…a smooth, flat rock with a natural hole in it. "Just in case you want to leave and they don't want to let you."

"That's very generous of you. Thank you." He pulled out a shilling. "For your trouble."

Her eyes lit and she wiped her hands down her skirts. "Well now. It was only a friendly-like bit of advice. But…" She wavered only for politeness' sake it seemed, before snatching it out of his hand. "For the children," she said. Not that there was any sign of children in her caravan.

He and Mingli took their leave, and Mingli offered to show Leopold a faery ring. He wasn't enthusiastic about seeing it, but he followed without complaint.

They plunged into the cool darkness of the dappling forest surrounding the camp, forging paths through the fern. Nervous, Leopold looked back the way they'd come.

"I say…I don't see a path back." His voice was higher than he liked.

"Don't worry. I can find our way."

Through the fern they came upon a deer path, and even though he felt a certain level of anxiety out in the wilderness, he could also take the time to appreciate its beauty: the sunlight through the trees painting the edges of leaves in gold; the sound of a brook lapping over stones; the gentle sway of high branches in the wind; and birdsong answering back and forth from tree to tree.

The tension in his muscles unwound. "How is it you know about this, Mingli?"

"As I have stated before, I have made a study of various magical disciplines. It helps to know a little about a lot of things."

"I suppose I've ignored the other disciplines to become a master of the one."

"That's admirable in its own way. Though limiting."

"Very limiting. I am seeing how much of a mistake it's been."

"You've had no mentor. I've had many."

"I doubt they teach that in Oxford."

She glanced sidelong at him. "You just have to know the right professor. Ah! Here we are."

They came to a dappled clearing where the trees themselves were mere saplings. Leopold at first thought that the clearing itself was the ring, but he slowly began to notice a wide ring of red-capped mushrooms in the center.

"They say," said Mingli as softly as one might speak in a church, "that the faeries dance in a circle and *that* is where the mushrooms grow. But, being an amateur mycologist myself, I know that the mycelium of the fungus will generate from the center, and when it has consumed all the nutrients available it will die, thereby forming a living ring of even more mycelium-producing spores. Thus, a faery ring seemingly out of nowhere."

"You do have knowledge of the queerest things."

"True. But even though there is a scientific explanation, it doesn't mean it is somehow *not* produced by faeries. Faeries do rely on the fungus for food and fuel, after all. It makes it the perfect gateway for their coming and going."

"So...one merely has to step into the ring?"

"Yes. When one has a proper invitation."

"I wonder in what form that will take."

She shrugged. "Madam Hui Ling is a mystery to me. I have known about her for ten years but have never before known her name."

Leopold made a tentative circuit outside the ring, examining it, and stopped when he reached Mingli again. "I can feel a pulsing of Earth magic here."

"Interesting. Have you never felt Earth magic prior to your recent encounter?"

"I can't say that I have. Though..." He shook his head, thinking deeply. "It almost seems..." Whatever thought he had was gone, vanished. He gestured vaguely. "I obviously used it to create Miklos and had no knowledge of it."

"Could it be that the Gehenna magic has interfered with the other?"

"Now that's an idea. I'll have to research it."

"If there is time. Do you...still have adequate magic?"

He didn't even have to reach deeply. It was there, simmering on the surface. It tingled the ends of his fingertips, strong and alive. Earth magic. "I do. The Earth magic is steady in me."

"Strange. No Gehenna magic at all?"

He shook his head. "I've had no congress with a daemon. But even the presence of Suchah helps. It doesn't stay for very long. Dash it. I feel like a damned fool."

"You have been walking a tightrope and haven't even known it."

"Is that the source of your own magic? I...didn't want to ask before. To pry. It somehow didn't seem polite. Though now that we are engaged..."

She turned away. "I don't know the source of my magic. Yes, I am a student of all disciplines of the magical arts, and yet I don't know the source of mine."

He was about to open his mouth to tell her about her daemon heritage when she raised her face to the treetops. "It's late. I suppose we should be getting back. Might your uncle supply us with some tea and other refreshment?"

Frustrated and at the same time relieved to put off the conversation, he replied, "Well, to call it 'tea' is a great exaggeration, but I'm certain he can produce a suitable repast."

They found Yanko at the campfire with the other men, smoking his pipe, his wild gray eyebrows dancing up and down depending on who or what he was discussing. But when he saw Leopold approach, he rose. "You must be hungry. Time for tea, eh?"

They retreated with him to the caravan and, as he made their tea and produced a loaf of brown bread, a plate of butter, and a pot of jam, he urged Mingli to tell him of her law-enforcing adventures. Leopold couldn't tell if her abbreviated tales of London police work were fabricated or not, but he was grateful that she left out any mention of the supernatural. Instead, she spoke of gruff arsonists and crafty child-stealers.

Yanko turned toward her with teapot in hand and a skeptical expression on his face. "You couldn't have rousted such a big burly man. You are just a slip of a girl."

"Shall I prove it to you?"

With mouth open, Leopold's glance flicked between Mingli and Yanko. He hoped she wouldn't throw the old man. God knows he'd deserve it, but Leopold surprised himself that he didn't want him hurt — or worse, humiliated.

His uncle finally relented with a hearty laugh. "No, I think I believe you. I see how you handle that umbrella. It's not to be trusted."

She pulled the sword out halfway with a dimpled grin.

Yanko laughed again, elbowed Leopold hard, and set the tea and tray of bread in the middle of the table.

Leopold couldn't remember a more enjoyable meal in Yanko's presence. Munching on the slightly stale bread, the sweetness of the jam and the rich butter, he was only beginning to experience what contentment felt like. Perhaps because he was older and the old man couldn't truly hurt him anymore. Or maybe it was the presence of Mingli, for though there might be chaos around her she always brought a semblance of civility and, to Leopold's disordered life, that meant a kind of serenity.

"What is the date you have chosen to post the banns?" asked his uncle as he shoved a thick slice of bread into his mouth and bit off a hefty chunk.

Mingli buttered her bread with delicate movements. "We haven't chosen a date yet. Presently, we have much hard work to do that is getting in the way of it. But be assured that the wedding will likely happen before the end of the month."

Leopold choked on his bread, coughing and holding his serviette up to his face. "End of the month?" he rasped.

"So soon?" said Yanko. "But the banns..."

"As you know, banns are to be proclaimed to make certain there is no canonical or civil impediment, a pre-existing marriage, lack of consent, or that there is no prohibitive degree of kinship between the two parties. We are both free to marry, there is no lack of consent, and I think if you examine our faces, you can readily agree that there is scarce chance of Leopold and I being related to *any* degree."

Yanko laughed again. He thumbed back at Mingli. "I like this one, Leopold. I think she can keep you in line."

He felt his face blush, but he couldn't help but smile. "Oh, she very much does. And I am content in it."

————— ◆ —————

AN HOUR PASSED. And then two. The whole camp knew what was coming, and the anxiety ran through them like an electric wire. Leopold could tell by the way everyone had half an eye on him and Mingli, and half on their work. Even the goats and wandering chickens seemed subdued.

As the day went on, and the sun grew closer to the surrounding distant hills, more and more gathered by the campfire. Someone played a plaintive Hungarian tune on a parlor guitar, but no one sang with it.

The smoke from the fire seemed to grow heavier as the sun receded. Everyone shared a rabbit stew from the large iron kettle hanging above the smokey flames, but no one seemed to have much of an appetite.

The hour grew even later. Children were put to bed, but the scruffy dogs in the camp seemed to sense something and they paced restlessly around the perimeter. The horses murmured to each other, and the goats moved about on their tethers impatiently.

The starfield was replaced by cloud cover and an icy drizzle began. It was the excuse they all needed to retreat into their caravans. Even the guards stayed close to shelter. No one, it seemed, had any intention of accompanying Leopold on his evening's mission.

It was when most had retreated to their lodgings—though their lamps were still lit behind curtains or broken shutters—that Zsófia Antalek emerged from her caravan with a lantern, a cape over her shoulders, and a hood protecting her head.

"It is time," she said.

Leopold grabbed Mingli by the hand a little more tightly than he had wanted, and followed the woman into the gloom of the damp woods.

CHAPTER TWENTY-TWO

THEY FOLLOWED THE lantern light as is bobbed over the fern and briefly lit the rough bark of trees around them. Zsófia followed a different path than Leopold and Mingli had taken earlier, and it led downward toward a ravine. Above on a trestle stood train tracks, following the distant, lonely call of locomotive whistles riding on the wind.

Zsófia stopped. "Now we wait."

The rain patted on the leaves and the forest floor. It was the only sound in the quiet wood, except for the occasional readjustment of Mingli's telescopic eye, whining as it wound in and out.

Then, together, they all looked to their left.

A sound deep within the forest. A resonating thud followed by the hiss of a piston. It wasn't long till the clank of the metallic footstep rang out as it drew closer.

Leopold braced himself. He longed to maneuver Mingli behind him, but his ears fairly rung with what the stubborn woman would say to that.

A light shone deep in the wood like a gas torchlight, sweeping from side to side, and when the man finally emerged, it was those goggles that served as Miklos' eyes.

"You've brought him to me," said Miklos, his voice even more hollow than it had been before. "And now my revenge will be complete."

"Miklos," said Leopold, holding up his hand, partly in greeting, partly to fend off the disturbing light strafing over him. "I came here to offer you peace."

"To kill me, then?"

"No. To free you of this curse."

"So, you now admit it was you."

Leopold bowed his head. "Yes. But you must believe me when I tell you that I never knew I had done it. I was nearly unconscious. From a blow *you* gave me, I might add."

"That's a lie."

"Miklos, is this really the time for falsehoods? Don't you think—"

"I can barely think!" he bellowed. "My brain...is nearly gone." When he raised his hands to his head, Leopold noted that the entire dome was now covered in metal plates with small rivets. The long, braided plait was gone.

"Miklos, I'm so sorry. I hadn't known I'd done it. It was an accident. Random magic that surged to protect me. But I can undo it. Won't you please let me try?"

"Why should I trust you? Look at me!"

"My son," said the plaintive voice of his mother. She was near to tears. "Let Kazsmer try. Please."

Gears ground as Miklos settled his feet. "If you try and fail," he said slyly, "then I kill you. That is my bargain."

"NO!" said Mingli. "After all this time, Mr. Kazsmer's magic may not be able to undo what has been done."

Leopold stared at Mingli. What was she saying? Did she know and had not wanted to say earlier? Without taking his gaze away from her, he said, "I agree to your bargain, Miklos."

"No, Leopold..."

He shook his head. "*I* did this," he said softly to her. "It's abominable. It should not have happened, even to save my own life. How can I live with it?" And suddenly, he was content with the decision. Even though it meant losing her. Even though it meant losing his father. The guilt of the thing ate at him. It didn't seem fair that he should get to live his life and Miklos—as cruel a boy as he had been—had had no chance at a life at all.

Mingli breathed hard, saying nothing.

"If I...if I die, Mingli, promise me you will save my father. Promise that you'll try."

She licked her lips. "I will."

"And Raj. Someone must take care of him."

"Leopold…"

"I know you will. He likes you."

"You have agreed," said Zsófia grimly, cutting off any further conversation.

Leopold gestured toward the lantern. "Come into the light, Miklos."

The clank of metal. He stood between two trees, a hand on each trunk. He pushed, grimacing, and both trees tilted with a crack out of his way. He stepped into the meadow.

Leopold looked him over. The lantern light reflected off the many — too many — brass surfaces visible on the man; his scalp, his arms under slashed sleeves, his legs, for the trouser legs were torn and he no longer wore shoes for the metal feet. What human was left of him?

Miklos postured before him, brass fingers curled into fists at his side. "I'm waiting, Kazsmer."

"If you'll pardon me, Miklos, I must…I must touch you."

The clockwork man shied away. "Why?"

"I must examine the extent to which the…the damage has been done."

He stepped up to Miklos and discovered that they were of similar height. Miklos had seemed so much taller, so much bigger when they were children. Though Miklos was a few years older than Leopold, nothing much about his face had changed…except for the goggles and metal plates. The man clutched that fearsome axe but kept it low by his side…for now.

Leopold was careful as he reached up to touch the outer rim of the goggles. "Can you tell me, Miklos; what is it like when a part of you turns to metal?"

"What is it *like*?" he growled. "*What is it like?* It is like Hell on Earth. Like my skin is being stretched on a rack. Like my bones are being realigned."

"I see." He ran a finger delicately over the rivets of the plates on his head and cheeks. "Does it happen overnight, or immediately?"

"Why are you asking these questions? Only to torment me more?"

Zsófia wept softly in the background.

"No, Miklos. To test the bounds of the spell. To understand it."

"You cast it, you fix it!"

"I didn't *consciously* cast it, and that is the problem. I was very young. I can understand more of it now but..." Leopold touched both hands to the man's chest and closed his eyes. God help him, but he could feel the cadence of the mechanical heart as some sort of escapement inside releasing a gear over and over to make the tick, tick sound. It was horrifying. How could it pump the blood in and out of his heart? How was the damned thing keeping him alive?

How could he reverse what he had done?

He thought of sheep to clear his mind. And when the green pastures and the slow-moving wooly creatures were in his consciousness, he sought the magic. Instead of his reaching for the magical tendrils, amazingly, they reached for *him*, as if they had been waiting for him to call out to them. He let it stream into his limbs, his fingertips. They tingled with each tick, tick of that mechanical heart.

He thought hard on muscle, blood, sinew, bone as the rising surge of magic coursed through him. He felt it travel from his fingers through to Miklos, who shuddered from the sudden intrusion.

The sensations were strange, stranger than any other magic from Gehenna that he had used before. It was as if the fields of magical forces were reflecting back to him what they were doing inside of Miklos.

Leopold jerked from the pain. His heart felt tight, as if bands of metal were wrapping around it. Is that what Miklos' heart was like?

He opened his eyes and to his surprise, he was hovering above the proceedings and looking down. He could see the strain on his face as he experienced the slow unwinding of the curse in the clockwork man's body. He saw the anguish of Mrs. Antalek's face as she squirmed with her son's pain, saw Mingli standing stiffly, breathing harsh breaths with anticipation. Leopold could barely feel a connection to himself as he drew farther away. He could scarce understand what he was feeling, what he *should* feel, why he should be there at all.

But looking at the beautiful woman in green suddenly made him linger. She was something important to him. It seemed to transcend his mission to leave, to fly away. And what was he to make of the strange metal man before him, standing before his own fleshy body? And didn't *that* fleshy body look strange? Thin, in a dark suit, a well-tempered mustache, and nearly using up all its strength at a strenuous task that Leopold barely remembered.

It would be equally strange if his flesh body were to fall over, diffused with the mechanism that kept the clockwork man alive. It seemed they were switching internals. The mechanical man was less mechanical, but Leopold's own fleshy-self seemed to become more mechanical, switching, becoming. One becoming less, the other becoming more.

He sensed he should care, and wondered vaguely why.

Leopold would have to make a decision. If he were to fly away, he wouldn't need to experience the pain and suffering or the choice to take it on or not. But then...there was the beautiful woman who seemed to be calling to him, not in a voice, but in different layers of pleading, in the aura she was exuding, in the way she stood, the way her magic spoke to his. He'd never see her again, never experience all the things he had yet to experience of her. That would be a shame.

Still, the pain. The choice. The choice itself intrigued. He could choose to *be* the clockwork man. He could allow it to consume him. Switch places. Let the other live its natural life. Let himself be something other. Yet, wasn't he something other already?

A voice whispered to him. Told him that this choice must not be. That the cycles and connections would not allow it, would not, in fact, work as it *should*, how it was *decreed* to be, and that he truly *had* no choice but to return...

And when he opened his eyes a second time, he was back into himself, into his flesh body, feeling the anguish and full force of the pain as they tried to switch, pulled on each other's life forces, while the magic drew at them both, and finally took away his choice and decided for him.

He screamed and fell backward. The other cried out too and fell back, while they were forced apart by a blinding flash.

There was nothing but mist until Leopold slowly came to himself and realized his head was lying in Mingli's lap. She stroked his wet hair, for it had not stopped drizzling. "Leo," she said softly. "Are you back?"

"Where did I go?" But he soon remembered. He sat up suddenly, and looked to the treetops. He'd been up there, looking down. Had she known?

Zsófia Antalek also cradled her son when he suddenly jerked to his feet. "Nothing! Nothing has changed. Now I kill you."

"Wait, Miklos."

"No. Are you a liar as well as a thief for stealing my life? You must die, Kazsmer. I don't care what happens to me now, but I will find my peace knowing you are dead."

Fear was an awesome mistress, he decided. For now, that his death was imminent, his fear was a hundredfold. With this mark upon his wrist, what would happen to his soul? He never truly considered before, never asked Eurynomos the question, but now he feared finding out. There was no going back once he was dead, no undoing what he had given away.

He untangled himself from Mingli's embrace. He *had* promised Miklos. Time to be a man and pay for what he had done. His father would have had him do no less.

"I tried Miklos. The magic wouldn't let me."

"You lie. How you lie." He raised his axe, hefting it in both hands. "I am glad I am doing this before my mind is completely gone. I want to remember this for as long as I can, that it was I who dispatched you. You...you bastard!"

Leopold clutched his hands into fists. He trembled as he stood tall, but at the last moment, he shut his eyes. "I love you, Mingli," he whispered and waited for the axe to fall.

He flinched, thinking he felt the wind from the axe coming toward him. Was he being a coward for keeping his eyes shut? *To Hell with that*, he convinced himself, and kept them closed.

Still he waited.

After a longer interval that should be, he cracked open an eye.

Miklos still clutched the axe, still held it above his head, but his arms began to tremble. His brass teeth clenched and his brass jaw flexed. "Damn you, Leopold. Damn your soul." His voice broke, and slowly, he lowered the axe to the ground. And when the axe head hit the leaf duff, he let it go. He turned to his mother and bent his head. She embraced him and rocked him, singing an old Hungarian lullaby.

Mingli was at Leopold's side instantly, embracing him and holding tight. She said nothing as he turned and embraced her properly, sliding his cheek against hers.

He breathed again in long tangled breaths. He inhaled her lilac scent, and it began to calm his wildly beating heart. Not a heart of metal with its tick, tick, but a heart of blood and muscle. He still wasn't certain he could live with what he had done, but he was sure he didn't want to die without…this. This embrace, this woman, this sensation.

When he opened his eyes and looked over her shoulder, he saw a small glow in the middle of the meadow.

"That's strange," he said and gently pushed her back.

She turned. "Leo…"

A small glowing figure was standing in the center of a ring of red-capped mushrooms, tilting her head this way and that to stare at him. She was barely taller than a hare, and her face was strangely elongated, with a long shapely nose, and pointed ears reminiscent of the goblins' though delicately piercing the veil of her straight tresses of silver blonde hair. She seemed to be arrayed in leaves pressed into spiderwebs on her torso and she wore no shoes on her strangely extended feet. She fluttered gossamer wings.

They all stared back at her, not moving.

"Leopold Kazsmer, Mingli Zhao, and Miklos Antalek," she said in a softly echoing voice. "Your request to enter the faery realm has been granted. Please come now and meet our king."

Leopold moved first. "Er…I thank you." He bowed. "But…erm…" He looked back at Miklos.

"Why?" the clockwork man said. "Why do they want…me?"

"You three are to come now," said the faery impatiently.

Mingli lifted a hand to Miklos. "You'd best hurry."

"I don't want to go."

The faery frowned, her slanted silver brows furrowing her forehead. "You are requested. Is your life here so perfect that you will not forsake it, even for a little while? Come now, or forever regret it."

Miklos faced his mother, taking both her hands. "I will go. What have I to lose now? I love you."

She reached up and kissed his metal cheek.

Leopold wondered if he could feel it.

Miklos moved toward him and Mingli. Together, they approached the faery, who stepped aside but still within the faery ring.

"Why are mortals so slow?" she muttered, gesturing them onward.

Leopold grasped Mingli's arm and then he hesitated only a moment before he linked arms with Miklos. "Are you ready?"

"No," said Miklos.

They stepped over the mushrooms and entered the ring.

CHAPTER TWENTY-THREE

THE FOREST AND the night vanished around them. It was daytime. A preternatural sun shone down on the windswept hill of green, swaying grass. The sky was blue without a cloud in it. Birds sang melodiously and darted from hedgerow to trees.

Miklos crossed himself. "Are we dead?"

"No," said Leopold, a little uncertain. This world was different, ethereal, soft and slightly blurred, but not nearly as disquieting as Gehenna, where all was chaotic. No, this was considerably better.

Mingli looked around them. "It's fascinating."

Leopold couldn't help but smile at her. He agreed. And perhaps they could save the world once more by offering their services.

"The king will soon come," the faery explained. "Now stand quietly. Don't. Move."

They obeyed. Leopold inhaled the scent of flowers though he could not see any among the sea of waving grass. The air itself seemed to shimmer. And then he realized why. A structure in white, tall with strange towers and arches, emerged from the very air itself. Leopold had seen many castles both in photographs and in person, but this matched nothing like his experience. He supposed it could be characterized as a castle, if he were a woodland creature like a faery. The proportions were odd, the size was deceiving and fluctuating. At first it was immense, but then, on looking at it longer, it was almost something a child might play in.

The air continued to shimmer with sparks of magic here and there like will-o-the-wisps dancing in the currents, but there was no question that the castle had become a solid presence, though it had settled into something like a grand folly.

"You will come," said the faery, and strode forward toward the large arched opening.

The humans exchanged looks and slowly followed. As they got closer, the strange castle was still in flux and getting bigger, but finally appeared to be not quite as big as a proper castle. They passed under what would ordinarily be a portcullis but wasn't, and not into a courtyard, but immediately into the structure. The hall was continuous and high-ceilinged, vaulting upward. He could see no torches or windows, yet the white walls were lit by some means. As they walked, they could hear music in the distance, and it was music unlike he had ever heard; sweet and melodious, a tune that made him want to sing along just as lyrics suddenly sprang to mind.

He smelled the fragrance of food and suddenly his mouth began to water.

"We mustn't eat the food," whispered Mingli to them both. "Nor drink the wine. Remember that."

Miklos looked on in wonder, barely acknowledging what Mingli said.

They turned the corner, and entered into a banqueting hall alight with faeries dancing, singing, serving one another from a long table covered with a white shimmering cloth. The food was served in acorn cups, on leaves, in basins made of carved-out stone. The faeries all wore similar clothes, if they could be called such, of leaves and moss pressed into spider webs. The women in short dresses, the men with spider web loin cloths. On first glance, it looked like an assembly of beautiful children, but as Leopold looked, their faces took on the strangeness of the faeries, with elongated noses and chins and exaggeratedly pointed ears.

A faery male sat on a throne of gold, with a crown of what looked like sharpened sticks encircling his head. Leopold was beginning to think Saint Collen had something there by bringing holy water.

Suddenly, their revelry stopped—the music, the dancing, the hoisting of acorn cups—and they all turned to look at the newcomers. The king gazed upon them with lowered lids and his chin raised, as if bored by the proceedings. "You've come," was all he said. He rose and stepped down from his dais, strode through his revelers, and walked up to them. He was no taller than Leopold's knee, but he was no less intimidating with his bare chest and leaf loin cloth.

Leopold and Mingli bowed. Miklos did so belatedly.

"You are welcomed to my banqueting hall, Mortals. I am King Gwyn ap Nudd. What do you say to that?"

Leopold hesitated. He knew he must tread carefully so as not to insult. "Sire, I am...awed by your presence and these marvelous surroundings. And we are grateful that you accepted our request."

His answer seemed to satisfy the little king and Gwyn ap Nudd began to walk around his table and court. Leopold and company followed a discreet distance behind. "You see our court and its finery, Kazsmer? You see how content we are. And yet, death has come to our people. Death is not part of our existence. It has come because of our mortal enemies, the goblins."

"Yes, sire, I know."

"That is why you are here. We must do battle with the goblins. But we cannot because of this strange power they have. My people...I worry over the decimation."

"What can we possibly do for you, your majesty?"

The king glanced back at him. He nodded. "We are pleased you wish to serve. When confronted with our people, most Mortals only think only to ask for favors for themselves. They are selfish in that way. But not you."

"Well, I would ask for one favor, sire."

The faery frowned. "Oh. We had hoped you were not like the others. Is it gold you want? Power?"

"Oh no, your majesty. The favor I ask is not for me, but for Miklos here." He gestured back to the mechanical man.

The faery king flicked a gaze toward him before turning his attention back to Leopold. "You made him."

"I did not mean to. I did not mean to cause him harm."

"Hmm. Well, this is nothing to us."

"But it is a great deal to him. Yet understand, we will help you whether you can cast away the curse on him or not."

A small smile curved one edge of the faery's mouth. "We will see. Come. Dine with us."

"Oh, sire, we mean no offense, but…we mustn't."

The king laughed. "That is an old wives' tale. Will you believe the prattling of old women?"

Leopold looked once at Mingli. "Being a superstitious lot, mortals must believe such tales. Just to be on the safe side."

The king laughed again. "Suit yourselves." He returned to his throne and beckoned to them to join the revels. Leopold and Mingli sat before the tables groaning with food of various kinds: roasted pheasant, asparagus swimming in butter and lemon, marrow with toast points, hardboiled eggs cut into wedges, oysters on the half shell, leeks with scallops and prawns, raspberry tarts, lemon cake, steaming rolls, and other delicacies Leopold wasn't familiar with.

Miklos seemed unable to sit upon the ground as they were doing, and so he stood above them, a solid presence just over Leopold's shoulder.

Leopold's mouth watered. Such a feast he'd never seen before. Oh, he'd been invited to a few parties to entertain the wealthy, but as the mere entertainment he had not been invited to feast with the guests.

He glanced at Mingli. Her face was set with a wary but interested expression. He supposed she was ecstatic to be in the faery realm, but her scientific nature would not allow her to openly revel in it.

He wondered if the food was what it looked like, or if it were transformed from something else, something not of this world.

Mingli leaned toward him and whispered, "Do not be deceived. The food is far more than what it appears."

"I wondered that. What is it, do you suppose?"

"Mushrooms, I'm sure. Transfigured to appear as these delicacies."

"For our benefit or for their own?"

"It is difficult to know. I've never —"

"Whispering?" said the king. "What are you up to, Zhao?"

"Do forgive me, your majesty. We were merely speculating. Mr. Kazsmer and I were naturally wondering what the food was made of."

"We assure you, it is quite delicious."

"Of that, I have no doubt. We were merely wondering the nature of it."

"Would you like to see it as it is? All of it?"

"If it wouldn't be too much trouble."

The king rose from his seat again. He watched his people revel for a few more moments before he waved his hand.

The castle disappeared, the bright lights, and even the windswept hill and the sunlight. They were in the forest, a dank and dark wood, with the silver light of the moon painting the revelers. There was a soft drizzle, and he and Mingli were already quite wet. The faeries didn't seem to mind the rain and looked even more foreign than they had done. They were tinted with a darker brush, for their silvery hair was silver no longer. Their hair was dark, their faces more insect-like with elongated noses and blank, almond eyes, their skin dirty and sallow. The banquet was made of mushrooms and moss, as well as grubs, and cream in cracked jugs they must have stolen from humans — for tales had it that they were particularly fond of cream, and it appeared to be the truth.

The fine kingdom of bright and shining arches and shimmering light was now shadowed and dredged in mystery and danger. Even the music was atonal and unpleasant.

Leopold shivered.

"Have you seen enough?" asked the king. He was also arrayed differently. Instead of a bare chest, he wore an open drapery of black and dusty cobwebs that seemed infused with an adder's venom, all sticky and infested with dead bugs. His face was more of a muzzle, and his crown was made not of twigs but of animal fangs; sharp, yellowed, cracked.

"Yes," said Leopold breathlessly.

The king waved his hand, and all was restored. His company were no longer wet from drizzle, or at least felt dry. Leopold sighed his relief.

"Yes, we set a fine show for mortals when they stumble into our realm. We make them welcome. They can see this…" and he gestured with his hand at all they surveyed… "to please them. Especially…if they become our permanent guests."

"You give them the dream?"

"Because they are frightened of the reality. But I suspect that you and Zhao are not frightened of the truth."

"Oh, sire, I am just as frightened as any man would be. But…I have seen a great deal of different worlds. I will not judge yours."

"That makes you different from other mortals, Kazsmer. Perhaps that is why you and your company were allowed through." He stared at Leopold for an uncomfortably long time, unblinking. "Come to our chamber. We will talk with our privy council."

They rose and followed him, with Miklos' metal feet clanking behind them. It was not a door the king passed through, but something like cobwebs. Leopold ran his fingers over it as he passed under the arched portal, and it was not sticky but silky. He wondered if it were part of the dream the faeries wove for their benefit. Perhaps nothing could be trusted.

A long table shaped like a leaf, even down to its veins, was spread out before them. Various faeries, both male and female, greeted them with round eyes and solemn faces. There were three chairs left empty for their visitors, but they were too tiny to sit in.

King Gwyn ap Nudd took his place at the head of the table at a throne that looked to be made of the twining limbs of a sapling, and sat. "Our mortal guests, please take your seats."

Leopold eyed the chairs warily. "I fear we might break them."

"Do you think we are fools in the Faery Realm. Sit!"

Fearing the worst, Leopold pulled it out and gingerly levered himself down…and found that the chair had grown to accommodate him. "Oh."

The faeries of his privy council chuckled to themselves.

"It has come to our attention," Gwyn ap Nudd began, "that you have visited the goblins, our enemies."

"If I may," said Mingli, bowing low from her seat. "We discovered the plot concocted by Gilpin Horner."

There was a rumbling among the council as the king frowned. "We know this miserly creature. He calls himself their king now. We wonder what he did with his predecessor. But we suppose it doesn't matter. What did you discover, Zhao?"

"That they took advantage of mortals to acquire enough funds to create a railway to run along the alignment lines. And the particular railway they acquired has been in use for some time for the transport of mortal corpses."

They cross-talked with some alarm. The king leaned an elbow on his throne's arm, his chin resting on his hand. "We see."

"Yes. And two nights ago—"

"Corpses arose from their graves and killed your citizens."

"As the railway tracks have killed your own," she said somberly.

Leopold couldn't control his impatience and blurted, "Horner's plot is to lay waste to the human *and* faery people of this land…and *all* lands if he succeeds."

"Yes, Kazsmer, we understand. That is why you are here." He turned to Mingli. "But last night and this night, the dead of your kind did *not* rise."

Mingli lowered her face but looked up in that way she had of doing so through her lashes that left Leopold confounded. "We destroyed their treasure room."

The faery council stared at her with widened eyes.

The king smiled under hooded eyes. "Well done."

Leopold was glad that Mingli understood these creatures, as it only just occurred to him that faeries might have treasure as well. But by the looks on the faeries' faces, that didn't appear to be so.

The king watched the humans for some moments before he rose, sauntered beside the long leaf table, until he arrived—not in front of Leopold or Mingli—but in front of Miklos. "You are…unique."

"I'm a monster," he said, his voice unsteady. "And I would rather die than be this thing."

The king cocked his head, openly perusing the accoutrements of the clockwork man, the brass arms, hands, and fingers. The brass plates riveted to his scalp. The curious goggles for eyes.

"You will not die. You will be useful. We have chosen you, Antalek, for what you have become. You will be our weapon against the goblins."

CHAPTER TWENTY-FOUR

"I SAY," SAID Leopold, somewhat puzzled. "Do you care to elaborate?"

"I am not a weapon," growled Miklos. "I am a cursed man."

"Yes," said the king. "Cursed with Earth magic. It is very strong magic. That is why it is being used against us in the way of a railway on an alignment line."

"I will not be a warrior for your kind. What do I care if faeries die? What do I care if humans die? They are nothing to me, as I am nothing to them."

"You will not be our warrior. You will be a conduit."

"I don't understand."

"I'm beginning to see," said a breathless Mingli. "Because he was created with raw Earth magic…"

"He can serve to accentuate our own, just as the alignment lines heighten goblin magic."

"I don't understand," Miklos growled again. "What nonsense are you saying?"

"Miklos," said Leopold. "They wish to use the magic within you. You are like a…a battery, with stored magic. It is more powerful than magic on its own. At least, that's how I interpret it." He glanced at the king who confirmed this with a nod. "But there is something I wish clarified," he said to the king. "I tried to undo the curse. The only way to do it, it seemed, was to switch places with him, for me to take on the clockwork mechanism that had grown in him. But it wouldn't work. In fact, I...well. I heard a voice telling me that this was not decreed. That it must not be—"

"That was our voice you heard," said the king.

"But...how did you..."

"Do you think we are not aware of the magic around us? You with your strange magic of a dread place that you use to entertain other mortals? We have been aware of you for some time, Kazsmer."

"Oh. I see." This information did not at all calm his nerves.

"You now wonder if we are pleased by what we have seen." The king smiled a faery smile—not quite merry, but sly and dangerous. "We have been...amused."

Leopold twitched a glance at Mingli, who kept her face confoundedly neutral.

"More importantly, we have felt no danger from you, Kazsmer," the king went on. "Your entertainments might have involved your daemon Eurynomos, but we did not fear him either."

"You...you know about him?"

"There are few magical folk who do *not* know of the denizens of Gehenna. But we have no congress with them, nor they with us. But the worlds..." He looked up into the arches of the ceiling—that was really no ceiling at all. "They are crossing. It is not a good sign. The goblins are only the beginning of what is to come. You—all of you—will help us fight them."

"No," said Miklos. "I have no fight with you. My fight is with Kazsmer."

The king sighed, bored. "You bargained with him. He lost the bargain. You tried to kill him. You could not. Now you will work for us."

"No! I do not agree to this! I—" Miklos froze in mid-sentence. He could not move his mouth, his eyes, his arms.

"Don't hurt him," cried Leopold, stretching his hand out to the king.

The king seemed wary with a hand raised, but he didn't stop Leopold, who dropped to a knee before King Gwyn ap Nudd. "Please, sire. Please don't harm him. I have done enough harm."

"We will not harm him any more than necessary."

They both looked at the frozen man. "Let me talk to him, sire. Let me make him understand."

"Take all the time you like. I'll give you five minutes." The king waved his hand, turned his back on them both, and strode to his council chair.

Miklos broke free of the spell and nearly stumbled. He glared at Leopold — or at least Leopold assumed so. His eyes had been absorbed by the strange goggles, and there was nothing left of them. He seemed to be changing ever faster. Miklos was right in that soon he would be *all* mechanical clockwork, without a human brain left.

"We can't reverse the curse. I'm sorry. I would never have consciously done such a thing. Perhaps your time is short. Would it not be better for your soul to do what you can for others? It is small comfort, perhaps. But I swear to you that you need not fear about your mother. I will take care of her. She will never want."

The mouth grimaced even if the eyes could not scowl. He took a moment to look Leopold over. "Why are you doing this?"

"Because it is the right thing to do."

He didn't move, and Leopold worried he couldn't. Finally, he turned away and walked a few clanking steps. "I used to watch you," he said, his voice low. "Everyone knew your tale. That your mother left us to become a *gadja*; that she married a Jew and forsook her Catholic teachings; that they both died, and you had nowhere to go but the camp. We mocked you, made fun of you. You were easy to mock, easy to punch and kick, for you were alone, no one to stand up for you."

"I remember," Leopold said stiffly.

"But you never gave up. Your uncle punished you for your books. You read them anyway. He punished you for summoning that daemon, Eurynomos. You did it anyway. I watched you. Couldn't understand why you were such a little fool. Getting punched every day. Getting beaten. Such a fool." He lowered his head. The sound of metal scraping metal made Leopold cringe.

"But look at you now. You never gave up. You have become a rich man. This woman stands beside you. Even your daemon friend still comes to your aid. And what have I become? Never mind this...this clockwork. What would I have become without it? I tell you what. I would have been hanged by the rozzers. I stole. I killed men for their money. I am no good, Kazsmer. I was not punched and kicked daily. I was not alone but instead with plenty of friends. But I was exiled from my own people. And I blamed them for that. I blamed you. But it was me. Me, all along. I'm no good, Kazsmer. I've been everywhere. On the continent, all over England, and what have I ever done worthy of praise? When I came back, my mother had to secretly feed me in the dead of night so that no one would see me. In the dead of night! My mother! And now you say, when I am gone, you will protect her? Well…that is good. I never brought her money. Of all the money I stole and lost, I never once thought to send any to her. You would have been a better son to her."

He stopped speaking and stared off into the corner of the room. "I cannot even weep with these eyes," he said in a small voice.

"Then…do this one thing, Miklos. For everyone. Everyone you have ever hurt."

"I will be dead soon. Or at least…what I used to be. I won't be human anymore."

"I am so sorry, Miklos."

He shrugged. "I deserved it. I know that now." He raised his hand and as gently as he could, lowered it to Leopold's shoulder. It weighted him down, and he struggled to keep his balance.

"I forgive you, Leopold."

Leopold couldn't speak. He looked into the face of the man—all goggles and brass and rivets—and could only express his gratitude with watery eyes.

Miklos slowly turned away and clanked to a far corner.

Mingli was suddenly at his side. "You're a good man, Leopold Kazsmer."

"I don't know about that," he said, wiping his eyes with his sleeve.

"Have you done with your mortal emotions?" asked the king, suddenly at his side.

Leopold scowled. "For now."

"Good. We have work to do."

———◆———

ACCORDING TO THE king, the faery realm had corresponding locations to the mortal world. In other words, they could find the Saint Collen Club's site from the faery kingdom without ever leaving it.

The king called forth a faery lieutenant he called Meddyliwr, so that the king could—presumably—carry on with his kingly duties.

Meddyliwr wore the typical leaf/cobweb garment with the addition of a hollow goat horn hanging from a strap over his shoulder. He was a waif of a creature, with jet black eyes, dark gray hair, and ridiculously thin arms. Leopold dreaded to think what he really looked like without the glamour.

"We must strike the goblins in the heart of their operations. But more importantly, we must destroy that alignment line."

"How is that possible?" asked Leopold.

"Won't it disrupt all the other alignment lines?" asked Mingli.

Leopold wasn't certain if Meddyliwr was smiling or grimacing, for his sharp teeth overlaid one another in a strange way and his lips peeled back just so. "We must be careful not to."

Leopold felt the fool again for not knowing more and had to ask, "And, er, what happens if they *are* disrupted?"

The faery grimaced/smiled again. "The world will tear apart."

"Oh. That's...that's not a good thing."

"You mortals. You have a gift of understatement."

"Only the British ones," said Mingli, matter-of-factly.

Leopold stroked his mustache. "Then...how do we proceed?"

Meddyliwr plucked a stick from one of the saplings that served as the castle's archways. The stick sparkled and extended into an elegant spear. "We go to the goblin lair in your world. And we begin to set the trap."

He walked through the arch and only glanced back once to entreat them to follow.

Leopold hung back to walk alongside Miklos.

"You don't have to try to convince me further, Kazsmer. I've set my mind to it. What does it matter if I die doing this thing?"

"No one said you were going to die."

"Only death would be a relief. How could Hell be worse than this?"

Leopold didn't want to say. *Sitra Achra* was a terrible place. Miklos would have to have been a terrible man to end up there—though he admitted to killing men just for their money. But how could Leopold judge what Miklos had already suffered to the suffering in *Sitra Achra*?

"I won't let that happen," he said quietly.

"And who are you to say? You've condemned me once, Kazsmer. Why should I be surprised if you do it again?"

He could say nothing to that. Instead, he simply walked alongside the man, keeping his strides longer to keep up with the swift whirr of gears and governors.

Meddyliwr led them out of the castle and upon the windswept hill. He stood a moment, smelling the wind. He swiveled and pointed his spear upward. "There."

The blue in that part of the sky became gray as if clouds had gathered, but it transfigured into the gray streets of London before the Saint Collen Club, like looking through a window.

"Is that it, Kazsmer?"

"Yes. But it is far below that mortal structure. It might be better to divert from the front door and go round the other way over the tracks..."

"But that is an alignment line. One that has been perverted by the goblins and the souls of mortal men. Faeries cannot traverse there."

"Oh, I see. Well then. I suppose we must storm the gates." He offered a brief smile to the faery, but the creature remained expressionless. "Once inside, what then?"

"We will see. Climb, my friends."

Climb? Climb what? he was poised to ask, when a transparent stair shimmered into view, leading up to the portal of the window in the sky. Leopold girded himself by straightening his waistcoat and stepped tentatively onto the first riser. He supposed he shouldn't have been surprised that it felt solid. If one simply ignored the ethereal essence of the thing and stepped solidly in a leap of faith, all was well. He looked back, and Mingli was the next to follow him. Then Miklos, and then Meddyliwr.

When Leopold reached the blurry mist between the faery realm and his own, he reached a tentative hand forward and felt proper sunlight, not the stagnancy of the faery world. He pushed all the way through and stood on the pavement below the steps to the Saint Collen Club. And though he was in his world again, he still wasn't quite entirely there, for a man on the pavement passed through him, and Leopold gasped in alarm.

"Meddyliwr! What is this?"

The faery arrived and the hole to the faery realm seemed to close up again. "We are in a portal between worlds. The people of your world cannot yet see you. This makes our passage easier and stealthier."

Leopold assessed their troupe and shook his head. "I'd feel more comfortable with my own reinforcements."

"There will be faery soldiers coming through, Kazsmer."

"And that is for later, as you said. For now, I want my own men."

The faery sighed and leaned against his spear. "Very well. Do so quickly. If they can find you."

That was the crux of it, wasn't it? How was he to call them? Until he looked at his marked wrist. He pressed a finger to the eye and declared, "Suchah!"

The imp popped into place and stared at his companions. "Suchah has come, Leopold Master. But who are these? And what is that?" He pointed a clawed finger at the faery.

"He's a faery—"

"You wish for Suchah to kill it?" He seemed ready to pounce to do just that.

"No! He's on our side."

Suchah's shoulders drooped, and the little bat wings at his shoulder blades flapped sadly.

"I want you to get my friend back at my flat to come here. Can you do that?"

"Suchah can," and he disappeared, but no sooner had he done so that he reappeared, with Thacker and Raj in tow.

"Why did you bring Raj?"

"You said bring friends, Suchah brought friends."

"I said... It doesn't matter. You are welcomed, of course, Raj."

"Welcomed to...where?" asked the automaton, looking curiously around him.

Thacker pointed at the faery. "What the bloody hell is that?"

"These are your *friends*?" The faery postured with his spear.

"Well, yes. This is Inspector Thacker. And as you can see, he is a ghost, a spirit. And this is my trusted friend Raj, who is a living automaton." He spread out his hands. "These. . .these are my friends." He felt foolish explaining it to—as Thacker would put it—a bloody faery. "And this," he said to his friends, "this is Meddyliwr, an officer to the king of the faeries."

Thacker and Raj nodded a bow, while the faery acknowledged them with barely masked disdain.

"Very well, Kazsmer," said the faery lieutenant. "It is not for me to question you. Let us go on."

But Miklos pushed his way forward and stepped up to Raj. "What are you?"

Raj placed a hand on his chest. He was still not wearing trousers, and his brass legs jutted from below his shirt and tailcoat. "I am the Amazing Raj, the Automated Man."

"Did Kazsmer make you too?" he growled.

"Certainly not. I am hundreds of years old. My origin is a mystery even to me. But I consider Mr. Kazsmer a trusted friend. He has saved my life two times now."

"Saved your life. And left you like this?"

"As I said, I was created by another, an *unknown* other. And I am happy in my existence which has recently been enhanced by the discovery of these legs." He lifted one to show the man.

Miklos didn't seem convinced, but he turned his head to stare at Leopold.

The faery tapped his spear staff on the ground. "There is little time for this idle conversation."

"I beg your pardon of course," said Leopold. "But a few lines of introduction won't seem to hurt anything one way or the other. I must explain to them what we are up against."

"Leo," said Thacker, "no one seems to see us. Are *you* doing that?"

"No, it is faery magic. We were in the faery realm. It's too long to explain, but we have agreed to help the faeries fight the goblins."

Suchah smacked one hand into the palm of the other. "Finally! We kill goblins."

Meddyliwr's eyes were hooded when he glanced at Suchah. "I generally despise demons, but I like this fellow's attitude."

Suchah got up eye to eye with the faery. "Suchah no like faeries. But Suchah likes to kill. Faeries, goblins, it matters little."

Leopold stepped between them, edging Suchah back. "Never mind that for now. As long as we are invisible, we must enter the club once more. Spense, can you lead us in the best way to the goblin caverns?"

"It would be easier if you could all go through walls."

"We can," said the faery, clutching his spear. "Get on with it."

Thacker blinked and commiserated silently with Leopold, then shrugged and stepped boldly through the walls of the Saint Collen Club.

CHAPTER TWENTY-FIVE

THIS IS STRANGE, thought Leopold for perhaps the hundredth time that day. They all followed his ghostly friend through the plaster, brick, and wood of the walls, seeing every layer, every little niche and rat skeleton, and yet feeling none of it as they passed. Thacker moved ever faster and descended, until the manmade portion gave way to hewn rock caverns and a warren of tunnels and holes made by the goblins.

Meddyliwr had them stop so he could assess. He sniffed the air in strangely animalistic movements.

Suddenly he turned toward Leopold. "Take me to the place where you saw the alignment line."

Leopold nodded to Thacker, and the ghost moved forward through the rock. This was, perhaps, the most disconcerting of all, for this was not like piercing the walls. Leopold saw parts of his own body disappear and reappear as he moved through the solid stone. He longed to reach back for Mingli's hand, but he feared that it might somehow disrupt their progress in inexplicable ways.

Finally, they emerged to the familiar narrow path and the cliff edge overlooking the tracks below. Leopold felt an intense pull toward those tracks — of course, it wasn't the tracks at all that compelled, but the line of power beneath them.

He noticed Meddyliwr looking at him intently. "Kazsmer? Do you feel a tug toward the line?"

"Yes," he gasped.

Mingli was at his side. "Be careful, Leo. You should not get close to that alignment line again. I don't think it would be healthy for you."

He was able to tear his eyes away from it and smiled. "With you at my side..."

Raj cleared his throat...or at least made the sound of it. "So that is the alignment line. Master Meddyliwr, how do you propose to stop the goblins and leave the line of power unharmed?"

"Can't we just kill goblins now?" asked Suchah, bouncing on his heels.

"I applaud your eagerness, my friend," said the faery to the imp, "but we must wait, take our time. As for our method, Master Raj—" Leopold felt a twinge of envy that Raj should be styled "Master Raj" while he was simply "Kazsmer" "—we must make certain to gather the goblins as close as we might. If they scatter too wildly, our magic will never find them all."

"Then it seems to me," said Thacker, "that the little devil Suchah and I should herd them into one spot."

The faery smiled. "Yes. You should do that."

Thacker poked Suchah on the shoulder and was effective enough that the imp seemed to feel it. "Let's go, you."

"We trick goblins? Yes!"

They both disappeared with a muffled pop.

Meddyliwr stretched his neck to peer over the ledge to survey the sludgy river, the tracks, and any stray goblins below. "Soon, I will call my faery army and put your clockwork man in place."

Leopold moved to stand beside him and peered over the edge as well. "I say, Meddyliwr, I can't count myself as a strategist of martial matters since I never served myself, but it seems to me you mean to...to wipe out the goblins. Am I misinterpreting that?"

The faery never acknowledged Leopold in his nod.

"Well now. I don't know that this quite sits well with me. I mean, you're talking wholesale slaughter, aren't you? I know the little beasts are terrible, but is it wise or even cricket to wipe out a whole race of beings?"

Meddyliwr seemed frozen to the spot, until he slowly turned toward Leopold and even rose from his crouched posture to face him.

"And you object to this? May I remind you that their very intent was to wipe out *your* entire race from the planet, as well as ours? Such beings cannot be allowed to continue."

"Oh, I know that. But…it just seems to me that we're doing the same damn thing as they are. Pardon me for my language, Miss Zhao," he muttered, touching the brim of his topper to her.

The faery eyed him most unpleasantly. "You have a strange view of the worlds, Kazsmer."

"And that reminds me. It's *Mister* Kazsmer."

The faery had not stopped eyeing him, and it was easier to see that superimposed insect face over the glamoured one. He said nothing more, but Leopold was certain that the faery now saw *him* differently as well. Was this such a good idea allying with the faeries? Thinking back on the walking corpses, he had decided there had been no choice—not with what the goblins had plotted against mankind and faerykind. Maybe Meddyliwr was right. Maybe such beings *should* be wiped out. After all, they had no wish to live peaceably with mortals, unlike the faeries. Still. He wished he could speak with Mingli about it. Alone.

A deep boom shuddered the entire cavern, and Leopold concluded that it must be Thacker and Suchah. Oh, such strange bedfellows he'd accumulated!

Raj touched Leopold's sleeve, and he felt the automaton's excitement. "Leo," he said quietly. "What is it *I* can do for this enterprise?"

He shook his head. "I haven't the faintest idea, old friend. Frankly, I don't know how this will play out."

"I am preternaturally strong," he said. "And I might be immune to their type of magic. At least I have that feeling."

"Then you may be very useful indeed," said Meddyliwr. "You may be needed to guard the clockwork man from interference."

Raj glanced back at Miklos. "That, my friend, I can do!"

Leopold watched Raj on his new brass legs gracefully turn and stalk back to where Miklos was standing like a piece of machinery. How he dreaded this whole thing! This waiting…

Another boom, and they heard the sound of many feet, many voices.

The goblins were coming.

Suchah popped in next to Leopold and Thacker appeared right after, rubbing his transparent hands together in anticipation. "They're on their way, me lad."

"Suchah ready to kill," the imp agreed.

"Then it's time to bring my brethren," said the faery. He took the horn from the strap over his shoulder, brought it to his lips, and blew.

The strange, ethereal sound resonated unpleasantly in Leopold's gut, but he sensed that it reached the faery realm. He shot a glance to Mingli and she, too, appeared to feel it. They locked gazes but he could not tell what was in her mind.

It didn't seem to take long for lights to appear through the rock behind them. The lights formed into faery warriors with spears in their hands, wearing what looked like enlarged acorns and snail shells as helmets.

Two by two they began to form a wide line with three, then five, then ten deep and still growing.

Meddyliwr turned toward Miklos and pointed his spear at him. "You. Clockwork man. Now is the time to position you."

Miklos turned his head toward Leopold and looked at him with empty goggles. "Are you sure about this, Kazsmer?"

Leopold glanced back at the faery and all the faery warriors and shook his head. "I must be honest with you, Miklos. I'm not. But..."

"What do I have to lose?" He seemed to gird himself and raised his chin to the faery commander. "Where do I go?"

"You follow me, down to the alignment line. We must be in position before the goblins arrive."

He began to follow the faery as he made his way down the steep trail.

Raj, with mincing clanking steps, strode down the trail to keep up, and soon the three of them disappeared.

Mingli sidled up to him. She had her strange gun in her hand. "You are wise to question this slaughter," she said. "Though I am not interested in the antics of goblins, I, too, wince at the destruction of an entire race of creatures. But I can't say I have the least idea how to negotiate a truce with them."

"That Horner chap seemed fairly angry with our race. And he wasn't wrong, dammit. We have blasted the whole of England with sooty engines and decimated the forests."

"Perhaps a compromise could be reached…"

"I don't think you are remembering the history of the empire, my dear."

She swore softly in Chinese. "Yes, I suppose you're right. The whole thing is a bloody mess."

"Miss Zhao!"

She quirked a smile. "Mr. Kazsmer, we find ourselves on the eve of battle. I think the occasion calls for a bit of…creative language."

He agreed. His belly was tied up in knots, and not only were his hands tingling with Earth magic but his tattoo had begun to throb in little stabs of pain. He rubbed it through his cuff.

"I…I want you to stay out of harm's way, but I know it will be a useless exercise telling you so."

She reached up and kissed his cheek, much to his delight. "You seem to know me so well."

It surprised him how much that sentiment thrilled him, that he should know her, and that she should know him. He'd never been this close to another human being since his parents died. He hadn't thought it possible.

She gave him a smile. "Don't pretend you don't enjoy this as much as I do."

Damned if he didn't. The Earth magic was still strong in him. He wouldn't have minded Eurynomos at his side right now but in truth, he didn't need him for his magical abilities. Leopold was flush with it. And he wondered, looking at his tattoo, that if he wanted Eurynomos at his side, if he needed to…

The sounds of hundreds of feet.

He was glad Raj was guarding Miklos, but he began to wonder if he shouldn't be down there, too. He peered over the edge, and Meddyliwr — standing well back from the tracks and the line of power — directed Miklos to straddle it. Raj stood beside him, a strange figure with his spindly legs and proudly raised chin.

The clockwork man's metal fingers curled into fists and he, too, stood proudly: chest forward, head raised to meet whatever came, goggle eyes suddenly ablaze with the clockwork light within him, strafing the area like a search-light.

The faeries never so much as moved a muscle, all waiting for the signal.

Leopold heard it. Down below, the goblins were gathering, emerging from the darkness of the tunnel in sporadic groups until they seemed to notice Miklos, Raj, and the faery lieutenant beside him. Some stopped, and the ones coming after them bumped and jostled the ones before.

"I have to get down there," rasped Leopold. Mingli gave a nod and, as Leopold made his way down the narrow path, she followed, gun held high.

Leopold hadn't even drawn his Webley. What was the point? He was so flushed with magic he knew he wouldn't need it. In fact, the closer he got to the alignment line the more confident he felt…but he knew he mustn't trust that. It was the power of the Earth magic urging him on, as if it were a living thing, cheering for him to succeed. But of course, it couldn't. It might not even have his best interests at heart. It might, all things considered, be a reckless and malevolent force, only using those fortunate — or perhaps *un*fortunate enough — to be lured into its power. If only he knew more! If only he had studied *all* forms of magic!

Oh yes. And that was why he originally thought it was malevolent magic he felt coming from Miklos. In a very real way, it was.

By the time he reached the bottom of the cavern, the goblin hoards had swollen to incredible numbers, and there in the lead was Gilpin Horner himself. He still wore his frock coat and vest, with its gold watch chain, but he also seemed to have cobbled himself a crown out of what gold bits and pieces had escaped Mingli's destruction of their treasury room.

Horner spied him and shot an arm forward, pointing at him with sharp teeth bared. "You! Kazsmer! You destroyed my treasure!"

Leopold, scared down to his toenails, nevertheless lifted his topper. "Sorry about that, old man. Couldn't very well have you send more living corpses about London."

"I will eviscerate you. I will gnaw on your bones and sinew while you yet live so I can savor your terror."

"I say." He stuck a finger in his collar to loosen it. "That's very…vivid."

"I shall not spare your Miss Zhao. Oh no. She will find a tortured death, lingering between pain and revulsion at what mass of blood and bone she will be reduced to."

"Now you've done it," said Leopold. In his hand formed a flaming sword. He looked at it in surprise, since he had not consciously conjured it. "Now you're talking about the woman I love. That is unacceptable." He postured and raised the sword over his head like some ancient warrior, flames rising and crackling from the enchanted blade.

When he looked at Mingli her face was perfectly composed as she raised her weapon straight-armed, aimed, and fired.

Whatever it was that came out of the gun, it hit Horner in his shoulder and he flailed backwards, thrown to the ground.

She lowered the gun with a smile curling her lips.

But Horner wasn't down for long. He scrambled to his feet, throwing off any goblins who tried to help him. "You've sealed your fate, Miss Zhao."

"Pish tosh," she said, aiming her gun at him again. "I've heard that before."

Horner grabbed the goblin nearest and shoved him in front of him as a shield. The shot hit the other goblin and Horner tossed him aside. "I have many more goblins to shield me," he said gleefully.

The goblins beside him didn't appear as gleeful.

"What is this?" He gestured toward Miklos and then pointed at Meddyliwr. "Him? You bring this damned faery to *my* kingdom?"

Meddyliwr sneered and lightly touched Miklos with his spear. "Now," he said.

Miklos stood confused, looking from Raj to Leopold standing several yards away. He hadn't a clue as to what he was supposed to do…until he suddenly stiffened.

Leopold felt the thrum of the alignment line come to life, felt it hum in his bones, his gut. He took a step back.

Miklos threw his arms and head back. A pillar of light burst forth from his face and speared into the vaulted roof of the cavern. His whole body glowed, and he roared. In pain? In confusion? Leopold couldn't tell.

A pulse of power boomed from Miklos' body and knocked everyone off their feet. Leopold crawled toward Mingli and helped her up.

"What was that, Leo?" she said, staring at the clockwork man.

"I don't…I don't…know…" But even as he said it, he *did* know. He felt it. Miklos, because of the raging Earth magic within him, was being used as a conduit for the magic pulsing through the alignment line. No wonder the faeries couldn't draw too close to it. But Miklos could be used like a human battery, storing and multiplying their magic. They'd use him till there was nothing left of him.

"Must get to Miklos," he shouted to her over the rushing noise of the magic as it continued to pulse and throb all around them.

"No, Leo! You mustn't draw near the line."

"It will kill him!"

"No," she shouted back. "Find another way."

Find another way? How could he? He only had to glance up to the ledge above to see the faery phalanxes gently floating down to them, much to the chagrin of the goblins, who tried to form their own muddled lines of defense. They conjured whatever weapons came to mind, mostly clubs.

The only help he could think of was Eurynomos, but he dared not draw his own blood and put himself in danger. Not this close to goblins.

Unless…

He pushed up his left sleeve, grasped his tattoo, and, calling upon the Earth magic in him, he summoned Eurynomos in his mind.

Light burst up from the ground and Eurynomos rose like an opera baritone through a stage trap door. He glared at Leopold from his great height, not even paying attention to the chaos around him.

"You summoned me," he said, perplexed. "You summoned me...and you didn't draw blood."

For once, Leopold stood tall in front of the daemon he had summoned and felt no weakness, no draw toward the depths of Gehenna. He felt nearly as strong as the daemon himself.

And vaguely, he now wondered that he needed to summon him at all.

CHAPTER TWENTY-SIX

"EURYNOMOS, WE HAVEN'T time to discuss it." He gestured toward the onrushing goblins.

Eurynomos looked at them, looked the other way toward the faeries surging forward, and reached out both hands to grab Mingli and Leopold's arms to drag them out of the way.

"What in Gehenna is going on here?"

"The goblins created an enchantment with their railway," said Mingli in a rush, "that raised the dead, who in turn killed the living, thereby making more dead to rise to kill."

"That's...ghastly," said the daemon. "Wait. I seem to recall...yes, something peculiar was going on with dead souls of late. I never could have imagined this."

"We've aligned with the faeries, Eurynomos," said Leopold. "But I'm not certain we haven't traded one Hell for another."

The daemon's eyes scanned all the doings. "Is that your clockwork man, Leo? And...good heavens. Raj has legs!"

"Never mind that! Can you help?"

"I'm afraid, old bean, that there's very little I can do. I'm not allowed to strike dead supernatural creatures *en masse*. It just isn't done. I can kill to protect you, Leo...which brings us back to how the devil you summoned me without sacrificing your blood."

"Earth magic. It's...it's so powerful, my friend. I...I feel so different, so light as opposed to the heaviness of the magic from Gehenna."

"Ah," said the daemon, narrowing his eyes. "So, you have discovered it."

"What? Are you telling me you knew this all along?"

"I suspected. But I wasn't certain. The ways of your world and my world are so confoundedly different."

The faeries broke the goblin line, and suddenly goblin and faery were at it hand to hand. Elf shot arced into the air over their heads, pelting the goblins, and many fell under the magical onslaught.

But goblins had their own weapons, and fiery rocks hurdled into the air back at the faery lines. Some fell, while others were burned, their wings damaged beyond repair. And yet, even the severely burned rose — half their faces blasted away, their fair hair singed to the scalp — and hefted their spears to rush the goblin lines again.

Leopold spied Suchah darting here and there, his tiny wings flapping and barely keeping him aloft as he twisted the heads from the necks of goblins. He laughed, licking their blood from his spattered face with his forked tongue.

And all the while, Miklos' roaring and the magic tumbling off of him and his pillar of light seemed to fill the faeries with a magical advantage. There seemed so many more of them than goblins, and they flew over the teeming hoards, through them, beneath them, wreaking havoc.

Eurynomos shook his enormous horned head. "Look, old man. The best I can do is get you and Miss Zhao away from here."

"We can't go. We must stay and see this thing through. I gave my promise."

"Then what shall I do?"

"Keep Mingli safe." She scoffed loudly in disgust. "And keep your eye on Miklos. I gave my promise to him too."

Even as Leopold said it, he saw a cadre of goblins making their way around the faery line toward the clockwork man.

Eurynomos barely turned before he flicked the air with his fingers, and the goblins tumbled away as if in a whirlwind. Faery spears took care of them for good.

"Also," said Leopold, "the faeries wish to entirely destroy the goblins. I can't have that."

"What? Why? That is the solution to your situation, surely."

"I can't abide a whole species of beings simply wiped out. It's...it's inhuman."

"Well, not to put too fine a point on it, old man, none of the players are human to begin with."

"I don't care. It's wrong. I feel it in my gut."

"And your gut hasn't been wrong yet," he sighed. "Well, then. I'll see to it that some of your goblins survive. In the meantime, I'll do my best along the perimeter, shall I?"

"Thank you, Eurynomos."

The daemon departed, taking long sauntering strides, his horned head rising like Satan himself amid the smoke and ash of the battle. A group of goblins, who seemed to have been waiting in the background for Eurynomos to leave, suddenly moved forward toward Mingli and Leopold. They roared, clubs raised high.

Mingli postured with her pistol, but Leopold raised his hands and summoned the magic within him. It took so little effort he hadn't realized that it was accomplished before he opened his eyes again. The creatures were flattened, leaving little more than a stain on the ground.

"Leopold..." Mingli stared at him as she lowered her gun.

He looked down at his hands. He hadn't even broken a sweat. "This power...it's so strange, yet so natural."

"And you summoned Eurynomos with it. Earth magic is your proper destiny."

"If I survive this, I'll definitely need to research it. But for now, we must get closer to Miklos." He saw her solemn face and offered a brief smile. "Don't worry. I can resist the pull of the line of power. I know I can with you beside me."

She seemed doubtful but she rushed forward with him anyway.

Leopold used his magic to set a perimeter around the clockwork man, a perimeter that even forced the faery lieutenant back.

"Leo," Mingli shouted. She was pointing at Miklos. "Look!"

Miklos was surrounded by blinding, pulsing power, but when Leopold looked beyond that he noticed how the man had changed. Where before he had metal plates covering his entire head, they now appeared to be gone. His long plait had returned as well as his bald scalp. Even one of his hands had returned to skin and muscle rather than mere metal.

"My God," he said. "The line is draining the magic in him."

"Not only a conduit," said Mingli, "but it is using him up. But not the human part; the magic."

"Do you know what this means?" His eyes welled. "He will be returned to normal."

"As long as he doesn't go beyond his capacity."

"Yes. You're right. We must make certain of that." Now, more than ever, they had to watch over Miklos. When the time was right, they'd have to pull him from the alignment line. But would it destroy the line if they did?

He didn't voice this to Mingli. They would have to try regardless.

The faeries continued to fight with a seeming advantage, but Gilpin Horner rose from the battle to stand upon a rock. His fine clothes were in tatters and there was much black blood spattered on his face from goblin and faery alike. He raised a curved sword like a scimitar and spread a malevolent smile across his face. "You faeries think you have the better of me and my men," he shouted above the din. "Think again." He speared his sword toward the cavern's roof and it sparked and exploded above their heads. Leopold saw little result from that—until he glanced at the ground.

Small mounds of soil erupted and soon, faery corpses rose from their graves.

Horner laughed and cackled from his perch. "Kill us and more soldiers will rise!"

The faery forces stopped and drew back. Their expressions were full of horror at facing their own dead brethren. Not only corpses from when the railway was begun, but the recently fallen began to rise. And they all moved straight for the faeries.

Leopold froze from the terror of it. But Raj was suddenly at his side. "Leo! We must redirect Miklos on his course. Tell him how to kill the enchantment over the dead."

"I don't bloody well know how to do it *myself*, Raj."

"But you can, Leo. I'll help you. And Miss Zhao, too."

Mingli bit her lip. "I don't know how to direct my own magic so specifically, Raj."

"Together then," said the automaton.

He grasped both their hands and nearly heaved them toward Miklos. "Make a circle around him. We must join hands."

Leopold didn't question it. They formed a circle around the clockwork man — while Leopold was careful not to touch the alignment line nor the tracks — and clutched each other's hands as if their lives depended on it.

Leopold closed his eyes and reached out, feeling for Raj's magic. He'd never done it before--hadn't ever thought about doing so, truth be told. But when he met the mysterious force inside Raj, he felt it like a familiar thing, like an old pillow or comfortable footstool. What Raj had couldn't quite be called magic, but it nevertheless melded with his own, strengthened him, bolstered his power. He could feel it directing him, offering a map of what he should do, what turns to make, what hills to climb.

And with that information, he then reached out to Mingli...and jerked back. Her magic was completely foreign to that of Raj's, but not unfamiliar to Leopold. After all, she was part daemon, and he had dealt with their like and their magic nearly all his life. Even so, her kind of daemon was unlike anything he was completely comfortable with. It churned with the strength of an ocean and seemed to be holding back, as if waiting for the signal to release. He had to be careful with this one. He didn't wish to unleash something she wasn't prepared to control.

He moved his magic around hers like a cat's sinuous brushing around its owner's legs: gently caressing, coaxing, coming to terms with it. Mingli's hand in his clutched so tight it nearly cut off the blood supply, but he let her, allowing her to become used to *his* magic.

When Leopold opened his eyes again, Miklos was even less of a clockwork man than he was before. His legs were now human and the goggles for eyes had fallen away, leaving him blinking in perplexity.

Sustained by Raj and Mingli's magic, he reached out. *Miklos*, he said. Or had he? He hadn't used his lips or breath, but said the name in his head, using Mingli and Raj's magic to reach into Miklos' mind. *Miklos, you are becoming human again.*

What? Are you in my mind, Kazsmer?

I am.

The enormous power that Miklos channeled suddenly stumbled. Perhaps Leopold's disembodied voice made him lose concentration.

The faery line fell back, and the creatures looked at one another confused and frightened.

Miklos, you must keep the magic strong. The alignment line has worked through you, draining you of the magic I had enchanted you with. You will be yourself again soon. But we still need you to fight the goblins.

I will fight, Kazsmer. I will fight with all my being now. I shall be myself again!

It is not without risks, Miklos. Follow my magic. Do you sense it? Can you see it in your mind?

Yes. Yes. I can see it. It...it's amazing. It's like a geometric pattern. Like a maze.

Yes, like a maze. Follow the maze, Miklos. We must destroy the goblins' enchantments. They mustn't be allowed to raise the dead!

He felt Miklos tentatively follow the path he could see in his mind, Leopold's magic like a maze. And Leopold felt his twists and turns, his taking of dead-end routes, until he seemed to become accustomed to it and its vagaries and became more sure of himself.

Leopold, on his part, directed Miklos, bolstering the faltering areas weakened by his becoming more human. Leopold particularly sought the enchantments that raised the dead. Yet probe as he would, he could not seem to find it...

Until the familiar magic of Gehenna joined his, and he looked up to see Eurynomos had joined the circle. He said nothing, but the daemon grinned, sharp teeth lacing over one another. The daemon, too, reached into his mind.

Leo, you must seek out the souls of the dead. Here is what it feels like.

Leopold shuddered as waves of icy sensations poured over him. Dead souls. Souls of the inhuman as well. His magic touched it with probing tendrils, getting the feel of it. His senses shot forward, seeking, delving until he found it. It was a sickening thing, like something from the depths of *Sitra Achra*. Malevolent and full of evil intent. Yes, it was now easy to find as it hid in the crevices of the earth, forming in the shadows of grief, and molded into black stickiness. Leopold marshalled the magic of his companions to punch holes in it, to pierce its fleshy membranes, and crush it into the ground.

Horner cried out as the enchantments fell, one by one. "No!" he cried. "Stop it!"

The faeries seemed to sense that the offensive had fallen, and they surged forward. Elf shot, spears, and acorn bombs lobbed over the heads of the goblins and decimated unit after unit. They began to scatter.

Horner, still standing on his perch, flushed red and shook his fists at his own men. "Cowards! Stand and fight! Return to the line!" But few listened to him. Even those that seemed to serve as his bodyguards leapt off the rock, leaving him to fend for himself.

He swung out with his sword and killed his own deserting men. "You are excrement, Phinneas. I should have eaten you long ago." He turned toward the faery line and screamed out his frustration, shaking his sword.

A streak of red zoomed by and an imp — webbed feet perched on the goblin's shoulders — grabbed his bald head and sunk his teeth deep into the skull.

"Get off!" Horner squealed.

But Suchah, eyes ablaze, sank his teeth in again and again. When Horner cast about for help, none came.

Leopold shuddered. Some other force was coming.

Raj's voice suddenly sounded in his mind. *I fear that Miklos — whether intentional or not — has summoned something. Something surging, churning.*

I feel it too, said Mingli.

They all fell silent as they concentrated on the sensations, trying to discover what it might be.

Something is happening, said Miklos. *Something is coming.*

We can all feel it, said Leopold.

Upon my word! cried Eurynomos. *I do believe...yes. A locomotive is coming! He's summoned an engine!*

Leopold snapped open his eyes and searched ahead into the long tunnel back toward London. Yes. He could feel the rumbling along the tracks as it used the alignment line's power. A mindless machine rushing forward from the Piccadilly station!

And it was coming directly for Miklos.

He glanced up at the man who had been nearly a mindless machine himself, but who was now almost completely human again.

Miklos, we have to move you from the tracks…but not yet. You've almost lost all your mechanisms.

I can feel it, Kazsmer. I can feel it. But…not all.

You must stay on the tracks until it is complete. He looked down the tunnel. The headlamp from the locomotive shone as a bright dot that was steadily growing larger.

Leopold signaled to Raj and Mingli that they should be ready to drag Miklos away from the tracks.

What is bringing the locomotive? asked Mingli.

The magic itself, he answered. *Or Miklos. More unintentional magic? Or the magic itself seeks to protect Miklos, but…* Clearly it couldn't stop in time if Miklos didn't leave the tracks.

Leopold watched Miklos steadily, watched for his clockworks to finally dissipate completely. Yet at the same time, the engine grew closer and closer, roaring in the echoing tunnel.

Eurynomos, as the goblins are dispersed, make certain some survive. Please!

He sensed exactly what Eurynomos felt about that, but the daemon left their circle to satisfy the needs of his friend.

The locomotive's powerful engines churned, smoke and fire belching from its stack. It was like a demon in its determination, in the fire that spewed into the tunnel. Its headlamp was like an angry eye, glaring down all comers. It was closer, far closer than he anticipated in so short a time.

Still, Miklos was not entirely free of clockwork. Leopold felt the tick, tick still in his own gut, waiting, waiting to pull him free.

He listened hard with all the magic he had, and finally, the clockwork heart had faded into muscle and there were no more gears, no mechanisms left save for those that nature gave him.

Pull him now! Leopold cried, just as the locomotive neared the cavern's entrance.

Meddyliwr was suddenly before them. "What are you doing?" he demanded.

Gasping, trying to speak—which seemed so much slower than speaking in his mind—Leopold rasped, "Freeing...Miklos..."

"No. We need him to continue."

"He's done his job. If he continues, his life force will be drained."

"What do I care of that?"

With a grimace of effort, Leopold yanked with all his might, and Miklos suddenly fell forward. He was smaller, not as broad-shouldered as his mechanical self. His eyes were the brown eyes of a human being, and his hands, feet, face, arms were of human skin, muscle, bone, and sinew.

The faery screwed up his face in anger, but with the roar of the oncoming engine, he snapped his head around. His eyes widened as he leapt out of the way. Leopold grabbed Mingli on one side and Raj on the other. "Run!" he yelled, making sure Miklos followed.

The locomotive, all fire and smoke, chugged at full speed into the cavern. Frightened faeries flew upward, getting clear of the danger.

But the goblins weren't as fortunate.

Gilpin Horner's face paled and Suchah, still biting his head, looked up in alarm. The imp quickly vanished just as the engine barreled forward. The tracks had run out and the spitting, steaming locomotive flew free of the tracks, momentum carrying it forward with driving wheels still chugging, straight into the goblins.

Sparks flew as the flying engine tipped forward taking out first Horner and then a huge swath of his fellow goblins before it slowly upended in the air. It soared upside down for what seemed like minutes until it finally fell, skidding and sparking spectacularly onto its smokestack and steam dome through the rest of the goblin line. When the boiler exploded, sending red hot coals, fire, and hot metal into the air, the rest of the retreating goblins were no more.

Twisted metal sang as the great machinery spun what was left of the driving wheels to bits, its progress slowed deep into the goblins' dark cavern, black smoke billowing, embers hovering, until if finally came to rest with an exhausted release of hot steam.

CHAPTER TWENTY-SEVEN

ONCE LEOPOLD'S COMPANY was free of the choking cavern and looked down from the ledge above, it was Mingli who told him that much of the Saint Collen Club was likely compromised, being mostly glamoured. "We shall have to put our resources into repairing it before anyone raises the alarm."

"Not until we leave the faery realm. I feel we are still within it."

"I think you're right. Just because we seem to be on our plane again, doesn't mean we are in reality."

"I do not trust the faeries," he said quietly. "We must make haste to get Miklos back."

Raj trotted forward. "I shall collect Inspector Thacker and Suchah, with your permission, Leopold. I fear to stay longer is to draw us under the undue attention of the faeries."

"You're right, of course. Get Suchah to return you to our lodgings the same way he transported you here. We'll meet you back there soon."

Eurynomos strode up to them, just as Raj fled back down into the caverns amid the smoking wreckage. The daemon looked back at the automaton and shook his head. "Many strange things afoot."

"Did you manage to save them, Eurynomos?"

"Yes. I sent them far from here. I doubt they will be happy about it. At the moment. Later, they will see the boon I have done for them. What of you, Leopold? That was certainly an exciting climax to the affair."

Leopold peered down at the debris. He couldn't believe they had been able to escape it. Even though he was still partially in the faery realm, he had no expectation that he would have escaped unscathed had he not gotten out of the way of the locomotive. "As you can probably see, I'm not exactly 'here'."

"Yes. I *can* see that. What is going on?"

"A promise fulfilled, my friend."

The large taloned hand rested on his shoulder. "I can see that, too. My heart is filled with joy for you, Leopold. But you're not out of the woods yet."

"No. If you can stay, go back to my lodgings with Raj, Suchah, and Spense. I'll explain it all when we return."

"Very well. If you need me…"

He smiled. "I know I can summon you…without ill effects."

"Yes," said Eurynomos thoughtfully. He turned and ran to catch up with Raj.

"How do you feel, Leo?" asked Mingli.

He heard the concern in her voice and it was not without merit. His coat smelled of coal smoke and ash, and his sleeve was singed on one side. He said to her—truthfully—"I am well, my dear. I…I seem better than well. And I also possess all my faculties. You needn't fear I am mesmerized by the line of power." He glanced back at the tracks. No, it held no sway over him, much to his relief. He didn't feel like letting go of himself and flying into the rafters like a celestial being. He chuckled. At least, not today.

———◆———

MEDDYLIWR STOOD ON the underside of what was left of the engine. It was the last place Horner had stood. He was decidedly gone now, having been effectively exploded by an enchanted train, one of his own devising. Leopold felt it was a fitting end.

The faery lieutenant directed his faery army to march back through the solid stone to the faery kingdom. They had laid to waste any living goblin, and had the solemn task of carrying their own fallen on their shoulders back to their kingdom.

Except for the still steaming engine, the late battlefield smelled better than it had when the goblins were in charge. It seemed fresher and purer. But Leopold sensed the glamour of the building would not remain long. He had a lot of work ahead of him.

Meddyliwr hopped down from his viewing place and conferred with several of his soldiers, nodding at what they told him until he seemed satisfied and sent them forth. When he they had gone, he faced Leopold—never looking at Miklos, who had done the bulk of the work. "My king will be pleased to offer his thanks. Come now...*Mister* Kazsmer."

Meddyliwr didn't look back as he led the way. Leopold offered Mingli his arm and she took it. Miklos, quiet and solemn, followed behind.

Through the solid rock they went, and onto the misty staircase down from the window in the sky. It was still sunlight in the faery realm, at least in the glamour they had enchanted for their visitors. There was no sign of the faery army when they entered into the shining castle and once again joined the court revelry in the king's hall.

King Gwyn ap Nudd sat atop his throne, eyes following their company as they entered and stood before him. The songs and music stopped, and all the sounds of reveling faeries ceased.

The king leaned forward on his seat and appraised Leopold. "You have done well, my mortal friends. You have saved our kind and yours. You will, no doubt, wish a reward."

Leopold doffed his hat in an elegant sweep of his hand and bowed low. "Your majesty, we need no reward, for our reward is our friend restored to himself."

The king glanced once at Miklos and then dismissed him. "So we see." He clapped his hands. "Come, bring chairs for our guests at our table."

Chairs were brought, once again much too small, but Leopold led the way to sit in them and, just like the last time, they grew to accommodate.

The faery king held out his goblet and a faery servant poured him wine.

"My friends, we celebrate a great victory. It has been hundreds of years since we last fought the goblins, and this victory was sweet indeed, though it is not without loss to our own." He raised his cup. "To the brave fallen!" he said and drank his cup.

The other faeries drank theirs, while Leopold and Mingli studiously did not partake.

Leopold glanced at Miklos who was bringing his small goblet to his lips.

"No!" shouted Leopold, but he was too late.

A thunderclap sounded. The faery glamour shimmered, blinked out once, before it restored itself, briefly showing the dark forest and the insect-like faery faces.

Miklos froze, looking about him, his goblet trembling in his hand.

The king rose and sauntered toward them. "Ah, Mr. Kazsmer. You did not warn your friend."

"I did. He...he must have simply forgotten. O great king! You must not hold it against him. He suffered for so many years as a mechanical man. And now he has only just been restored. He was instrumental in winning the day. Surely...surely..."

"There are rules in our realm, Mr. Kazsmer, as you well know."

Gwyn ap Nudd stood before Miklos and studied him almost too closely, barely inches from his face. "You have consumed something of Faery. You may not now return to the world you knew."

Miklos tried to rise but one look from the faery king and he stopped dead.

"You are mortal again now, Antalek, but if you left our kingdom, you would revert back to the clockwork you were."

He turned to Leopold. "Is this true, Kazsmer?"

"I'm...I'm not sure, Miklos."

"But *you* are sure, are you not, Antalek?" The king put his finger under Miklos' chin and held his gaze. "You know this is true. Return to your realm and succumb to a fabricated existence...or stay with us as a mortal man and learn the secrets of the faery world."

"Miklos..." Leopold could barely breathe. He had been so close. So close to leaving. Yet, was it true what the king said? He had no way of knowing.

"Perhaps you and your Miss Zhao would also wish to stay," said the king. "We only trust certain visitors. We can learn much from one another. And that tattoo you bear, Kazsmer, we can eliminate that too. If you stay with us. The wine is far more extraordinary than your own. The food that much more delicious to consume. And so much magic. So many enchantments to learn. It would be a delight to teach you far more than you could ever learn on your own. So many things to learn, Kazsmer…"

It was tempting… But wait.

He shook out his muzzy head and looked around. No, it wasn't tempting at all! To lose all his friends, his life in London, his life to be with Mingli? No!

He shot to his feet. "No! I shall not. And Miklos cannot remain."

"But he drank, Kazsmer. You know the rules. He drank of our enchanted food. He must not leave. None of you must leave."

"So, this is a faery's gratitude? To go back on your word?"

"We gave you no word of mine. We swore you no oaths."

Faeries were emerging out of the shadows and creeping closer. He didn't dare take his eyes off the king, but the prickle at the back of his neck told him they were all around them, converging.

"None of you must leave," said the king in a soft, cooing voice that almost made Leopold want to succumb to it. Almost.

Until he remembered the hag-stone.

He thrust his hand into his frock coat pocket. Fingers touched, curled around the smooth river stone, teased the natural hole in the center of it. He glanced toward Mingli but she seemed mesmerized, and likewise Miklos. They both seemed to be losing their own will.

Leopold quickly linked arms with both and took out the hag-stone, revealing it to the king.

Everything happened at once.

Gwyn ap Nudd hissed like a cat and snarled, baring suddenly sharp teeth. The glamour winked out, leaving the dark, cobwebbed forest, the mushroom debris from their banqueting feast, the insect-like faces and rags of the faeries. The darkness fell about them and Leopold whipped around with his companions and ran for the arches of trees that served as the doorway from the banqueting hall.

He held tight to their arms and yanked them onward, stumbling with their sluggish steps. He closed his eyes and gathered the magic within him.

He heard the hundreds of feet pursuing them, pelting the mossy ground, but he concentrated and ran until he broke through the barrier.

The sudden quiet and cold assaulted him and he opened his eyes. He stopped and pulled back on his companions just in time before they toppled over the edge of a steep and rocky ravine.

It seemed to have awakened the sleepers and Mingli touched her head. "What...what has happened?"

"Kazsmer," gasped Miklos. "Are we free?"

Leopold looked about. No faeries, no faery kingdom. Only the cold darkness of the English countryside. He looked up into a sky filled with stars like a ladies' sparkling ball gown, smelled the damp of the woods, with just a hint of coal smoke rising from his coat.

"Yes. We're home." He looked Miklos over. He was human again. Human for good. The faery had lied. "And you, my friend, are free at last."

———◆———

LEOPOLD SAT AT the campfire in the Romani camp, hands clasped together, arms resting on his thighs. Miklos had run the rest of the way ahead of them and they heard the screams of his mother and then the rest of the camp as she tugged him into the firelight.

Mingli sat beside him, a chipped mug of tea warming her hands.

There were many congratulations, much back-slapping, and even Miklos took him into an embrace. The elders seemed to have forgiven Miklos, for who could blame the man who had suffered the life of a living machine?

After a time, they stopped fawning on Leopold and some of Miklos' old friends gathered round him instead, laughing like old times. Except that Miklos seemed more subdued, less inclined to join in with their jokes and pranks. Leopold wondered how long that would last. Would he go back to his cruel ways, or was he changed for the better? Only time would tell.

A shadow fell over Leopold, and when he twisted to look, it was Yanko. His uncle said nothing, only stood behind him and carefully laid his hand on Leopold's shoulder. His fingers squeezed and then he moved away.

But that one gesture of affection had meant the world to Leopold.

———————•———————

LATE IN THE night, after declining the offer of lodgings, he and Mingli trudged to the main road in hopes of finding a cab. The best they could do was to hitch a ride on a milk cart. Leopold was dead tired, but he found he didn't mind at all when Mingli's head, drooping with sleep, fell against his shoulder. He leaned his head against her damp hat, and briefly slept himself.

Near three o'clock, they were dropped off at Oxford Street and had to walk the rest of the way to Leopold's flat.

Once they'd wearily climbed the steps to his door, he unlocked, unwarded, and opened it for them with one sweep of his hand.

He'd nearly forgotten he'd told his friends to meet him there, and was greeted by the loud exclamations from the ghost, the imp, the automaton, and the daemon.

"Maybe tomorrow, my friends. I fear I can't keep awake one more moment." He flopped onto the sofa and kissed Mingli's hand as she drifted off to his room to sleep.

It was only in the sunshine of late morning when Mingli joined him — and after his guests hid themselves when Mrs. Granville brought his breakfast — that he explained, between mouthfuls, all that had happened.

"So, you think that the Saint Collen Club was glamoured?" asked the daemon.

"I can't imagine that it wasn't. And dash it!" He looked at his pocket watch. "I meant to rise early to fix it before anyone saw."

"Don't worry, old bean. I'll go myself and fix the problem."

"Will you? Oh, that's awfully good of you."

"Not a bit of it. I miss doing a little architecture. Who do you think helped King David build his palace?"

Leopold buttered another piece of toast. "I never know quite when you are joking."

"I assure you I am not." He turned to Mingli and took her hand delicately into his enormous one. "Miss Zhao. Allow me to say how delighted I am that you will make an honest man of Leo."

"Eurynomos!" hissed Leopold.

"Ta! I'll see you back at the theatre, won't I?"

"Yes, I've got a lot of explaining to do. I've sent a message to the Templeton sisters, but God knows if they'll come."

"Good luck," he said with a wink before he vanished with a curling puff of smoke.

The patter of webbed feet. "Suchah take gold man back to theatre?"

Raj gave his version of a smile. "It is quite the unique form of travel. I do enjoy it."

Suchah rubbed his hands together. "Race, Thacker?"

Thacker straightened his ghostly bowler. "Just don't cheat this time—" But Suchah had already vanished with Raj. "The little blighter!" Thacker winked out too.

Leopold ate the last of his toast and sat back. "Well! I don't know that I've ever been as hungry. May I escort you back to your flat, my dear?"

"No thank you. I have several stops to make and it's getting late. *You'll* have to get to the theatre."

"It's really no trouble." He rose as she made her way to the umbrella stand to retrieve hers.

She glanced at him up through her lashes before darting in to give him a peck on the cheek. "I'll try to be back early here to have supper with you."

"Oh! Yes. That's...that's fine!" He straightened his waistcoat and his topper.

———— ◆ ————

HE WAS CLOSE enough to walk to the theatre and took his time, whistling the music to his act, and throwing his cane forward as he nearly skipped along the pavement. Such friends he had! And the magic. He was flush with it and felt marvelous! He felt as if nothing could go wrong today.

But as he arrived at the theatre, a feeling of doom began to descend. The poster with his name on it had been torn down. And when he got inside by the stage door, workmen crowded the wings. He'd forgotten that Miklos and Eurynomos had made a mess of things fighting each other. Some of the stagehands glared at him with blame clearly written on their faces, and some seemed to refuse to even talk to him.

"Dear, dear," he muttered. Clearly, he needed a conference with the theatre owner Barnabas Dawes.

He took a peek past the open curtains, and there were more workmen replacing the floors that Miklos had destroyed and where his metal hands had dug into the apron of the stage. Singed seats were being replaced, and others were still covered in dove droppings. What had happened to his doves? He hoped they'd flown back to the dovecotes on the roof. He'd have to check that.

He trudged a little less cheerily to his dressing room. No one had removed his wardrobe. He supposed *that* was something. But now it was time to pay the piper and face his assistants. What was he to say to them? Eurynomos suggested the truth, but were ordinary folk prepared for the truth? Well, *he* was once "ordinary", and *he* had handled the truth well enough. After a fashion.

He left his dressing room for his rehearsal room, the one the theatre owner had set aside for him after their contract negotiations of six months ago. He supposed he might be sacked again.

He touched the lock, expected it to be closed, but it had been opened. Tentatively, he pushed the door open and peered inside.

Raj sat in the corner, legs hidden behind his table again. And there were the Templeton sisters, Agnes and Aimee, sitting with arms crossed over their chests and looking at him expectantly and none too happily. *Átkozoh!* he thought.

"Well, we're here, guv," said Agnes, her auburn hair piled artfully atop her head…identical to her silent sister. "I hope you bloody well have an adequate explanation for all that. Because you can't tell me that was a conjure. Oh no. I told Aimee here that I won't believe none of that. Something queer's been going on here a long time, and you owe us an explanation. We were in danger of our lives, weren't we, Aimee?" She took a breath to look to her sister. "Of our very lives, that's what. Now you go ahead and tell us true, Mr. Kazsmer. It's the very least you can do."

Leopold took off his hat and set it aside. He slowly sank into the chair before them. "My dear Miss Templetons. I...I have no excuse but to say that I was afraid you would run in fear if you knew the complete truth. And I am well prepared to offer you extra payment so that you can find another situation without harm to your livelihood. It's true, it was dangerous, and I shan't blame you at all if you wish to leave."

"Then go on," urged Agnes. "Tell us."

"Well...it started long ago when I was a boy. I learned to perform true magic..." He swallowed. "By s-summoning daemons."

"Ow!" Agnes jumped to her feet. "It's far worse than I imagined, Aimee." She looked ready to leave...until she stopped and slowly sat again, placing her hands folded in her lap. "But, of course, we agreed to let the guv get it all out in the open before we left, didn't we?" She gestured to Leopold. "Go on, then."

"I learned to summon daemons — the friendly kind, not the damning kind — from my father. And I thought, 'wouldn't it be fun to include a little *real* magic in my act?' It started like that. Just little things. Until...well. It became bigger things. Like Saint Paul's."

"Didn't I tell you, Aimee."

"Er...would you like to meet the daemon."

"Crikey. You don't mean to say he's here."

"Well, he can be. I used to have to summon him by cutting my arm. Blood sacrifice, you see. But I don't anymore. I simply..." He pushed up his sleeve, touched a finger to the tattoo, and a shaft of light erupted from the floor. The women screamed and grabbed hold of each other as Eurynomos emerged from the light, quite meekly and the size of an ordinary man.

He bowed to them. "Do forgive me, ladies, for frightening you. I assure you it was never my intention. Only to help my dear friend Leopold."

Agnes straightened her hat and, still panting, slowly rose. She took a tentative step forward. "What about God and his angels, eh? Did you come from Hell? Are you the Devil?"

"Oh no, dear lady. I have come from Gehenna. It isn't Hell as you've been led to believe in the Scriptures. And my name is Eurynomos, at your service."

"The service of damning our souls!"

"No, I assure you. I don't damn anyone. I'm quite a congenial fellow. Really, I am."

"Well…you don't sound like no devil. 'A course, that's just the kind of thing the Devil would say, innit?"

Eurynomos' face wore a sorrowful expression. "Look, why don't I set a tea for us all and we can further discuss it." He waved his hand, and a table with tablecloth and full pot of tea, saucers, cups, and sandwiches on a plate appeared. There was even a cut crystal decanter and small stemmed glasses. The daemon tittered as he gestured toward them. "Sometimes tea is not quite adequate to the occasion." He pulled out two chairs for the ladies and, once they sat, he delicately pulled out his own.

Somehow, his horns were not quite as imposing as they usually were. Leopold was taken aback at his formality and graciousness.

The daemon poured for everyone. "Do you take sugar, Miss Agnes?"

"You know our names?"

"I'm afraid so. Leo is most accommodating. He tells me everything. I've even made suggestions for his act. And I must say, some of your *own* suggestions have intrigued me. I've told Leopold he should take them up. No sense in letting the act go stale now, what?"

Agnes, slowly warming to him, took the offered cup and saucer. "Which suggestion?"

"Oh, the costumes of course! Two lovely ladies such as yourselves should be arrayed in the finest. Your beauty is the thing that keeps the punters attention misdirected, after all."

"That's what I told the guv."

"And you are absolutely correct." He turned to the silent sister. "Miss Aimee, can I interest you in this little cake? It's lemon. I heard that was your favorite."

It didn't seem to take long before both assistants were charmed down to their shoes by Eurynomos and his manner. After a long while of talking, Eurynomos rose. "I hope you will both excuse me, but I do have to run. Please don't make any hasty decisions as to whether you will leave or not. You see how unique Leopold and his act truly are. A remarkable and, I might add, *lucrative* situation it is for you all."

"Yes," Leopold hastened to add. "I was definitely discussing with Eurynomos to raise your salaries. After all, once you knew the truth, there was far more you could do to make the act that much more spectacular."

"Good-bye, old friend," said the daemon, waggling his fingers. He stepped back into the lit doorway that had emerged and, once he was inside, it closed with a snap.

"Well!" Agnes set down her cup and saucer and looked at Aimee. "He's a right polite daemon, ain't he? I can't say I expected that."

"And he means every word. He's saved my life many times. And he loves playing cards. I'm sure he'd like to play a hand with the two of you sometime."

"Well ain't that something, Aimee? Who would have thought, eh?"

Aimee set down her saucer and cup, and straightened her bodice.

They both rose. "If you really meant it about raising our salaries—"

"Oh, I do!" said Leopold, rising too.

"Then…maybe we'll stay. With this new information, we can make a right proper show of it, is my thinking."

"Yes, I think you're right."

"Then we have a deal!" She extended her hand in its lace glove. Leopold took it and shook on it.

She was at the door when she paused and looked back. "That Raj fella." She thumbed at him over her shoulder. "He's alive, ain't he?" she whispered.

"Er…well…Raj?"

Raj suddenly came to life and rose from his table.

"I'll be damned!" she cried, clutching the arm of her sister.

Raj bowed. "My very dear ladies."

Agnes hesitated before she let go of her sister to stand before the automaton. She took a breath and beamed. "I always thought you were lovely."

"And, if you will forgive my boldness," he said softly, "I have always thought the same about you."

She burst into her tittering laughter. "Go on with ya!"

"No, it is true."

"Well!" Her cheeks blushed with a bright pink color and she pushed at her hair. "Then we shall have many conversations in the future."

"I should be delighted."

She spun on Leopold. "I suppose the ghost is real too."

Thacker peered around the corner of the Proetus Cabinet. "Er...Inspector Despenser Thacker at your service." He raised his bowler.

This time it was Aimee who stepped away from her sister. "You're an inspector? A *police* inspector?" She spoke slowly and carefully. It was the most noise Leopold had ever heard out of her.

"Well, dear lady. I *was*. Before my untimely demise."

"I should like to hear all about it," she said boldly.

Thacker raised his widened eyes to Leopold.

It couldn't have gone better, thought Leopold. Not in his wildest dreams.

CHAPTER TWENTY-EIGHT

EXCITEDLY, HE TOLD Mingli all about his new agreement with his assistants as they sat down to their first course of soup. Through the fish course, he exclaimed how they could improve his act with much more magic, and elaborated on it through the main course of rosemary chicken, merrily pouring Mingli more wine.

"That's remarkable!" she said, eye shining. In fact, her whole face beamed. Her black hair sheened blue in the gaslight, and she seemed as flushed and excited as he felt.

"Do you know that a great weight has been lifted off me? I had no idea how much keeping secrets kept me on tenterhooks. And they both have some marvelous ideas of things we can do that no other magician can *ever* do! We'll be touring Europe in no time at all."

"I'm so glad, Leo."

"Me too." He poured more wine for her. "I feel that...that for the first time, I'm truly moving forward. That maybe everything will be all right after all."

"I think it might. You have many unusual friends."

"I do, don't I." And wasn't it only a few short days ago that he lamented that he didn't have any *human* friends? What a difference a few days could make!

He drank and then looked at the wine in its crystal glass. His excitement dulled slightly when he said, "I just have to rescue my father, and all will truly be well."

"A toast, then." She raised her glass. "A toast to you and your friends. And to working together."

They clinked glasses and Leopold drank, savoring the deep berry flavor of the red wine. He was a little light-headed. He supposed he had indulged a little too freely with the wine during dinner, but maybe it was more than that.

When dinner was finished, they moved to seats by the fire. At first, Leopold sat in a wing chair, but as Mingli settled on the sofa, he rose and meandered toward her. "Would you mind terribly if I sat beside you?"

"I should be delighted."

Those dark lashes of hers. That eye that gave him a coquettish glance. Her hand lay on the seat cushion and he gently took it up, kissing the fingers. Before he lost his nerve, he whipped out of the seat and knelt on one knee before her. He took a small box from his waistcoat pocket and opened it. He took out the ring and showed her the blood red stone in it. Mingli offered a satisfying gasp.

"This was my mother's ring. She had nothing but a beautiful marriage with the man she loved. And I'm certain she would want the woman who made her son so happy to wear it and cherish it as she did."

"Oh, Leo."

He slipped it on her finger...and of course it fit her perfectly. He kissed her fingers once more and gracefully moved to sit beside her again.

Mingli examined the ring, turning it this way and that to catch the light. "This is very precious to me. You are a most unusual man."

"To love a beautiful and exquisite woman? I'm not so unusual, but instead the luckiest of men."

"And so very sentimental."

"I think it a strong suit. A magician, as well as any man, must know how to comport himself. Empathy, understanding...love. How can it be wrong?"

"How indeed?"

His cheeks reddened with the full flush of his emotions. He wanted to tell Mingli that perhaps they didn't have to wait for their wedding to... Oh, but it was all so embarrassing. He didn't wish to sound as if he were *begging*, after all. How would she take his change of heart?

She'll laugh at me, is what she'll do, he thought, but even that didn't vex him. And she had said she had wanted him, too. The very notion set a coal burning inside him that caused his blood to simmer. She was to be his wife. What did it matter if they consummated now or later?

But how to initiate it?

"M-Miss Zhao...Mingli...I wondered if..."

"Leo," she said, her voice dark and rich like velvet. "Do you recall when I offered you a...well, alternative to a relationship?" She turned to him fully and reached up to touch his collar.

His mouth suddenly went dry. "You mean...before you agreed to allow me to court you? Your...offer?" He squeaked the last.

"Yes. You flatly refused me. Far too honorable for you own good." Her hand slid up over the collar to his neck causing goose flesh there. "But I wonder, under these new circumstances, if you won't reconsider. We *are* to be married, after all."

"Do you mean to say..."

"I *mean*, what does it truly matter if we consummate now or later?"

Had she read his mind? He wondered if she could. "Do you...do you really think it would be all right?"

She shifted closer still and snaked her arms around his neck. He seemed to flash hot where she touched him. Even the closeness of her breath warmed his face. "I don't see how it could possibly be wrong. We *are* pledged to one another, aren't we?"

Her face was now mere inches away, her lips almost touching his.

"Yes," he whispered, before he leaned forward and took her lips.

Bliss! Her kiss had begun slow but quickly transformed to something more sensual. If he had held back before, he gave in now.

The rest was a blur of moving to the bedroom, of miles of ruffles and lace and...*corset*! And of her unbuttoning his shirt...

Oh, what wonders! He, touching her with trembling fingers. She, touching him with expert hands and lips in unimaginable ways...

At last, when he lay beside her, flushed and damp with perspiration, he was completely unable to control the smile on his face. He stared at the ceiling, hands laced behind his head.

He could feel her gazing at him. She had turned on her side and rested her head on her hand. "I don't think you've stopped smiling since we began," she chuckled. Her eye patch had been removed long ago, revealing her "galaxy" eye. Her unbound hair tumbled all around her. *And* he had finally seen her tattoo in its entirety; touched it, kissed it—and a beautiful work of art it was—but not as beautiful as the rest of her, and soon that tattoo had been utterly forgotten.

"Because it was so amazing," he sighed. "Why aren't people doing this all the time?"

She laughed. "They do. You just don't know they are."

He shook his head against the pillow. "But it's incredible. Especially with one that you love. Why in God's name do men go to brothels? It's—" But suddenly he remembered and sat up, aghast. "Oh, my dear. I'm so sorry to have brought that up. It's so callous of me."

She gave him a sad smile and rolled to her back, bringing the sheets up to cover her chest. "You mustn't worry about that, Leo. It was long ago, in my past."

"But still. I would never wish to remind you of anything so unpleasant."

She lay silent for a time, pensive, and Leopold was suddenly terrified that he'd ruined everything.

Finally, quietly, she said, "Leo, there's something I need to tell you. And it might mean that you wouldn't wish to marry me after all."

"Oh no! There is absolutely nothing you can say—"

"Wait until I have told you all." She took a deep breath and stared up at the ceiling as she talked. "When I worked in my uncle's brothel, he...he gave the girls potions and hurt us with unpleasant surgeries. He wanted to make certain we couldn't become with child. It was permanent. I cannot have children. Ever. I know that men value that in a wife, and I should have told you sooner. But I never quite imagined the depth of your feelings for me. It never seemed to matter before." She tilted her face toward him then, and he saw fear in her eyes—a fear he'd never seen throughout all her brave deeds. His heart broke.

He scooped her up in his arms and held her close. "It doesn't matter, my love. I don't think that the life we will live will be fit to raise a child in, but even if we should change our minds on the matter, there are so many orphaned children in London. Surely we would have a place for one of them."

She pulled back and stared at him, eyes wide. "You would adopt a child?"

"Why not? We've done more amazing things, you and I, have we not?"

She pulled him in and hugged him tight.

"Anything to make you happy," he whispered to her hair.

When she slipped from his arms again and lay down on the pillow, her hair cascading over her shoulder, across her cheek, and curling around a breast, she shook her head at him. "You are truly a most unusual man."

He smiled, so filled with love was he.

Yet, it didn't take long for a shadow to cross over his heart. She still didn't know. And he had to tell her.

He scooted to a sitting position and sat back against the bedstead. He turned away from the beautiful vision of her in the gaslight, both golden and shadowed. "Perhaps this is not the most opportune time...Dash it! There is no right moment for this."

She, too, sat up to prop herself beside him. "What? What do you wish to tell me?"

"Well...when you first appeared, you might recall that I never quite trusted you. At first."

She smiled, reached over, and kissed the outer edge of his mouth. "But you trust me more now, don't you?"

He took her hands and made her look at him. "This is important, Mingli. Well...as I said, I didn't quite trust you so I...I had Eurynomos investigate you."

She stiffened. "Oh *did* you now?"

"Yes. I mean, after all, I thought you were trying to kill me. But...my dear, he discovered that you are...that you are...Dash it. I'll just come out and say it. He discovered you are part daemon."

She didn't move, didn't speak for a long moment. Until... "This is a jest. One in very poor taste."

"I assure you it is not."

She wrapped the blankets about her and turned away, throwing her legs over the edge of the bed. Her naked back faced him, that long, sinuous tattoo that marked her as the servant of the Ghost with a

Grievance, forcing her into the life of righting wrongs. "What have you to gain by telling me this?" she said, her voice low and expressionless.

"Nothing," he pleaded. "Nothing whatsoever. I meant to tell you far earlier, but you were gone for six months and then when you returned there was scarcely a free moment. It wasn't anything to simply blurt out in the midst of tea!" He ran his hand up into his hair. "Oh damn. I'm doing this all wrong. I wanted to tell you as soon as possible, before you found out on your own and then learned I had known all along."

She glanced at him over her shoulder. "So, you've known for at least six months."

"Yes. I'm sorry."

She sat that way a long time, fuming, he supposed.

He scooted marginally closer. "Please. Mingli? My dear? Talk to me. I've no idea if this is good news or bad."

"It's bad, Leo," she whispered. "It's very, *very* bad news."

"But my love. Let me help you in whatever way you need. Together, we can search for a reason, for understanding it."

She whirled about and stared at him. "Wait. You *knew*. All this time. You knew. And…you still loved me?"

"Of *course* I did! I do! I've never stopped. Why should I?"

Something seemed to dawn on her face with a beautiful light. "Why *shouldn't* you? Oh, so many reasons. But not you. You truly don't care one way or the other, do you?"

He looked at her perplexed. "No. You are still my Mingli. My love."

"You are the most amazing man!" She leapt at him, throwing her arms around him and kissing him soundly, as she had kissed him most of the night.

He gladly moved to succumb again to their marvelous lovemaking, shifting to slide atop her…when his tattoo abruptly blazed with hot, searing pain.

He screamed and fell back. The heat swept up and down his arm. Vaguely, he heard her asking him what was wrong, but he could not answer for the all-encompassing agony that rolled over his body. He writhed on the sheets, holding his arm, shouting out his anguish.

When it finally leveled off to stabs and prickles and a throbbing ache, he caught his breath. But only for a moment, for it was then that the voices of the Unholy Hosts rippled the air about them.

"LeopolD kAZSmEr," said the chorus of voices. "THe time HaS cOME for yoU to sErVE USSSSS!"

To be concluded in LIBRARY OF THE DAMNED

AUTHOR'S AFTERWORD

WE HAVE RETURNED to a yesteryear that never quite was. A history skewed to include a world operating on steam…and a little magic.

My style of steampunk or historical fantasy or gaslamp fantasy — whatever you'd like to call it — is to adhere as closely to the *history* of the time period and then twist certain elements. In that way, a faithful foundation makes the reader feel that the rest is all the more real, that the fantasy that seeps into it, is real and livable. Being a historian, I found the *real* time period interesting enough to use rather than loading the story with unnecessary mechanical contrivances. There's no need, in my opinion, to have steampunky machines at every turn — a nonsensical doorbell, for instance — just for the sake of steampunking it up. Maybe the average reader of "steampunk" does not favor this, but it is the way I prefer to write this series.

As for the "mechanical contrivances", yes, they had elevated trolleys that ran on steam and later electricity. No, they didn't have dirigibles at all for travelling.

And so…the railways, engines, stations, and all that are in them are accurate to the real Victorian time period.

Sans the goblins.

In 1836, for instance, the stationmaster Thomas Edmondson of the Newcastle & Carlyle Railway invented the ticket system that we would recognize today, with a printed card of the destination and hand numbered so it couldn't be used again.

By 1900, you couldn't enter a railway station without noticing the W. H. Smith newspaper and bookseller.

Refreshment Rooms where railway travelers could obtain food and libations were run by railways companies, but Spiers & Pond were the contractors that made them palatable by the 1890s. In 1867, even Charles Dickens commented on railway-owned refreshment room fare; "The pork and veal pies, with their bumps of delusive promise and their little cubes of gristle and bad fat...the sawdusty sandwiches, so frequently and energetically condemned..." makes you shiver. Like today's packaged gas station food. Gas station sushi, anyone?

And it wasn't until the early 1890s that toilets were even included on train passenger cars. Think about *that* for an unpleasant moment.

In case you wondered, the alignment lines I spoke of are more commonly known today as "ley lines", a term coined by English antiquarian Alfred Watkins in the 1920s. His pseudoscientific belief proposed that these lines seemed to be straight alignments between either prominent landscape features or were the sites where ancient structures were erected because of "earth energies" found along the lines. But because the term first appeared in the early twentieth century, I wasn't able to call them "ley lines." As to their "earth energies", I leave that up to the observer.

I can't speak for the community of faeries and other magical creatures. Their existence is pure speculation. Although Sir Arthur Conan Doyle of Sherlock Holmes fame was certainly enamored of the little fellows and was a fervent believer.

A few notations of terms used that you might not be familiar with:

Sprats — Fish eaten at breakfast, like kippers.

Elevenses — Snack time at around eleven o'clock.

Punch Cartoon — Punch was a magazine in the 1800s and made popular the term "cartoon", mostly of an amusing and often political nature. Sometimes faces of real people might have exaggerated features much like the editorial cartoons of today.

Bootblack — A person who shines shoes; a shoeshine boy.

Bloater — A pickled herring

Saveloy — A bright red sausage similar to a frankfurter.

Gimmel Ring — A ring used for betrothals, sometimes designed in multiple rings to be put together only for the wedding.

Gwáilóu—Literally means "Ghost man." A disparaging term for white person from the Cantonese perspective.

Folly—A structure in one's garden of no practical purpose, designed to look like an ancient temple or crumbling castle tower. Popular in the eighteenth century.

And finally, because I am trying to remain true to the time period, I do use the often disparaging terms that were employed at the time for certain minorities—"Oriental" for anyone of the east like Raj, Arabs, and Chinese people. "Chinaman" and "Chinky" were also used disparagingly, and, of course, "Gypsy" for Romani people.

Now "Gypsy" is a complicated term. At the time and to some current Romani peoples, "Gypsy" is not necessarily a slur (much like the term "Indian" for Native American peoples). The Oxford English Dictionary defines the word as "a member of a traditionally itinerant people originating in South Asia and now found mainly in Europe and North and South America", also known as Roma, Romani, or Romany. The earliest form of the word, *gipcyan*, is a shortened form for "Egyptian", coined because the people who first appeared in England near the beginning of the sixteenth century were believed to have come from Egypt, and many Romani did not choose to disabuse those who thought this.

In actuality, according to genetic findings, the Romani people seemed to have sprung from a single group that left northwestern India in about 512 CE.

In various following centuries, a plethora of terms came to define men and woman of this Roma origin in both disparaging and non-disparaging terms. For instance, if someone is termed a "gypsy" (in lower case), it is only meant that they are a wanderer without any negative connotations.

Unfortunately, as time went on, Romani people were almost universally vilified by outsiders, and in the twentieth century, Hitler had them rounded up and put in concentration camps as "racially inferior". Tens of thousands of Romani were killed in the German-occupied territories of the Soviet Union and Serbia and thousands more at the concentration camps under Nazi Germany.

And so, thank you, dear readers, for following along with the series. Leopold is coming to the dramatic conclusion of his tale. In his last adventure, LIBRARY OF THE DAMNED, Leopold and Mingli make the perilous journey to the Library of the Damned, a structure fluctuating between the worlds, filled with the archives of the centuries. They must find a way to rescue Leopold's father from an uncertain fate. It is at this treacherous juncture when the worlds are imbalanced that the Unholy Hosts call upon Leopold to fulfill his promises. Because he is bound to them, he has no hope but to obey, and it seems that what they desire most is to destroy Leopold's world. If he stops them, he might be trapped himself in the depths of *Sitra Achra* for all eternity, but many surprises await in this final chapter of the Enchanter Chronicles.

As always you can find me on Facebook and Instagram and sign-up for my paranormal newsletter from my website, JeriWesterson.com.

Thank you for reading. If you like a book, consider reviewing it. It is much appreciated.

ABOUT THE AUTHOR

JERI WESTERSON is the author of the critically acclaimed Crispin Guest Medieval Noir mysteries. She also writes historical novels and several paranormal series. An award-winning author, her medieval mysteries were also nominated thirteen times for national mystery awards, from the Agatha to the Shamus. Jeri lives in Menifee, CA, mother to a gray senior cat and a laconic tortoise.

JeriWesterson.com

www.ingramcontent.com/pod-product-compliance
Lightning Source LLC
Chambersburg PA
CBHW050357260626
47156CB00003B/766